CORPUS

ı Irvine was born in Scotland and brought up
d. She is a journalist who has written for the
ɣ *Telegraph*, the *Sunday Times* and the *Independent*.
married and lives in London. Her first novel,
was published in 2008 by Quercus.

CORPUS

Susan Irvine

Quercus

With thanks to Charlotte Clerk, Jon Riley,
Georgia Garrett and Andy Vella.

First published in Great Britain in 2009 by Quercus
This paperback edition published in 2010 by

Quercus
21 Bloomsbury Square
London
WC1A 2NS

ISBN 978 1 84916 163 3

This book is a work of fiction. Names, characters,
businesses, organizations, places and events are
either the product of the author's imagination
or are used fictitiously. Any resemblance to
actual persons, living or dead, events or
locales is entirely coincidental.

10 9 8 7 6 5 4 3 2 1

Printed and bound in Great Britain by Clays Ltd, St Ives plc.

For 'B'

CONTENTS

CONCEPT I

Interviewer: Tell us about yourself.

Artist: I am an artist. I am thirty-five years old. I live in Nottingham.

Interviewer: And you have a son, Tom?

Artist: Son is not the description I would use.

Interviewer: But he is a little boy that you gave birth to?

Artist: Yes.

Interviewer: Wouldn't it be true, then, to describe Tom as your son?

Artist: My job as an artist is to challenge apparently self-evident truths that contaminate quotation marks, reality.

Interviewer: So you never think of Tom as your son?

Artist: I conceived of Tom as a question about the societal norms of designation for this type of work, so it would not be appropriate for me to describe him as my son.

Interviewer: How old is he?

Artist: You would say he was six. I started working on him seven and a half years ago.

Interviewer: And how would you describe Tom if not as your son?

Artist: As a work of art. Specifically, Concept I, a work in progress.

Interviewer: Why did you choose that name?

Artist: This work is the first in a proposed series of exstallations produced out of my body, hence to be numbered one, two etc., but in Roman numerals.

Interviewer: Don't you feel that it's unfair to give your boy a name like that?

Artist: It's fashionable now to call children after American states like Montana, or vehicles like Ford or Harley, and concept-names are becoming popular. Destiny, Liberty. I know a Californian boy called Leisure, Lee for short.

Interviewer: How did you arrive at the name?

Artist: In Spain they have a girl's name, Concepción; Conception in English. Conception refers to the fertilisation of the egg in the womb, or the engendering of abstract ideas in the mind. It's a suggestive name for what I'm trying to do with this piece, but because I've chosen to sex my piece male, I've opted for the version, Concept.

Interviewer: Might the numbering not be considered demeaning to the child's sense of individuality?

Artist: Here I am following the American upper-class custom of numbering sons – never daughters. For example, William Richard Franklin I . . . William Richard Franklin II . . . William Richard Franklin III.

Interviewer: What about Tom, how does he feel about it?

Artist: He has the nickname, Tom, which is how I address him and how his teachers and friends address him, and, it would seem, how you prefer to refer to him. He is not yet aware that this is not his real, in quotation marks, name.

Interviewer: What about the more obvious nickname, Con?

Artist: I considered it, but it could be detrimental to how the piece is perceived.

Interviewer: Does Tom know that you claim him to be a work of art?

Artist: He is no more aware that he is a work of art than a Rembrandt self-portrait is.

Interviewer: How do you think he will react when he discovers that he is a work of art, real name Concept I?

Artist: I'm looking forward to that moment. This is a highly sophisticated and, one might once have said, avant-garde piece though also an example of the oldest and most primitive work of all. But the moment when it becomes conscious of itself as a work will hardly be a unique moment. Historically, most humans thought of themselves as works of art, it's nothing unusual. What's exceptional in this case is the entity claiming to be the artist.

Interviewer: Aren't you afraid it might damage Tom's sense of his own identity that he is categorised as an artwork?

Artist: It's possible, this is a risky enterprise, but then the value of any work of art is predicated upon what it risks.

Interviewer: You are willing to risk your child's emotional well-being to make some kind of point?

Artist: Obviously I take very good care of Concept I. I also manipulate the material as a means for embodying ideals and ethics as well as my implicit criticisms of our culture. This is common practice. I go further than most parents in the direction of quotation marks, truth, end quotation marks, that's all.

Interviewer: And you see Tom as your own work?

Artist: Tom is a collaborative piece like many works of art, but he's my responsibility, I am the auteur, or, in a manner of speaking, the mother of this work. In Tom's particular case there is no father apart from in the biological sense. Tom was conceived artificially using anonymous donor sperm.

Interviewer: Did you conceive him that way because you couldn't have children any other way?

Artist: I conceived him that way because it allows the questions I am raising with the piece to be foregrounded.

Interviewer: You mentioned earlier that you chose to have a male child. Wasn't that out of your control?

Artist: There are several ways in which I could have determined or sought to determine the work's masculinity. Considering that gender is now seen as a cultural construct rather than something at least partially delimited by the body, I could have allowed the sex of the child to be randomly selected and then raised, say, biological 'girl' as cultural construct 'boy' and seen how that impacted on the work. But for this particular exstallation I'm not interested in interrogating gender in that way, so it was simply a question of asking the IVF doctor to insert only male embryos into my womb.

Interviewer: That's not legal in this country.

Artist: Tom wasn't conceived in this country. There are many countries, for example the United States, where sex-selection is a legal and fairly common part of genetic screening. In this country screening is only used to discard genetically disabled offspring.

Interviewer: Are you worried that sex selection is a step on the road to designer babies?

Artist: I'm interested in that question. Parents are already crafting children with regard to sex and disease. In future, they will be able to make many more choices. It is already scientifically possible to design children to be blue-eyed or brown-eyed, to have straight or curly hair, and you could select for traits like vivacity simply by interfering with the thyroid during gestation. Then there is the Pax6 gene, which is the master-regulator for the presence or absence of eyes. This same gene selects for eyes in both mammals and insects, even though their eyes have such different structures. For example, it is the expression of Pax6 in multiple locations that ennables spiders to have numerous eyes. Manipulation of this gene in humans is very close to being possible now, and could lead to some intriguing aesthetic outcomes. But most traits are not controlled by a single gene. In fact many, like high numeracy or musical talent are the result of a precisely orchestrated reading of perhaps thousands of genes. The whole text for say, numeracy, must be read in the right selection of cells and in the right part of the body as well as at the right time for the text to become performative. This makes such traits impossible to include in the design of a work in the conceivable future. A more fruitful area to explore for now might be cross-species hybrids. Scientists have already created these, and it's probable that artists will eventually do so as well.

Interviewer: Does that probability trouble you?

Artist: There's a satisfying circularity in returning to the basic material, flesh, in order to evolve as artists. In the nineteenth century the potent media for art were paint and the novel, in the twentieth the perfect expressive medium was film, in the twenty-first century it is flesh.

Interviewer: But unlike film, words and paint, flesh is alive. Do you accept there are sinister implications in your view, implications that would remind some of the Nazis?

Artist: Certainly this form of art can be seen as sinister as well as liberating. But I am not advocating a eugenics programme where some characteristics or races are promoted, and others suppressed. On the contrary, as an artist, I am interested in multiplying the creative possibilities for human flesh, not narrowing them.

Interviewer: What kind of creative possibilities do you have in mind?

Artist: Imagine if artists were permitted to create what's known as a surgical chimera, a creature with some of its cells completely human and others fully animal. Surgeons already do this, with pig valves in human hearts. Recently scientists located the part of the bird brain that contains birdsong. Theoretically, this part could be implanted in a human brain, and with some tweaking of the vocal cords, a human could sing like a nightingale. He or she might, however, lose the ability to speak, that's an unknown factor at the moment. But it would be an exceptional piece of work.

Interviewer: Would you have made Tom a cross-species chimera if that option had been available to you?

Artist: Art thrives on crossing the line to go beyond what's acceptable by convention and the art establishment. It is conceivable that in future exstallations, I may find creative possibilities in chimera and new genetic technology. Concept I is just the beginning of my work with this material.

For now I wanted to limit the pre-birth artistic decisions to a biological-only father and to choosing the gender. In this way, I have made decisions about Concept I that a growing number of parents worldwide make about their children. In all other respects, Concept I arrived as a readymade.

Interviewer: It's almost a hundred years since Duchamp gave us the first readymade, the urinal. Isn't the idea somewhat hackneyed now?

Artist: The readymade idea has fresh relevance in the context of my piece. Duchamp said that whether Mr Mutt – R. Mutt was the name with which he signed the piece – made the urinal or not was irrelevant, what was important was that he chose it and placed it so that its usual significance disappeared under the new title and point of view. Similarly, I have taken an object of which there are millions, billions of examples in the world. There is nothing more ordinary than the type of object I have chosen. But I have named and placed it so as to create a new way of thinking about that object.

Interviewer: So there is nothing special about your son?

Artist: That is a rhetorical question addressed to a mother. As an artist I can say that insofar as Concept I is a readymade it is both a replica of all other sons, and a singular work of art, ready-made at the point of birth, yes, but predestined by the particular reading and rewriting performed on each other by the two texts inherent in the origin of the piece to take a unique form both physically and psychologically.

Interviewer: You describe newborn child Concept I as a readymade with a form predestined by the intertextuality of two texts quotation marks, inherent in the origin of the piece, end quotation marks. I presume the texts you are referring to are his genetic codes?

Artist: Yes.

Interviewer: This would be true of any son?

Artist: Yes.

Interviewer: Fine, could you explain your exact definition of a son?

Artist: Son is currently used to designate any offspring of a man and a woman that bears male sex organs. A son begins to be produced when a sperm cell from a male throws some DNA and a few proteins into the egg cell of a female. A cell may be a living entity but it is also a text in the DNA language. The text of the egg-cell is cut and pasted with the text interjected by the sperm-cell to produce a new text: son. This son may be nothing more than a tissue of quotations, but what makes him singular is the way the new intertext is read. Some quotations are silenced, others are expressed or even emphatically expressed. The text also incorporates transcription errors. And what you have to realise is that this text is inately more poetic than any text humans have, so far, written. Of course the meaning of a text in a human language is ascertained to a large extent by its context, but arguably not to the extent a genetic text is. Let's consider a simple genetic stanza, the one which, when read, performs eye colour. Imagine if the word quotation marks blue end quotation marks completely changed its meaning depending on the day on which it was read. This is what happens with genetic text during the development of the embryo. Genetic text means something completely different when it is read in, say, week one, and when it's read in say, week twenty. Genetic text is a vital, rich, and above all, kinetic language.

The son produced by these readings and writings may be complete after the mother has extruded him from her womb but he is also a nascent work. A son – I prefer exstallation – is a complex piece of work, but only arguably more so than, say, a theatrical play. He continues to be formed by the exigences of the internal text that produces him, but also by his interactions with the environment and certainly until he reaches adulthood – and I would argue beyond – by the conscious and unconscious work of the artist upon the material that he constitutes.

Interviewer: And a son's father and his friends and his teachers, they work on him too?

Artist: Absolutely. This is is a collaborative piece. And naturally the material resists. This resistance of the material has always been a factor in art. However, Concept I resists the artistic process in a different way than, say, marble resists the sculptor.

Interviewer: But you feel that you as the mother are the most important factor in this work, more important even than Tom himself?

Artist: What is Tom himself apart from all the elements we have just been discussing?

Interviewer: But he is not just produced by you, the mother; why do you feel you have the right to sign this work?

Artist: Who signs the work is an interesting question, and one that I am asking with this piece. There are works of the same type as Concept I named as versions – in a sense you might say self-portraits – of a putative artist, in these cases, a father. Hence William Franklin I, II, III, etc. But I would argue that the son is the masterpiece of the mother.

Interviewer: But the son is made 50–50 of the mother and the father.

Artist: Not exactly. The cellular context is maternally inherited, including the non-nuclear DNA, mainly the mitochondria which are within the egg-cell. It is these mitochondria which generate the chemicals the cells of a body use as energy. So the energy system – you could say the life force – of the body is solely the legacy of the mother. In addition, the child is gestated exclusively in the woman's body – an uncomfortable idea for some cultures – and nourished, both physically and culturally, at her breast in the first formative years of his life. I am not saying that men, fathers, do not have an input into works like these. But I am highlighting what has been undervalued or left ambiguous through history: the role of the mother as artist.

Interviewer: It may have been true once that men were jealous of women's ability to seemingly create life from their bellies, but surely not nowadays?

Artist: That's a far more vexed question than you allow. The Christian Holy Family is an interesting case in point. This ideal type of the family has as its core, in the iconography, a mother and child. Rarely in the picture are the two absent fathers, one a spiritual entity whose divine text interacted with Mary's human DNA to produce the Christ-child, the other a father figure who hovers impotently in the background providing the child with a spurious provenance (you remember Jesus's paternal genealogy, though it has nothing to do with the genes he inherits, is given textual importance in the New

Testament). There's a great deal of male anxiety in this founding Christian myth.

Interviewer: Joseph's anxiety about whether or not he is the real father?

Artist: Rather, male anxiety about what being a father actually means, and its connection to physical reality. For example, in the past it appeared as if the mother's role in the production of a child was paramount. A dab of liquid from the male, something evanescent and prone to evaporate, was squirted into the female. Nine months later from, as it were, her studio, she produced a child. The position of the two fathers in Christ's story reflects male anxiety about this. Was a father's input to the child two rather abstract things: a name, and something tenuous that would quickly evaporate, becoming invisible? If so, to emphasise the superior claim of the father, the invisible part of the child had to be established as more valuable than the visible part, the flesh, thought in the past to be formed of the clay of the mother. You can see the body/spirit split right there. Views have changed, but such anxieties still function subconsciously.

Interviewer: Well I think that could be disputed.

Artist: Our culture has also failed to pay due attention to the role of the mother's womb in forming a child, a role which science is now recognising as subtle but significant.

I mentioned that the child is a work of art predestined by the particular reading and rewriting performed on each other by the two texts inherent in the origin of the piece. But this reading and rewriting is not purely the result of chance or unknown factors. The womb has a considerable influence in deciding which genes will be expressed and in which way. The womb is an invisible hand co-writing the new text, it has a role in deciding which elements of the old texts will be imprinted in the child, which deleted.

Interviewer: To return to your idea that the son is nourished by the mother in the formative years of life, women are emancipated now and men do care for children.

Artist: Yes they do, but childcare is still classed as women's work and overwhelmingly done by women, as mothers, as primary school teachers, as carers, as au pairs, as house servants. On the one hand, people pay sentimental lip service to this kind of work, but on the other, it is considered low-grade, dreary, even shameful. The name of Mother is both exalted and abject.

Interviewer: So is Concept I a feminist piece?

Artist: It's possible to produce political readings of the piece.

Interviewer: Is that why you applied for various Arts Council grants and museum bursaries to help you bring up Tom?

Artist: I applied for financial aid to help me continue my work. Most mothers in Europe do the same, receiving child benefit from the state. As I am producing a work of art, it seemed more appropriate to look for funding in the arena of art sponsorship.

Interviewer: And you have, in fact, received several size-able grants and bursaries?

Artist: Yes. The state funding for children as such is poor, whereas I am in receipt of substantial funding through state art institutions for Concept I.

Interviewer: You have been nominated for this year's Turner Prize and have chosen to exhibit Tom.

Artist: Yes. I am excited about the opportunities that would arise should I win the prize. The money would allow me to take Concept I in a new, experimental direction.

Interviewer: What do you have in mind?

Artist: I'd like to see how the input of private schooling would affect its ability to pass exams. On the other hand I'm interested in the three-dimensional shape of the piece and the potential for it to interact with space in more extreme ways. I am considering collaborating with a well-known gymnastic training camp in the former USSR.

Interviewer: But what if Tom doesn't want to do any of this?

Artist: I will consider that as much as other parents with special children do. If, as he develops, he resists such programmes strongly, I may compromise with the material, as other artists do. Or I may capitulate completely allowing the material to take the work in a new direction. For example, Concept I loves to watch TV. I would consider allowing him to control his own access to it to the extent of taking days off school.

Interviewer: Wouldn't that be detrimental to his ability to function in society?

Artist: Possibly, but it would possibly also give him a head-start in a society mediated by television.

Interviewer: Is there anything you wouldn't consider doing to Tom, however interesting, as an art project?

Artist: Well, I wouldn't consider chopping the piece's limbs off as has been the custom amongst beggars in some countries, even though this would have fascinating aesthetic consequences. Perhaps if I were a member of such a beggar tribe as well as an artist, I would consider this option. I use Tom to explore how my own culture operates and I've observed that by and large this precludes acts considered as grossly cruel within this culture.

Interviewer: How are you showing Tom as part of the Turner Prize exhibition?

Artist: My work is at the Tate Gallery with the work of the other nominated artists. There's a room of texts, photographs, short films, interviews, etc., around the project. And there's an interactive play area I have built where I display Concept I at weekends and most days after school. Sometimes he brings friends to play in the gallery as well.

Interviewer: Have any visitors to the gallery objected?

Artist: Yes, although others have brought their own children to play with Concept I in the play area. In fact this part of the work has become a phenomenal success.

Interviewer: You don't feel you are asking too much of Tom?

Artist: No. We leave when he's had enough or when it's time for his bath. It's a playroom. It would be different if we could conduct lessons there with his teachers, then he would have to stay whether he liked it or not, as in any classroom.

Interviewer: Do you love Tom?

Artist: When I conceived of Concept I it was because I wanted to make a work of art. This is widely held to be a selfish desire, a work of ego. In Concept I, I have some measure of immortality, for a time. Artists are often said to create for this reason, to beat death. However, my piece affords me a different degree of immortality, both greater and lesser than other art works. I live on in Concept I, since I am his quotation marks, mother, end quotation marks. He will soon die, whereas other works of art do not die, and though they may decay, many will endure for longer than a single generation. However, should Concept I produce offspring, I live on in them – in a way both more real and more uncanny – far longer than artists of more conventional works live on in some sense in those works. This residue of I, heavily hedged in question marks and quotation marks as it is, will be passed down. It could rapidly become more widespread – depending on how many children, grandchildren, etc., though it would also become diluted in each succeeding generation. If, however, at some point in the future, my great-great-grandchildren, say, were to interbreed – as was certainly common in the past – the percentage of the ghostly I in those offspring would actually increase. At any rate, once quotation marks, I, end quotation marks, has passed a critical threshold of dissemination, it is likely that I will endure as long as humanity endures. Here is a potent reason to make Concept I that has nothing to do with love for anything except me.

Interviewer: So you had Tom because you love yourself?

Artist: I loved the concept of Concept I before I conceived him. Once Concept I was physically born my feelings became dominated by something simpler. Now I would say yes, I love Tom, more than anything, and that is why I am making him.

Interviewer: What will you do when he reaches an age when you can't control him?

Artist: At that point I won't try to control him any more than a mother would. But my role in the work will not be over since it will be impregnated with thought patterns and beliefs from me and feel obligations towards me. Another interpretation of the piece might be useful here: Concept I as a work of environmental art, temporarily demarcated from the landscape from which it came, shaped by the artist, mutating in directions unforeseen by both the artist and its own self-awareness, before decaying and sinking back into the ground from which it came.

Interviewer: And if somebody wants to buy Tom?

Artist: All art can be given a transaction value nowadays, that's the nature of our culture rather than of Concept I per se. But I won't be selling him. He's my gift to the nation.

Interviewer: Thank you and good luck to you and Tom in the Turner Prize competition.

Artist: Thank you.

LATE

It is late. You have a few grey hairs, one sprouting in an eyebrow. You have crow's feet at the sides of your eyes when you smile. At your back you always hear Time's wingèd chariot hurrying near. You don't hear it until you reach about thirty-five. The chariot is too far away to hear before that, like a tsunami still far out in the Pacific Ocean. It is almost impossible to believe that this quasi-mythical tsunami will one day find and hit your tiny outcrop in the millions of square miles that is the Pacific Ocean. Then you turn thirty-five. You turn thirty-six. You turn thirty-seven. By that time you know what the rushing, roaring sound in the distance is – it's the chariot in the form of a tsunami. Looming, mounting, culminating, a wall of water swinging low out of blue sky to scoop you up. You begin to hear it behind all the everyday sounds. Every year it gets louder. Sucking up life with its drag. You get used to that sound. You hear it and it alters everything you do, everything you say, stupid things you start saying like, when I was young, which you say a lot more than people who are a lot older because it's still so shocking for you and you can't help it because it's obsessing you and you draw attention to your age the way fat women draw attention to their weight without meaning to, saying I know I look really fat in this, and people think you are fishing for compliments, for consolation, because you don't look that old, you're not that old, and you must be a sad, shallow woman to go on about it like that, but they don't know about those moments when you catch sight of yourself in an outside mirror in daylight, leaning forward on the street to check your mascara in the wing mirror of a parked Range Rover and seeing how your face has sunken like a cardboard box left out in the rain, how those wrinkles are not only there when you smile, they are, in daylight, permanently cut into your skin, and you straighten up quickly and you know that you are living an illusion of looking younger than you really look, an illusion that sustains you, but of which you are ashamed because in the modern world we are supposed to face up to our illusions and even plastic surgery is a kind of honest recognition that there is a problem, and as you straighten up you push your own face under the water at the back of your mind, you turn snappishly to the man at your side and you say to him, I'm tired, I wish we could go home right now, and he says something like, You are so beautiful, which breaks your heart because it's all gone, gone and a skull is beginning to press through the peaches of your cheeks and all the things you never valued, hated even, when you had them, are revealed by the toothless laugh of the Medusa – who, after all, is a worm-crowned skull – as a source of joy, freely given like water from an urban tap, just when you know for sure that your particular tap has been turned off for ever by the authorities. Whirling on your heel you hear the water roaring, gulping, you hear the wind shrieking at the back of the wave. You walk on. You know that all that remains to happen is the gradual convergence of you and the tsunami. One day you will not only be able to hear it, you will be able to see it approaching at around thirty knots over the surface of the ocean. Then before you can take it in, it will have taken you in.

That's how late it is in life as you leave the house this morning. In terms of the morning it is precisely one hour and fifteen minutes too late. In that hour and fifteen minutes, you could have been halfway to achieving what you had set out to achieve today when you put your head on the pillow the night before. Last night you told yourself: tomorrow I will start afresh, I will just do it, I will begin tomorrow, it is never too late, Gaugin was still a banker at thirty-five, and I am thirty-eight, which maybe means it is too late, but it's in the Gaugin ballpark, just, and get this, there is no benchmark after Gaugin, after Gaugin it's just banking and its grey corollaries for ever, a stasis that just looks as if something's happening until you reach the age of dribbly jumpers and Stannah stair lifts, then a post-show sadness as you face the end.

So tomorrow. Up at seven. In the café by eight-thirty with pen in hand, steaming cappuccino on the little formica table, head stuffed and ready to disgorge. That's what you thought as you laid your head on the pillow last night, even though events had already conspired, even though the plan was already challenged, so that what had happened was that instead of going to bed at around eleven as planned, you got into bed at one a.m., as was more usual, and you'd had around six glasses of something, maybe as a result of the feeling of liberation you had had all evening, and so you were wide awake at six-thirty a.m. and thought, yes, by God, I'm already awake to herald the great day, but the next second you realised you felt hungover, so you turned over and thought, just an hour more and I'll still be within schedule and then you wake again and it's eight-thirty, you've slept through the alarm and this is the precise moment when you are supposed to be sitting down in the café licking the end of your pen.

You lie on your back and stare at the ceiling and think, another day ruined, so why bother? but you pull yourself back from the brink with a great effort, you tell yourself I Will Do This and you turn on your side in preparation for getting out of the bed and stare at the carpet where it joins the wall and think, Right. But at that moment you sense something bumping against your buttocks like a donkey nosing an apple. You say, I'm late. I've got to get up. The bumper says, You always say that, you never want to have sex in the mornings, you're getting boring and staid, you've lost your passion and spontaneity, your lust for life itself, you don't love me any more, you don't love love, you're lifeless, conformist, why can't you just let yourself go for *once*, and so you thrust out your buttocks towards the bumper and you say to yourself, shutting off the carpet with closing eyelids, you say, this is what life is all about, and then you have sex with him, throwing yourself into it to show that you do have lust for life and love still in you, making right effort for the good – is that how your yoga teacher puts it? – doing what you can do now, today, to affirm life in the face of the tsunami, to show you are not heartless but that your heart is beating, beating away.

Then it is over and he immediately jumps up and into the bathroom locking the door and running a bath, a bath that you know from experience will last a good half hour and here you are, dazed among the sheets, your day in pieces before you have even got out of bed because you have not even got out of bed once again, and you make right effort for the good and it *is* an effort and you block the seething despair and say to yourself, it's OK, I can still do it, feeling shit, looking shit, feeling wine-fur on your teeth, sperm running into your pubic hair, it will make your pants sticky, but if you don't embrace that sticky feeling you can't embrace life, so get started, be single-minded, don't let Time's wingèd chariot get one over on you again.

You get out of bed and climb into some clothes and then, inspired, run into the kitchen and wash your face in the kitchen sink, wiping off last night's mascara with the dishcloth, cleaning your teeth with a forefinger and you scrape your hair back, wipe the wet dishcloth over the back of your neck the way men do in black and white films about the beleaguered working classes and leave the kitchen, snatch up the notebook and purse and make for the door.

As you reach the door he shouts from the bath Where are you going? like privacy is a crime in modern society, in the stupefyingly close embrace of modern love and you shout sharply back, Nowhere. What's wrong with you? he shouts. Nothing, you yell and you stomp out, banging the door and locking it behind you, but instantly you get out the front door key, open the door again and go and stand outside the bathroom door because you know that if you walk out like this you will feel bad all day and you need those magic words said in just the right way to bless you on your way.

– Baby, you say, I'm sorry. Just late and I'm feeling a bit shit from last night.

– Late for what?

Why the fucking nosiness, the finger always expertly inserted into the unprotected orifice?

– I've got a meeting.

– Who with?

– Who cares who with? Just a meeting.

– Well don't take it out on me. Christ, what have I done?

– Locked yourself in the bathroom for half an hour so I can't get ready, that's what.

– Well how was I to know, if you don't say anything, you're always so fucking secretive, like you're some kind of John Le Carré character, why are so you weird all the time?

– I'm not, you never— and you stop yourself, you marshal forbearance, you are going to have to be more mature than he is, again. We just need to start this morning again, my love. All I wanted to say – through gritted teeth with a smile thrown into the intonation – is that I really, really love you.

– So why do you have to say it in the voice you use when you mean you really, really hate me?

He asks too much.

– Because you're a selfish fucking bastard! You're so selfish you're not even aware—and he is shouting over the top of your shout, some shite about hysterical emotionalism fucking up the simple joys of every day. But you refuse to be subjected. You turn and leave singing La La La LA LA, banging the front door, down steps and out the house door and here you pause and lean your head on the doorpost for a second. Do Not Be Defeated. Do Not Be. You feel like filth, so you reach for filth in a homoeopathic kind of a way. You get out a Camel Light and light it. As you are taking the first drag, a window opens upstairs and he sticks his wet head out of the window and yells I love you.

The cheek of it, pursuing, chasing you down, so you start to slightly cry, so he can see, and start to run down the street in a jagged way as he yells louder and louder after you, I fucking love you, you bitch, I love you. You run fast, full of anger, but also fear that he will duck back into the house before you reach the corner where you will turn, look up at him and blow him a kiss. Only then will you be able to go forward and live the day instead of crossing it like a windswept marsh.

Hallelujah. It happens as your inner art director must have it happen. He stays at the window, he blows you a kiss back. You skip. You wave again, you call I love you, you turn the corner and you are alone again and you can, you will, rescue the day, this day of days, this first day of the rest of your life, you will carpe diem and realise your deepest, most onanistic dreams as Robin Williams urged the whole world to do, and you sing to yourself a little as you hurry up the road to the newsagent's. Victorious over adversity and it is only nine-thirty a.m.

Only. You are telling yourself that because no one said anyway that it had to be done early, although you are basing your new start on someone you know, someone who Did It and said he was in the café at eight-thirty every morning. He reads the papers, drinks a cup of coffee and then he starts. He only does two hours a day. That's the ridiculous fact of it. It takes up barely more time than other people spend going to the gym. And fuck it, you would be a pathetic human being if you couldn't find that amount of time and remember it's not that he's special.

You go into the newsagent's because that's what the Real Writer always does and you dutifully buy a newspaper, the *Guardian*. Dutifully but with trepidation because you do not read a newspaper every day and you ought, you really ought to be abreast of current affairs, who the Minister of Defence is, who is the President of the Democratic Republic of Congo. Someone called Des? Can it really be someone called Des? Something Kabila? Why does that word come into your head, Kabila? The *Guardian* is a gigantic compendium of facts, affairs, opinion, the whole world to catch up on before you write a word, but what use would a word be if you have no idea what is going on out there?

and it all changes so rapidly, you have to check on it several times a day to keep abreast and you have to read the Comment & Analysis section to see what clever, genuinely abreast people think about the problems, all the problems, and then lay out more problems, which drives you closer to helpless feelings, or gets you sending emails to your MP, though you always forget her name between emails and have to go to www.parliament.uk to look it up again. It is such a burden, such a trap but Other People not only have jobs, boyfriends, children even – and these are the real time-eaters and your own biological clock is ticking as if an IED not an IUD has been implanted in your womb – but they are abreast of the whole world, cresting the wave of it, conversant in the cacophony of it, serene in their views about it and they even have time to read *American Scientist* and know what superstring theory is and lap up the *LRB* like it was *Grazia* instead of big drab pages with no pictures and still write their novels.

Pacing rapidly towards the still-distant café you calm yourself, you bring your head round like a runaway jugger-naut with heroic skill and strength to the Now. You inhale prana, pure healing energy, you remind yourself that you do not have to write a great novel, not even a good novel, that way performance-anxiety lies, you just have to write something.

Something is better than nothing and maybe Yorick or Hamlet or someone said that. You pull round the jugger-naut and fold the *Guardian* and decide as you walk that your brilliant stroke will be reading it not before beginning on your story but afterwards in the afterglow of two hours of Writing. No, something is better than nothing and so your morning in the café will not be wasted although it will take a whole morning whereas the original plan – which works for Other People and Real Writers – had been to do it in an interstice before starting on your real job, a job you rarely start on time anyway and so are always still doing into the evening when he wants to go out and live life again, fuck your brains out, drink you under the table and be a proper spontaneous human being.

Be present in the now, just keep walking one foot in front of the other towards your goal. You are walking down the high street and you see a chemist on the other side of the road and this gives you a brilliant, life-affirming idea that will make this morning, the first morning of the rest of your life, even more brilliant, and so you cross the road, go in and ask for a toothbrush and a travel-sized tube of toothpaste. When you get to the café you will order a cappuccino – with an extra shot of espresso – and while it is being glugged up you will whip into the loo and brush your teeth to stainless pulchritude with the toothbrush and then emerge to your coffee and page one of your new life feeling shiny, fresh and with the ring of confidence. You pay and are turning to go when you see this girl you know, Emma, waiting to the side for a prescription.

– Emma, you say, hi, are you not well?

Emma turns a pale green face towards you.

– Oh hi, she says, it's you. No, I'm really not well. The doctor told me I wasn't to get out of bed, and I said fine because I didn't want to have to explain that Gary left me two days ago and says he's not coming back – her voice breaks – so not only am I quite seriously sick but I'm alone as well.

Emma sits down on a little chair by the prescription counter and everyone in the chemist looks at you to see whether you are going to behave like a proper human being, and you feel you can't just leave, you have to go over and extend the hand of friendship. You don't know Emma that well. You always thought she was a bit unstable, a bit leaky like now, spilling her guts about this Gary and how crap her life is. To a virtual stranger. But you go over and you crouch beside her and you stroke her back and make soothing noises which is a big mistake because the moment you do that Emma starts to cry and the moment she does that you are overwhelmed by a feeling as irresistible as a need to go to the toilet. The irresistible need to make it better.

– Hey, Emma, you say, don't cry. It's OK.

And then because Emma just looks at you with misery eyes through the teary veil, you rush in, saying Can I take you home? which is how you find yourself bombing down the road to the minicab office, bringing a cab back to the chemist – you must be a proper human being! – supporting the staggering, sweaty Emma into it, clutching the little paper bag with Emma's prescription, and driving back to her house. In the cab, you look out of the window and think, it must be about ten a.m. and once again some fucking emergency – leaking pipes, red bills, budgie dead, milk off – has come up and because you have to be a proper human being and not totally egotistical – you have to deal with it.

At the same time as you are looking out the window you feel:

• hate for Emma;

• despair that this virtual stranger has fucked up the first morning of the rest of your life and thereby, quite possibly, the rest of your life, throwing it off course like a butterfly with a wonky wing-beat in Brazil derailing a whole weather system in the North Atlantic;

• hate for yourself for these vile feelings towards someone who can't help being sick;

• anger at yourelf for being such a repressed middle class homosexual (metaphorically) that you have to go into the chemist to get a toothbrush as if you can't write your novel without clean teeth;

• hate for life itself;

• hate for Time's wingèd chariot;

• hate for Gary;

• hate for everyone you know with all their endless fucking problems dragging you down, always needing to talk, eating up your time with some sort of evil desire to accumulate more time to themselves, sucking your time away into their sphere, piling up riches of time for themselves while you, time-depleted, rush back home afterwards with only time enough to keep abreast of the chores that he pretends not to notice need doing, the chores that are every woman's lot.

You look at Emma trying to figure out if she is as sick as she says she is. Because if she isn't, then you have been had. You are a naive bitch too gullible to really have an identity. On the other hand, if Emma really is sick and you are reacting like this, it just shows the really bottomless extent of your egotism. You get to Emma's place and Emma crawls out of the minicab as you find yourself saying, It's OK, I'll pay for this, and handing over a tenner you can ill-afford. You help Emma inside, into bed. Get her water to take her pills, get her a basin with a bit of water and Dettol (why?) in it in case she throws up, make you both a cup of tea, have a fag outside because Emma can't stand the smell and then have to listen for three quarters of an hour, no, an hour while Emma sings you the ballad of Gary the Shit and how sad her life is now and how she's sick into the bargain. Like many women – you're being sexist as well as egotistical – Emma doesn't know how to edit the bilge-like stream of consciousness into palatable and pithy phrases, she lets it all come out willy-nilly, more, she actively draws it out, reaching in with her two hands and dragging out the endless stream of banalities and he said and she saids and I told hims, and you don't know what I went throughs, and trivial, minutely-delineated incidents supposedly proving what a mean shit Gary is. She pulls all this out like it is a big series of knotted-together sheets, pulls them out of her gaping mouth hand over hand till all the dirty linen of this mindless tale of boyfriend banality is out, because she wants rid of it, she wants this cleared away too with the cups and the saucers, preferably by having the other person swallow it all herself while dribbling out the sweet milk of human kindness for Emma to lap up in return.

After an hour of swallowing this you feel you've done enough and enquire how she feels now and she says you've been an angel and she feels much better so can you just draw the curtains, put her phone off the hook and let yourself out. You say no problem and add in a Tourette's Syndrome kind of a way that you will look in on her tomorrow.

Then you leave, you actually get out the front door and stand on the front step, then you sit down on it and put your head in your hands. As you do so you look at your watch and it is eleven-thirty a.m. You have work to do, job-work, survival-work, as well as this secret, important work you've wanted to do since you were twelve, and another day has been thrown on the trash heap that is your history by the willy-nilly irruptions of life, or was it by your lack of willpower and discipline, why are you so pathetic? And you wonder should you just abandon the first day of the rest of your life and try to start again tomorrow, making use of today to make inroads in your real job-work so it doesn't make inroads into your true work tomorrow?

Or – and this seems a far less attractive alternative as the day stoops towards the uninspiring hour of noon – should you just keep going no matter what – because that's what you have to learn, that phrase No Matter What – until you get to the café and when you get there you just sit down,

No Matter What, and word by grimly-won word, write your fucking book?

As if in a trance you get off the step and turn back the way you have come towards the café which is now a good three miles away. Not that far and you need the exercise, you tell yourself positive-thinkingly. You walk with a determined gait, your eyes staring unfocused into the middle distance. You are going to do this in the way you should always have been doing it, the way a man would do it. You are going to do it No Matter What.

You haven't got very far when you hear a sound of feet behind you and a woman in slippers runs up and puts a hand on your shoulder.

– You Emma's friend? she says, catching her breath.

– Yes.

– You'd better come quick, she's taken a turn.

You are just about to run back with the woman like a proper human being when you stop yourself. You harden your eyes.

– I can't, you say, I'm sorry.

– What do you mean you can't? says the woman, she needs help, she's calling for you.

– I can't help her. I've got to start writing my novel this morning, you say.

The stupid words grate in your throat, and you can only say it because of what you have suffered already, because you must do this No Matter What and this is the first test. The woman in slippers looks at you as though you're insane. Then she laughs.

– You what? she says.

– My novel. I've got to begin. You quickly add a useful modern cliche. I'm sorry but this is not my problem.

– Can't you spare even a few minutes for your sick friend?

– No I can't, you say.

– God help you and your kind, said the woman, starting to walk away.

You watch the woman walk away, feeling as though you have betrayed your proper human beingness, refused to shed the milk of human kindness, feeling anguish for Emma who has taken a turn for the worse, while you, her only friend nearby, refuse to heed her call of help because you have decided, quite arbitrarily, that this is the first morning of the rest of your life No Matter What. Emma could die and at the inquest you would be called, and they would ask, Why didn't you go back when she called for you? And you would say, I wanted to get started on my novel. Everyone would stare, Emma's mother and father, Gary her boyfriend, your own mother and father – how have we brought her up? – members of the press, and you would stand there alone, a pariah consumed by selfish desires, by aggrandised ambitions. And the thing is, you think, walking slowly, I haven't even started it yet. It's not as though I have to rush away to finish it, get the last word down before the Man from Porlock turns up to stymie me for ever. I don't even know what it's about yet. I don't even know if it will be any good, and given that it takes most writers twenty years to get good and I've started twenty years too late, what's the point? I'll be too old, in marketing terms, to be read, just as all the good stuff is starting to flow, the clean, pure stuff that I can't get to right away.

You walk on, trying to get Emma out of your body where she circulates like poisoned blood, poisoned blood with thousands of tiny, bloody lips mouthing help me! in every innermost organ of your body. You decide to cheer yourself up by walking along the canal which anyway is a short cut to the café where your new life, somewhat bedraggled, somewhat bloodied, waits for you next to a steaming cappuccino. The canal is green, quite soothing, and you walk along smelling the dog roses and wheaty grasses growing beside the path, and looking ahead you see some boys about thirteen, fourteen, with bikes, gathered round something on the path. As you get closer, you see that the thing is a young collie. The dog is thin, his tail between his legs, and his big, brown eyes are looking up at the boys who are trying to tie him with a bit of twine. As you pass the boys they get the twine round the collie's body and cross it over his chest and front legs, and you look over your shoulder as you walk by and see that the dog is down on the ground, whining, and you stop and say, What are you doing to that dog? None of your fucking business says one of the boys and the other boys laugh. They get the twine round the dog's back legs and they shout, Shove off, hag-face.

You turn and carry on walking towards your novel No Matter What and you have walked about twenty yards when you hear the whining of the dog louder behind your back. You turn again. The boys have picked up the dog and are shuffling with him towards the side of the canal. You watch, every bone in your body urging you to run back and grab the dog. But with an immense effort you say to yourself, This is not my problem, and force yourself to turn and continue walking up the canal. You hear a splash and yelping, awful yelping behind you as you push on up the towpath and a few moments later the boys pelt past on their bikes. From behind, a desperate yelping, increasingly smothered with water, comes from the young dog in the canal. Then silence. Tears start to run down your face.

I am a monster, you say. You walk on, wiping the tears. But I have to be a monster if I am to write my book. And you turn off the towpath and start walking up a side street to get to the café by another route and there on the corner it makes with the high street you see a protest march getting under way and you notice that it is a protest to save the Bushmen of the Kalahari, one of the very protests about which you have written so many emails to your MP, and letters to Ministers in the government of Botswana, and to under-secretaries at the UN and you think about how the Bushmen of the Kalahari will soon be forced to give up a way of life they have followed for 20,000 years because the Botswana government have filled their wells with concrete and chased them away to the cities where they are treated as an under-class. Last chance to save the Bushmen of the Kalahari! shout the protesters, This is their last chance! Join the march! And you veer away to the other side of the road. Hey, sign the petition at least, shouts a protester, can't you just give us one minute to save a whole culture from extinction? Sorry you shout over your shoulder, Novel to write!

You carry on to near the end of the street and here you are, back at stage one, passing the newsagent's, when someone comes out of the newsagent's. It is your mother in her apron, her eyes fixed on her daughter as you approach up the pavement. Your mother reaches out a hand to you, then lets it fall as you pass without a glance. She calls out your name and the sound of it plucks at you because when your mother says your name it sounds more like your real name than when anyone else says it. You keep walking No Matter What, but you can't stop yourself, you look back, and you see your mother standing there wringing her hands in front of the apron. You give her a wave and shout, Sorry Mum! Novel to write!

Now you turn onto the street with the café at the end of it. You are almost there. True it is past noon and this is not going to be the first morning of the rest of your life, but you will, you will ensure that it is the first afternoon of the rest of your life, and as you walk you look around you properly for the first time and you see that the city has been bombed while you weren't paying attention and an army has come rampaging through. The buildings have been reduced to pencils of brick, heaps of rubble and shattered glass everywhere, bombed-out craters, red pools of blood, and your path to the café and the first page of your novel is winding up the middle of them. Between the piles of rubble dozens of wounded and dying people are lying: raped, punched women, old men with their legs blown off,

39

children with bullet holes where their eyes have been and the blood draining from the sockets into the brickdust, burning babies that smell of melted fat and charred meat, and they are all groaning and screaming and calling out to you, Help me! Help me! Oh help me! stretching out their arms and catching at the leg of your jeans, and you look round at them as you walk up the road between them and stub your toe on a little girl lying right across your path in a torn pink dress with blood pumping out of her chest who looks up into your eyes with the last minute of life in her child's eyes and you call out to her as you step over her, Sorry, I've got a novel to write! Sorry I've got a novel to write! Sorry I've got a novel to write! Sorry I've got a novel to write! Sorry I've got a novel to write! Sorry I've got a novel to write! Sorry I've got a novel to write! Sorry I've got a novel to write! Sorry I've got a novel to write! Sorry I've got a novel to write Sorry I've got a novel to write Sorry I've got a novel to write! Sorry I've got a novel to write! Sorry I've got a novel to write! Sorry I've got

STORIES

His ears are full of tears was what I actually wrote. I went back and changed it when I realised. Then I put down my pen and looked out of the window. The church bell sounded once. The half hour. I picked the pen up again and held it over the page. Then I scribbled over what I'd written. Because what was there to say since he hadn't said?

His eyes were full of tears though not full exactly but the intrusion of even a single tear, if that's what it was, a more than usual level of liquid in his eye, unheard of in those eyes that had always looked on the world without tears, or at least, had always looked on the world in my presence without tears, was a bad moment. He turned his face away and stroked the arm of the chair.

The tape recorder ran on on the other arm of the chair. You could hear the tape running over the felt pad and slightly ticking as it wound onto the 'after' reel having recorded – as it travelled over the two tape heads under the 'before' and 'after' reels – nothing. Though not nothing, his silence, which though it was recorded, was, when I played the tape back later in my room, undetectable.

You could hear me chattering at the beginning, trying to put him at ease though he had seemed at ease, settling down in the chair with the glass at his side and the cigarette stuck between the two fingers that weren't like the fingers of anyone else. There were the nicotine stains there just below the top finger joints and the pits on the loose skin below the main finger joints out of which sparse grey hairs grew, and the dried-in-ness of the fingers. They were becoming more and more gnarly, the joints stiffer as if they were solidifying to some kind of lignate substance, and the wavy white scar that ran up the inside of one of them from the base to the nail.

When I was a little girl and sat on his knee, I used to hold the finger and pore over the scar and ask him to tell the story of how he'd got it. I'd go over the whole hand, and the other hand, asking for the story of this scar and then that scar. The one up the side of the hand. I had felt a lot of blood would come out of that scar when it wasn't a scar yet but just cut up the fleshy part of the hand. The curving scar on a thumb. The scars on the back of a hand that were fraying now like old ropes and harder to trace, something maybe to do with the way his hands had developed as he aged, droughty. Very little blood flowing through the hands, and to compensate, the veins had swollen to thick roots between which the skin sunk away and was then wrinkled up again over the bones of a skeleton hand pushing its way out through the flesh. Strong hands though, droughty but tough and able to live on with very little flow of blood. Of course I could never pick the hands up

42

and kiss them now, and I don't think I ever kissed them then when I sat on his knee, so I kiss them with my eyes instead.

Right, Dad, tell me about the time. He looks round. One of the hands comes up and touches the side of his face with shaky fingers. He looks away. The hand goes down and strokes the arm of the chair, just vestiges of strokes. Come on, Dad, don't think about the tape recorder, it's just so I don't forget. What about the time when you were young, you and your friend Macky Leish? I pick an easy one, a nothing story about the time they had the fight with all the Royal Navy boys in their fol-de-rol uniforms. It was war between the Royal Navy and the who exactly? The town boys? The Snakepit boys? Or was it the naval engineering apprentices versus the sailors? I needed the exact details because it could be any of those and still be him.

You and Macky Leish, Dad. Swing the lamp. He looks away and feels the side of his face with the shaky fingers. He hears the call but he doesn't give the response which is and I'll tell you a tale, To you a tale I'll tell, About the man called One-Eyed Dick, And the lass called Eskimo Nell. Sometimes we would say that bit together, me joining in on To you a tale I'll tell. He always did the next bit on his own. He'd take a sip and go When the nights grow cold and a man grows old, And the tip of his nose turns blue (rolling his eyes a bit), When he's bent in the middle, Like a one-stringed fiddle, He'll tell that tale to you. Not getting that last bit quite right. It not scanning. He'll something that tale to you. Aye aye, he'd say, mock old Jock

43

down a pub, if I could write a book. Me not realising for years about One-Eyed Dick and the tip of his whatever turning blue. Till some randy student sent me the Picador *Book of Erotic Verse* in the summer holidays and I hid it in the dog's basket only to come back with the dog and hear roars from the living-room and go in and see the two big chairs either side of the fire, tumbler on an arm of each, my dad and Uncle Sandy, one of them holding the book and them intoning together Four and twenty virgins came down from Inverness, And when the ball was over there were four and twenty less. Them laughing while I was standing there, all of eighteen, maybe wondering if I was doing things they hadn't, back in the day, been able to do at eighteen; or maybe they had.

Which is about all I know about the sex life of my father who wasn't a man who ever mentioned things like that, except then, via the four and twenty virgins, and when I was little with One-Eyed Dick and Eskimo Nell, a ballad which appeared in the Picador *Book of Erotic Verse*, well-known by everyone but me, and which, bowdlerised, was his preface to the tales he had to tell. His Hwaet! which is said like a north-eastern American saying What! but is actually Listen! and which was the signal from an Anglo-Saxon bard, the swing of the lamp that announced the story.

If I could write a book. Sip. Aye aye. Playing old mock-Jock down the pub. Abisa Abisa Abisa, I'd say, probably kneeling at his feet. When small, on his knee. When bigger, at his feet, sometimes resting my arm on the arm of his

44

chair and sometimes my head on the arm. Abisa Abisa Abisa. He'd say, Borracuri Borracuri Borracuri. Which might have been spelt differently or never spelt by anyone anywhere, Borracuri Borracuri Borracuri, a Hwaet! within a Hwaet!, a chapter heading. The adventures that happened there had a circle woven round them thrice. A different kind of adventure happened in Queensferry which was a very different place from Queensferry Queensferry Queensferry and even more from Kwensferi Kwensferi Kwensferi.

The lamp swinging Long John Silverishly above his head, the light sweeping over his head, also silver, and then onto the curtain and then back over the top of his head and over the carpet and then a nest of tables. Then swinging back again. At sea. Come on Dad, I say, what about Hungry Hogarth? He laughs. Faintly he says in Hogarth's voice, No, it stands for Happy Hughie. Shakes his head. HH on the funnel and nobody would sail on her. Looks away. The hand goes up to the side of the face. And the ham and veal pie in the freezer hold, seventy-five yards long? I say. A hundred and seventy-five yards, he says. He looks at me with eyes I can't work out. But that's not the story I want anyway, Hungry Hogarth, it's a little nothing story, just a lead-in. Old Scobie I say. He raises eyebrows like bundles of oose, taps the side of his nose. Was it old Scobie who ran off with the racing cup when you had the betting scam going at the dockyard? He nods. The tape runs over the nicotine-coloured felt pad. It ticks as it winds on the 'after' reel.

If I could write a book, he would sometimes say and shake his head, smiling to himself, his eyes candlelike, half for me, half for himself, what a life I've had, eh? What a life. The tape runs on. Now I'm feeling strange too, sitting on the carpet at his feet, kneeling maybe in a too businesslike sort of a way. I put my back to the arm of his chair so I'm not looking at him and stretch my legs out towards the coffee table. So, Dad, don't you ever wish you were away from this shithole and back in Africa? From behind: No way! The emphatic no that doesn't mean no, that means, if you knew all the things that happened there, if you knew about Abisa Abisa, and Dead Man's Island and how I knew it was time to leave, that first time, when I walked through Joe McMann's house calling his name and no one was there, and I went out the back and saw they'd hanged Joe from a tree. The questions I wanted to ask. What does a man look like hanging from a tree? How did you feel, Dad, to see your friend hanging? Not questions you could ever ask, it was set questions all the way. Dad, how long were you left in the jungle that time with no boat and nothing but the record player and the crocodiles at night? Set question. Were you lonely in Africa without us, Dad? Not a set question. Were you lonely in the months before we came, there and in the other countries? What did you think about, what are you thinking about when I come down the stairs some nights to get water and switch on the light and see you sitting there in the dark with the tumbler on the arm of the chair?

But I don't even want the not-set questions, I want him

to answer the call with his Hwaet! and swing the lamp over the old stories, the set stories that I love and that I'm scared of forgetting the details of, which I do already forget the details of, those stories of his youth. How he was sitting at the end of the jetty on the big brown river up the jungle with the generator and the one record, 'Rhapsody in Blue', which he played over and over day after day, when at last a boat came down the river with a Swede on it and Dad shouted, Hey can you give us a lift? and the Swede said, Jump aboard, and he did, leaving the record going round and round, 'Rhapsody in Blue' fading away among the cicadas and the mona monkeys, and when he got back to the town whose name I can't remember he walked in the office and up to the man behind the desk and socked him one.

Abisa Abisa Abisa. Dad? From behind me, nothing. The sound of the tape whirring over the felt pad and the ticking as it spooled onto the 'after' reel. Then I saw his fingers in claw shape go down to the other arm of the chair and run up and down it, just grazing, vestiges of strokes. I didn't ask him for the story, though it's a nothing story, of once when he was leaving. He never told me that story, my mother told it to me, but anyway I remember it, though I had to have been less than four years old, sitting on the floor playing with my doll when he was about to go for the train that would take him to another ship. I saw him lower his white forehead with the black hair that was swept off it with Brylcreem, and put it in his hands which were resting on his knees. I remember it, or at least I can see it as something that didn't come out of me, him putting his face down in his hands, and I remember I slightly turned away and lifted up my doll and talked into her face.

The voice over the shoulder, that male voice speaking from behind and a little to one side putting stories into my ear, came in the end not from him, but from another one near the end, one who was supposed to be a sort of father, a replay father, though I don't need another father to play back, and he didn't look like a father at all, that other one, more like a grandfather, not like the father I have, my own one with his black hair and his white forehead remarkably unsullied by all the sullying that had been done. Instead one day, coming in the gate to the flats where this other one lived, I looked up at the window to see a young man standing there in trousers and a vest. A young, tall man with such black hair and such a white forehead, doing something, maybe fixing something. When I got in the room the young man wasn't there, so I asked the old one, Who was that? He said nothing, that was his job. OK, I said, your son. He said nothing. Your lover? He said nothing. OK, I said, maybe some kind of workman, a plumber? He laughed. My son, my lover, and my plumber, he said, you have a rich imagination.

Saying nothing was his job though actually he said quite a lot while I lay there looking out of the window and round the room the colour of raw insides, a horrible, maybe meant to be comforting, colour that I hoped wasn't significant. Maybe meant to be womblike, which would have been appropriate in that particular way for the old man

with the fantastic name, especially for his job. It's suprising
how many people have the right name for their jobs like
my sister's dentist, Mr Gummer, and the nurse who lived
next door once called Mrs Death, she pronounced it Dee
Ath, and the old man like a grandfather more than a father,
whose name held the word womb chambered inside the
word tomb, and who himself was dying. Say anything, he
said, whatever comes to your mind. Though it was set questions all the way. What happened to your beautiful white
hair? Not a set question and he never answered it. Then
later on. What's wrong? I can tell something's wrong. And
then much later. So, did it work, is it all going to be OK?
Not a set question and I never asked it.

But I didn't want to ask the not-set questions, not at all,
I wanted to ask the questions with their answers that we
both liked. What's sea in Gaelic? An farraige. What did
Ireland do? She fought every battle but her own. What's
that poem again? And his voice from behind me and a little
to the side would cough gravellishly and say, We are earth-
worms of the earth, And all that has gone through us is
what will be our trace. Or else it would tell me the joke
about Paddy in the village who finally got married, a
terrible joke, or repeat the line of a Take That song as a
bit of advice to me in my fancied predicament. You're gay,
I said. Why do you say that? he said, and his voice quick-
ened behind me as though he thought he was onto something. Because no man who's not gay quotes Take That
songs, specially not at your age. He laughed though he tried
not to, and it turned out probably to be true, since for the

49

funeral he asked for not flowers but donations to a charity that gave shelter to young gay men and women who had been thrown out of their homes for shame. Though that's no proof of anything. The only other person I glimpsed in his flat all those years, way at the end of the long corridor with the other rooms off it, was a very old lady, doubled over and moving along slowly, her hand going out to grasp a doorknob, then opening the door and going through. Your mother? Silence behind me. Or maybe your wife? Silence. It's impossible to tell how old you are and I don't know if she should be your mother or your wife. Should? he said. Or your plumber, I said.

No dreams all those years. I gave him only the one dream, towards the end. At last I've got a dream I said, and it's about you. Silence behind me. We are in a house in the country, I said, and I'm in a room with a clock on the mantelpiece, looking out the window worried about you because you are sick. I want to go through the door to the part of the house where you are lying sick. I know others are tending you, your relatives and so on, but I know I'm not allowed to so I stay where I am, watching the clock and looking out of the window. Then suddenly I realise, the sickness has turned. You've recovered. I go over to the window and I see you come out of the house surrounded by beautiful young men. They hold your arms and put a wreath of flowers in your hair, and lead you through the garden, singing and dancing, to the sea.

His ears are full of tears, a slip which I naturally scribbled out with my pen when writing down the note about my father, which was only a very short note about how he wouldn't swing the lamp and tell me the tales. My father not telling me the stories as I faced away from him towards the coffee table with my voice going back over my shoulder to him, my voice which sounds on the tape recorder too piping and sharp, too impatient, and too English, which is a sharp, cutting sort of accent, though it unEnglishes itself the moment it crosses the border like someone coming back into herself, an animal bride maybe, but something lingers, a vestige, and I lack the native turns of phrase. My voice hurts me when I listen back to my questions, which seem too sharp and piercing, the questions of someone who doesn't understand how to ask questions, and his silence which I can't detect in the strangely loud mechanical sound the tape recorder plays back when nothing is said.

One of the last times I saw the old one more like a grandfather he told me a story about himself. Not the last time because that time, which I for one had no idea was the last time, neither of us said anything at all. But maybe the second or third last time he told me a story, which I was always asking him to do and though he sometimes dropped a line or two like Atalanta's suitor, he never told me a whole story except this one, which was about the time when he was young and he worked for the social services. Maybe he specialised in children, I can't remember now because I never wrote it down till now, but anyway he was sent off to this Orthodox Jewish woman, probably in Stamford Hill where the men have those fetching ringlets and the women have no hair at all, or at least not their real hair on show, only wigs, and not fabulous wigs of sixties singers, but drab sparrow wigs. This woman, a widow, had a son, a problem child who wet his pants and then even started to shit in them, at school, he was ten or eleven years old. So the social sent people round to try and sort him out, but they couldn't. The boy just got shittier and shittier and more bolshy and difficult. Then my one was sent round and he couldn't believe the state of the house, she was no housekeeper, the whole place was a mess. She said something would have to be done about the boy or she couldn't keep him, she needed pills, she was depressed, and life was coming down on her like a ton of bricks. Get me pills! she said. He sat there smoking for a bit and he said, Is there a matchmaker in your community? This is a true story, and it seems those communities do still have matchmakers, or did, twenty or thirty years ago because she said So what if there is? and What does that have to do with it? He said, You don't need anything I can give you, you need a husband. Which got her squawking and when the other social workers heard, got them squawking. This was unheard of, Is there a matchmaker round here? not being a set question for social workers. But he ignored them and her, and got in touch with the matchmaker, and after some to-ing and fro-ing, a man was found for her, unwashed as she was, with no hair, in a slovenly house and with a boy who peed his pants and even shat them. And when he went back to see her after the wedding, there she was, spruce as fresh linen, her house bright as a new pin, the husband sitting pleased as punch reading the paper, and the boy with his clean pants playing football in the street outside the door.

There, he said behind me and a little to one side, I'm giving you that story. I asked more questions about it, but he didn't answer them, even on this remarkably expansive day. I was trying to work out if he had told me the story because he thought it was somehow relevant to me but then he said, You can write that in a book if you want to, I don't mind if you do. I'd never written a book, only wanted to, but I said I would try and find the words one day to write it down. He laughed, thinking back about the woman and the son, and I laughed to show him how much I liked it but thinking, how will I get this down? Knowing that this was important, that this was the story that he wanted to pass on and that that was what I was there for, to pass it on, especially as he probably had no children of his own, I was thinking, because he was probably gay, though that's no guarantee, either for someone old like him or now. I'll write it down, I said, but what I knew was, I could never pass it on, even though writing is always somehow ghostwriting, I couldn't pass it on for him, it could never be written by me.

Though maybe that's what I'm here for, I thought as I went out of his door, to pass it on, to chronicle the stories like some weakly-diluted remnant gene of Homer's is expressed in me that means my ears are ready to receive the old old stories, stories of heroes, of Achilles and Odysseus, also diluted by the passage of time and the inevitable muta- tions from those golden days of yore. My ears ready to receive the stories that they wanted to pass on and anything that they wanted to put away in there as well. I knew I could take them in, but I also knew that, being so weakly diluted, the moment I took them in, the ghosts would start to fade and change, and that's why I got the tape recorder. Abisa Abisa Abisa. Kwensferi Kwensferi Kwensferi. Dad, remember the time you saved the sinking ship? After a while I heard, Yes. An unnatural voice, a tape recorder voice, from behind me and a little to one side. To my right I saw the hand go down in the claw shape of a hand whose joints are stiffening and stroke the arm of the chair.

He didn't tell me the stories, maybe because I was foreign, with more than a vestige of an English accent, and because I was his, and of course because of the tape recorder. He's always been about to die and now his about to dieness is gaining strength over his livingness and soon, and maybe even now, as I write this almost two thousand miles away on an island where the church bell rings — it's just now nine strokes of the twelve of midnight gone — he has died and is going away far down to vanishing, leaving only the skeleton hands splayed out on the arms of the chair. Has it ever occurred to you, people sometimes say to me, that you've married your father? As if this is a terrible revelation, like you wouldn't freely choose to marry anyone who had anything in them of your father with his white forehead and his very black swept-back hair, which my husband doesn't have at all. Why would it be cause for complaint? Since it would mean I could go on sitting at the foot of the chair, or on the knee, or at your side, my legs up over the arm of the sofa, or in a bar, our drinks in front of us, still able to go on listening to the stories that aren't told, and mulling over the few that do come out, when you least expect it, a line or two dropped like Atalanta's apples, and me holding, while we're talking, in some squirrelled-away nook of my body, the non-story of walking with my parents and my sister down Nathan Road in Hong Kong, on Kowloon side. My sister and me are holding hands and made to walk in front, so they can keep an eye on us without us hearing what they are saying, and then my father calls to us and we turn round and see that they are holding hands too – which makes my sister and me look at each other – and beckoning to us to follow them into a bar called something like August Moon, where the barman knows my dad by name to my delight. What we say in the bar I don't know, only how dark it is, the polished table, the clink of ice and the August Moon look of a slice of lemon in a glass of Coke.

A non-story that I've written down for no good reason since it can't mean anything to anyone but me and I don't know what it means to me, only that I've remembered it, while I've forgotten so much. Sitting here now waiting for the church bell to ring once for the half hour, which it will quite soon, and thinking, for a reason I think I know, how I hate Graham Greene. I know it's not fair for me to hate Graham Greene, really hate him, and get up and go raving round the room thinking about him going to Africa to research a book he wanted to write called *A Burnt-Out*

Case. He set off in that mythical writer way, or so he wrote, not knowing anything yet about the story, except some minor thing about the main character, maybe a moustache, and he headed for a leper hospital run by monks in the middle of the jungle thinking he might find what he needed to find the story out there. All of which he wrote about in a book about the writing of the book, *A Burnt-Out Case*, and which I had read. The half hour. One bell.

But what he hadn't put in the book about the book was something that somebody else wrote about in an article, something I read once and which has probably started to fade and change. This somebody worked at the leper colony, which he called a leprosarium, like aquarium or vivarium. He met Greene when he turned up with his notebook looking for colour for a story, background, flesh. He showed the writer round, noted how reserved he was, how nice to everyone, and then told how one evening when Graham Greene was sitting chatting with some of the Holy Fathers and maybe having a gin and tonic, the article-writer rushed in the door and told Greene that several of the local expats had got wind of his arrival and were heading over to show him their manuscripts. You'd be surprised, wrote the article-writer, how many people in the colonies have manuscripts shut away in a drawer. At which point Greene, the article-writer, and the Holy Fathers heard the sound of jeeps pulling up outside. There was no time for Greene to slip out the door, so he opened a window at the back and climbed out, no doubt in a safari suit or at least those beige shorts with knee-high socks and city shoes white men used to wear in the jungle. He headed out into the night and the jungle full of leopards and black mambas and lepers, so he wouldn't have to see 'the wretched manuscripts'. Before he left, the article-writer just had time to apologise to Greene for being put-upon in this way, then the writer was out the window.

Which was supposed to be funny but only made me get up from the desk and go raving round the room thinking damn you, Graham Greene, you collector of colour and flesh. Go to hell, which you unfortunately believe in, and where your punishment for all eternity will be to sit on a burning rock with queues of souls coming up to you, all the damned souls, queuing up to tell you their tales and hand you their manuscripts which you will be fated to read, you non-Dante you, and never recraft in your rather reserved, man-of-the-world style, since you won't be coming back to the world to tell your story in strings of tercets or a novel or a book about a book. One bell. One o'clock.

Swing the lamp. It swings, Long John Silverishly, over the carpet, over his head, also silver, and over the arm of the chair and then the curtain. Then it swings back. The tape moves over the nicotine-coloured felt pad and winds onto the 'after' reel, recording my voice and his silence, which is undetectable when I later play it back and hear the mechanical furring sound that a tape recorder records when no one says anything. And now, in this now, I sit at the desk almost two thousand miles away waiting for the next bell, which will also be one bell, and which I won't hear since I won't be sitting here writing, since he didn't say anything, and since anyway the moment you think of a phrase, think That'll do, that'll start me off, and you put your pen to your paper and start, you know that the story will never be written.

LOVE AFTER DEATH

When I'm dead I rise out of my bones. Out of my bones and up into the air. Air is thin but I am thinner. I rise into the air without displacing a single atom of it and glide, just as ghosts are supposed to do, my tips a bare inch above the graveyard grass. Picture me like that, propelled forward by nothing but thought. Picture me as a kind of Victorian bookplate ghost in a story about ghosts. See me in a white nightie though no one in the story sees me like this or like anything else. Gravity has no hold over me. I can go up or down propelled by the power of thought. My nightie also floats. It's like a nightie underwater, saturated with the substance it moves in, eddying round me like something absorbed in its own dream.

Air cannot pass through iron. I can. When I reach the railings round the graveyard, I pass through them as if iron bars were the insubstantial things, the merely thought. All the things that are real in the most obvious way when I am alive are immaterial to me when I am dead. I pass through the walls of buildings. I pass through people. It is not I who am immaterial passing through them, but they who pass through me.

It's night-time. I pass through lamp-posts and the pools of light they project. I pass through parked cars. I know these streets. It's raining. I turn my face up and feel it dropping through my cheeks. I pass one or two people hurrying under umbrellas or with the collars up around their ears. They don't see me rubbing my bodiless body against the sodden concrete of the housing estate. I cross a road and float up to the Thistle Barbican Hotel. A taxi waits by the entrance, its windscreen wipers clicking from side to side. I pass by along the side of the hotel and I see a cook sitting on a step in a doorway out of the rain. He is smoking a cigarette in his soiled white apron. He's young, in his twenties, narrowing his eyes while he takes a drag. He has blond hair a bit wet with sweat and cooking oil and rain as well. He pushes the hair out of his eyes then sits with his arms hanging over his bent knees. His jaw and throat are mottled where he shaved this morning with an old razor. He is watching orange strands of rain in the streetlight. He sticks his head out of the doorway to look up the street. It's empty. There is the sound of the rain landing on the pavement and further down on the opposite side of the road the lit-up sign of Chicken Cottage with its red and blue chickens. He withdraws his head. He has come from Poland to find a better life and here he is on the step just out of the rain. I come closer. His lips move and I kiss them. Picture it as he can't see it. The young Pole on the step and the ghost bending out of the air to kiss his lips.

60

I go on and float up for a few moments to meet a tree that grows out of the pavement. Its branches and twigs slip through me, I sink down. I go along one street after another. I cross streets without waiting for a red light and let the cars speed through me first one way and then the other way. Astronauts in space feel something like the way I feel. They fly weightless and free through eternity. They look down and see Earth, dear, familiar and far away as they have never seen it.

The rain sets in more heavily. It pours down through me. I glide in under a group of small trees in front of a tower block. A couple are sheltering here. They have been cycling. They are soaking wet and now that they have stopped she is shivering. He stands under one tree, and she's under the one next to him. He gives a short sigh. He is annoyed it's raining, he wants to get home. His programme is coming on. She is happy. They are stuck under a tree till the rain abates. They will have to do nothing, and not for a couple of minutes, maybe for ten, maybe even for twenty minutes. She looks at him when she thinks he won't notice. The rain is moulding round his face and dripping from his chin. This is a rubbish tree, he says. She says, Come in under my tree, it's bushier. She laughs. Come on, come in here. She reaches a hand from under her tree. It's OK, he says, I just want to get back. Why? she says, this is great, come over here and put your arms round me, I'm freezing. He doesn't move. I'm very close to his body. The surface of his skin is tense where the muscles have contracted underneath. The hairs on his arms are standing up and drooping all in the same direction like windblown wheat. I take him into me a little. I feel his heart beating in my chest. He moves out of me suddenly saying, I'm going. He runs to his bicycle with his head down. I can hardly see him for rain. It's rebounding from his back in spurts and filaments. He looks round at her. His face is swimming in rain. See ya! He puts a leg over the bicycle. Don't go, I love you, she says. Come with me then, he says. He rides away and she stays under the tree watching until he turns the corner at the end. She closes her eyes. I kiss her.

I go on, up one street and then another. I see no one, maybe because of the downpour. Then the rain falters, quietens. It slows to siftings that are fanned into shapes by an almost imperceptible wind. There's no rushing sound of it falling now, just the tock tock of drips from leaves and guttering.

A man comes out of a block of flats with a dog. He's a short man with a hard face and greying hair. At night, he walks the dog up and down the streets. He always wears what he's wearing now, a mid-blue zip-up jacket and light brown trousers. He always keeps the dog, a Rottweiler, on a short leash. When I was alive and passed him on the street, he would never look at me. He'd wait till I got near, then haul back on the leash as if reining in an almost unstoppable force.

The dog walks carefully so as not to get too far ahead of the man. He would like to be off the leash, to stop, to sniff, to wander from kerb to shopfront, looking over his shoulder from time to time at the man, showing that he loves the man and doesn't forget about him even while he is busy enjoying the things along the street. He would like to splash through the puddles with the easy gait of a free dog and stop for as much time as he liked beside each rubbish bin and drainpipe, reading the smells he finds there like an old man burying his nose in a newspaper. He cranes his head to sniff a fresh and tiny dogshit. But the man yanks on the leash before the dog's nose can take in the words, maybe the music that can be heard coming out of the dogshit, faint and alluring as if from the earphone of a miniature radio left on the pavement.

I go along with them for a while. We reach a small outdoor car park with hardly any cars. We go in and the man lets the dog off the leash. The dog wants to play, to savour every minute of this time off the leash. But no one else ever comes here except them. There's nothing to sniff, nothing to see except cars. The man doesn't throw a ball or a stick. He says something. Do your needs. The dog lumbers off, wagging his tail. He searches hopefully for signs among the parked cars. The man stands in the middle of the car park with his lips pressed together. More than his wife or his son who is grown up and gone, the dog is what he loves. I sink ankle-deep into the ground so we're eye to eye. I lay my forehead against his forehead. He looks through me. He watches over the low walls of the car park for any threat.

I move through him and away, thinking, in a way this night will go on forever, just as a door opens on St John's Street and girls spill out onto the pavement, all black, all beautiful and talking ten to the dozen. They are chilly in their too-short dresses, secretly happy with their bodies tilting on shoes that are nothing more than arched tongues. Happy, just for tonight, even the ones of them whose selves are pockmarked with anxiety. Beautiful girls with silver eyeshadow and shiny lips, holding glasses, some of them, that champagne spills out of onto the wet pavement. Maybe the dog will sniff it later, wondering what creature that's the perfume of. It's like a miracle has happened on the street taken over by this flock of women who are attending a birthday party in a bar, and who have spilled outside so their young bodies can feel the damp air, and be seen by ordinary mortals, though they wouldn't admit that, not to each other and not to themselves, the bit of them they permit themselves to see. If only you could see yourselves as I can now, as I fly from one to the other of you, bestowing kiss after kiss on this moment, perhaps the apogee of your whole lives, a moment when you rush out onto the street, spilling the excess of yourselves for others to inhale and wonder at, thinking, what creatures is this the promise of? You are laughing crow-laughs, chatting into your phones in loud, excessive voices that are really saying, here I am on this night at the apogee of my youth, dolled up just for the hell of it, waving my small gold bag at another girl for no reason and gabbing into my phone when I'm really communing with eternity. I can't get enough of these girls casting themselves about like largesse, but haughty too, proud girls who don't see, as I do, the boy who veers off the opposite pavement with his eyes out on springs, unable to believe that the night could offer him these cuspy girls, poised on the apogee, talking, stamping, spilling on the pavement.

How old is the boy? Maybe early twenties, a few years older than the girls, but nervy, white as well, skinny as well, and he's gone for one of the fashionable looks of this year, a look that involves floppy minstrel hair, a scrubby beard, and a jumper that's meant to express his soul in green and yellow mohair stripes. He must know, as he comes across the road like a boy in a trance, that there is no way this great swirl of girls who have landed here on their way to some Arctic feeding-ground of rarefied possibilities, will be disposed to hear what he, a boy with a scrubby beard and a green and yellow mohair jumper, has to say to them. It's a doomed encounter for the boy with a hairdo and the girls carried above him on stiff arched tongues. But as the boy weaves between the parked cars towards them, he knows he must hail these girls, must show them that he has seen them crossing the sky like a comet, and get down on his minstrel-trousered knees and serenade them with some indie white-boy tune, a tune that unlocks the secret passageways of beautiful girls, not because he expects – he's not stupid after all – that any one of them would listen to his rendering and take his offered hand, would say, Let's go away from here together, just for tonight, or for forever, just for a drink, or for a life, just to say here we are together on this night under these fantastic stars. He's not stupid, he knows things like that don't happen in real life, but precisely because of that, he must cross the road, getting whiter and whiter as he gets near, he must weave between the parked cars, a nonentity in a misjudged jumper that the girls have not yet registered as they blurt and stamp and spill champagne. He knows that, and he knows that he nevertheless has to expose himself to their ridicule or indifference because he must hail life in the multiple form of dazzling girls before they disappear back into the pub to talk to each other about their periods and their boyfriends.

He hails them. He ranges up and down the kerb shouting to grab their attention and I hear him say: She walks in beauty, like the night of cloudless climes and starry skies and all that's best of dark and bright meet in her aspect and her eyes. And they hear him say, Hey what's going on here? Hey girls, talk to me! They talk louder into their phones and when he weaves closer, deranged by sweaty boldness, saying, One shade the more, one ray the less, had half impair'd the nameless grace which waves in every raven tress, or softly lightens o'er her face, they hear him saying, Can I buy you all a drink? Hey! Hello? I'm talking to you, girls! And they look right through him and turn in their skimpy dresses and delicate jewellery and walk back into the Rising Sun.

He stands there a bit unsteady, feeling the sweat cool off under his arms. He shrugs. I think about the girls as I follow him down the pavement past the meat market where lorries full of carcasses are arriving and then past the hospital, heading east. I wonder if it would be better if they were white girls, which I wouldn't mention the colour of, then. But I leave them as black girls because black girls are what appear tonight as I drift along, maintaining a distance of three-quarters of an inch above the surface no matter what's revealed.

I fly just behind him. I kiss the back of his neck. He goes along the tunnel next to the Barbican and up City Road right by the graveyard and works through a maze of small, empty streets till he reaches Shoreditch High Street, where he turns off and enters a large building with a doorman, a members' club. Someone coming out stops him as he goes in, says Don't do it mate, it's a carnival of cunts in there. Someone who, although he is a member, wants to demarcate himself from the cuntish carnival inside. The boy stares, smiles stupidly, and gets in the lift with three other members. He presses the button for the top floor. I climb the lift shaft ahead of them, soaring up to the pulley-wheel and then down through the members in the lift to the basement where cooks are bent over gas burners up full, shaking frying pans, yelling orders, hashing vegetables and snorting coke. They all yell in various Englishes above the driving beat of a rap track on the stereo. I rise back up the lift shaft and stop in the lift where the four members are staring at the lift doors as if they might open onto the mystery of life.

The doors open onto a rooftop restaurant and swimming pool. Curved perspex walls and a retractable roof protect the diners from the weather. The swimming pool is open to the air. The minstrel-haired boy walks away from the main part of the restaurant. He goes down the side of the pool where tables are interspersed with loungers on which groups of people are lying drinking. He looks around as he's walking, trying to find someone he knows. The eyes he meets assess him and look away. He reaches the far end of the pool and sits on the edge of a lounger by himself. He orders a Mojito and stares into the lit-up water. A group of people come and sit at the table near him, open menus. They want to live, they want to experience what life is at its best before it's over, and they have to hurry and choose carefully from the vast options available because it will be over soon. So they sit at their table and as their first choice this evening from the vast options available they choose Roasted Loire Valley Foie Gras with Braised Carrots and Almond Foam, and also Embers Grilled Artichokes, Barigoule and Diabolo Sauce. I extend above their empty plates, their knives and forks. I have trouble seeing them clearly so I try to hear what it is they are saying. They are talking about their projects. One of them is doing location-hunting for a medium-budget film. One of them is designing sneakers. One has been paid by a Japanese games brand to check into a boutique hotel for a weekend and play the latest computer game. One has been sent by a children's charity to take pictures of children in favelas. One is a model. The first three mock their projects and themselves. The fourth tries to think of something meaningful to say about the children. The model leaves the table for a moment to give her credit card to the waitress. She is embarrassed at how much money she earns and wants to pay for everyone. They look at the cocktail menu like children looking at an ice-cream selection. They order a round of one kind of cocktail, then a round of a different kind. A third kind. The model sips tap water and slides her artichokes onto someone else's plate. I try to see them more clearly but they remain somehow unsatisfying. Maybe I'll see them another night. Maybe they will stay this way forever.

The minstrel-haired boy watches the blue and yellow light moving in the swimming pool. He listens to the sound of voices at the table next to him, their laughter, their ease. He thinks about himself. His mind slides away on the lounge music playing on the rooftop. He brings his mind back, wanting to think about how he can make things go better. His mind replays the worst moment of the scene with the girls and then slides away into lounge music. Something goes past his line of vision and into the water. It's a jet of vomit coming from a boy who has jumped up from the table next to him, still holding a glass half-full of Winter Garden. He drops the glass. The glass breaks and he heaves weakly into the pool again. The particles of vomit separate in the water. Some sink, drawn down by the suction of the pool's filters. Others float, possibly bits of braised carrots and crud that was once almond foam. The other people at the table stare as if they are watching a TV. The boy gets down on his knees with one hand on his stomach and the other round his throat. He retches like a lamb retching. The minstrel-haired boy stands up. Cunt, he says. He walks away to the other end of the pool and back towards the lift. I enter the pool so I can face the drunk boy on his knees. My nightie floats in water and vomit. I hold his head. His lips taste of acid and peach schnapps.

I let myself be drawn by the power of thought into the air above the rooftop restaurant and float away over the streets and buildings. I need to drift for a while, far away from people. I stay up in the sky a long time, thinking nothing, feeling low cloud moving through me and the lights of the city reflected off the underside of the cloud as well. Then I feel myself drawn down. I could resist but I drop down and enter a small terraced house. A man is sitting in an armchair in front of a TV where the picture is just vanishing. He moves to the front of the chair using the arms to manoeuvre. He pulls a Zimmer-frame towards him. He is light and thin. A teenage girl could lift him to his feet with one hand. He sets his feet against the bottom of the chair and pulls himself up with the help of the Zimmer. He is shaking all over. The Zimmer keeps him upright. He works his way towards the door and goes through to the hallway. There is a chairlift at the bottom of the stairs with its seat and its arms folded up. He makes his way to it, seeing by the streetlight coming in a pane of glass above the front door. He unfolds the two arms on the chairlift, then the seat. His hand creeps up the wall and rests there for a bit, trembling. He works his way round till his back is towards the chairlift and lowers himself halfway. He stays like that for a moment then lets himself go.

The chairlift whines and begins to rise. The man holds his slippered feet together to one side like a lady perched to take her tea. His slippers touch the edge of each step as he goes up. He reaches the top and hauls himself out of the chair. He stands shaking. Goodnight, Geoffrey, he calls. He makes his way along the corridor with another Zimmer. He opens the bedroom door. A voice speaks clearly in the dark. Goodnight, Alan. He goes through the door into the bedroom. There's a bed, a wardrobe and a plastic box of incontinence pads outlined in faint light from the street. The bedclothes have been turned back ready. He undoes his trousers with strengthless fingers and somehow pushes them off. He leaves the old pad by the side of the bed and works a new one half-in the side of his underpants. He can't get it to go all the way in. He leaves it as it is. He turns on his side still with his shirt and cardigan on and puts his head on the pillow. After a bit he twists his legs up onto the bed with the help of his hands. He pulls the bedclothes over. He lies with his eyes open and I stay there looking into them. I want him to know I'm here. But he can't see me. His breathing becomes slow. His eyes close and I kiss them.

I go through the wall. Another man is lying there in his bed. His eyes are closed but he's left the bedside light on. There's a book on the bedcover. He is old, not as old as the other man and not as thin. He looks as if he'll go on for some time. His mouth sighs in the pillow. He puts his hand out and feels for the light switch, switches it off.

I kiss him and go out through the window. I go down the streets till I reach the graveyard and pass through the iron railings. I pass through the tombstones feeling the cramped cold of stone as each one enters me, then leaves. I find my grave, the one I've chosen. Small birds are already pecking on it, looking for seeds. I see their eyes as tiny budding breasts in their feathered faces and I let myself put that in though I know I'll take it out later. I see the birds far away but dear, familiar. I love them with a love that has no shadow. I love them and all the others that I've seen tonight in a way I can't love when I'm recoupled to time's line, when the others see me as I see them, when I'm alive as they are and have to move with them again along time's line hour by hour, when I put down the pen that my fingertips have held a bare inch above the surface no matter what's revealed, and sink back down into my bones and up into air of this world.

YOUR SOUP-CAN CHANGED
THIS COUNTRY[1]

So much has been written about Andy Warhol and even by
Andy Warhol. The *Diaries*. 'Noble in its obsessiveness': *The
New York Times*. 'A remarkable literary achievement': *New
York Magazine*. (He dictated them down the telephone.) The
Diaries are pretty famous. I guess because they are studded
with the names of famous and glamorous people. Plus they
are sometimes kind of mean about famous and glamorous
people. Andy was a kind of Proust of the sixties. By which
I mean he just loved to be in on the social action of the
day, 'where it's at', as they used to say. Conveniently for Andy,
a lot of where it was at was wherever he and his entourage
were. He never went anywhere without a dozen people. A
cordon of jester-bodyguards, tripping, nodding out and

1. Hackett, Pat, ed. *The Andy Warhol Diaries* (Time Warner, 1991). Entry
for Saturday, October 29, 1977: 'She was on *As The World Turns*, and now
she's Phoebe in *All My Children*. She was Orson Welles's first wife in *Citizen
Kane*. She's very good. The first thing she said when she saw me was, "Your
Soup Can changed this country." '

73

speeding over the limit. A cordon of overgrown adolescents with attention-deficit disorders clamouring to impress this evil indulgent Father Figure. God were they glad to trade in their real dads for Andy. Even the way he made something out of old hair. Imagine if your own dad was going grey and he said to himself, 'I'm not going to fight it. I'm going to journey to the other side of grey.' Your dad with a bowl cut, and instead of Just For Men, a bleach bottle. (I am aware, in Andy's case, of the wigs.) Your dad in stripes that are not pinstripes or baseball stripes. Andy took that Breton fisherman's T-shirt and made it cool. If it had been cool already, wearing it would have been redundant. Andy's speciality was the opposite. He took the redundant and made it cool. Et cetera, et cetera, et cetera. His whole thing was like proto-punk. A teenage kick in the teeth to all the adults. Kicks in all the meanings of that word aimed by Andy, the first Father Figure Eternal Adolescent Amen.

Andy started out doing illustrations for fashion magazines. Things like shoes. That's key to understanding the Warhol approach. He'd blow up images of like a plane crash, someone being shot and falling out of their car, a car smash-up with bodies, the electric chair and so on, he didn't take the pictures. He appropriated them. He just flicked through newspapers, cut out the pictures and blew them up. So simple, so devastatingly clever. We all know now that art is not about technique, being able to do, make, anything. Making is over in the modern world because now we have manufacturing. Manufacturing is the making of now. Manufacturing, though, is usually followed by a bit of manipulating to show just enough that the tradition of making is encapsulated in the object. Otherwise it's harder to say it's Art, that word like a bottle of liquor where all the liquor's been drunk leaving just a slick of colour in the bottom. Or maybe you imagine the slick of colour. Andy blew the pictures up and then he screen-printed them with pretty colours. This was the part where the art came in, if you could call it that. That's not meant as a derogatory remark, by the way. It's a question. Could you call it that? Thing is, and Andy supposedly taught us this, the question is redundant. Once again, cool goes to redundant, redundant goes to cool. Remember those trajectories.

Andy was manipulative, so they say, in life. I've heard it said, and I can't personally comment on the truth of this, that the Reynolds Wrap wallpaper they put up in the Factory wasn't just a neat decorating idea. It was a practical solution like a wipe-down surface. It was there, right at hand, in case the Factory folk ever ran out of foil for smoking purposes. Check out the pictures, see how shredded and torn that wallpaper was in parts. Andy liked to watch people disintegrating around him. But you'll notice that ol' Shark Eyes never crumbled.

As in life, so in art, I suppose? He really did not move things much further than from A to B and back again. His contribution was to do less art to an appropriated image than ever before. You get a Campbell's soup can and you screen print lots of copies of the can. Well, actually, you get other people to do it for you. It's worthless and art is worthless and the joke is people think it's better art than all the rest for saying that and they pay through the nose for these

Campbell's soup cans, made something other than only Campbell's soup cans, made into authentic Andy Warhols – whatever that is because there is no authenticity to Andy Warhol and I mean that as something he would have regarded as a compliment – by some arbitrary symbol, numbering or whatever, his signature for God's sake.

In later years he took to signing cans themselves. My niece was taken to some exhibition in Miami in the eighties. She was just a kid who played softball, she knew nothing about Andy Warhol and she said he was sitting there on a barstool, this weird-looking old man, and people were lining up with cans of Campbell's soup, getting him to sign them. All condensed tomato, highly specific. She was bewildered. Why? she asked me. Is he in the Campbell's soup commercial? I suppose so, I said. Ha ha ha ha ha. He was a stand-up really. God he would have loved all this globalisation of big brands. What a goof.

All very well and good, all stuff you know, right? And what can I add to this pile? Don't worry, it's not going to be another 'I met Andy' style revelation. I never met Andy face to face. Which is crazy. Because we shared this thing in common. Well, in the end, it was much more than that. In the end, I'd say, his communication with me – he picked me – was his most profound, his most private, perhaps, some would say, his most embarrassing communication. It was dynamite. Or then again, perhaps not. With Andy it's just so hard to know. Read the *Diaries*. Page after page after page. It becomes shocking, the blandness. You are flicking through it and you're thinking, could anyone really be this shallow? He was this smooth manufactured surface: The Undead. That was what he projected. And because he was undead, he could play with life. Read the bios, all that exposé/hagiography hype. What's worse is that with Andy you know he's alive even though he looks dead. It is no surprise that his name breaks down to War and Hole.

– Where's Andy?

– They put him in the war hole.

– So he's dead then?

– No. It's worse. He's probably still alive down there.

So there we go. Trash, art, celebrity, cynicism, drugs, pretty vacant, gaping warhole. All the modern stuff. Andy worked it. As a result he's probably the most famous American artist of all time and he's rated. The one thing about being an artist today, I would say, is that you have to be willing to throw your life away, to spend it for a gesture. Not for Art; for a gesture. By definition it's got to be something trivial. Being an artist today is like how it was to be a gentleman in Pushkin's day. Art is the modern equivalent of the duel.

For years, Andy used to rent my grandmother's house out on the island. During the summer, on and off, and at odd weeks other times. I could never second-guess when he'd want to go. I used it myself at Christmas and at Easter. Plus I used to go out there, when I was young and doing my thing, for a month at a time. It was lonely out there but no one bothered you. My mother left me the house when she died and every year I nearly sold it. I was broke for a long time. Every year I held on to the old house just for another year. And every year Andy would be back out there again, unknown to anyone as I discovered later.

I'd been to art school with someone who later hung out at the Factory. He would ring me up and say, hey, Andy needs to get out of town can he rent your old house? Later on, I just let him have it for free. He was famous, it didn't seem right to ask for money. By the time he was famous I thought maybe I should meet him and then I also would have an Andy story to tell. It was kind of what gave a point to your life back then to have an Andy story. I asked Vince about it. He said sure, why not? but he stalled. He'd pass on messages from Andy about how great the house was, or, could I get the furnace fixed? About how he was dying to meet the grandson of the woman who grew those trees shaped like giant chickens. Then I'd say, hey Vince, come on, he's been going out there for like five years, can't I just come by the Factory? I want to meet my tenant. Though he had long since ceased to pay for the privilege. Vince said that ever since that crazy chick shot Andy he wouldn't let just anyone come to the Factory. I said that seems fair so let's meet out.

Meetings were set up after interminable arrangements. Sometimes these were handled by Vince, but later on by a woman called Angst. I'd turn up at the appointed hour at an art opening or a bar, a fancy hotel or a dive – it was always different – and I'd wait and wait. Andy would never show. Sometimes I'd get phone calls from Angst letting me know he was held up, gee he was sorry, he'd be there in an hour, he was just leaving Halston's, don't go away, he's

78

not feeling good, he would have to postpone, he sends his best regards but he has to work on through the night. That kind of thing. Next day there would be flowers – always those flowers that look like giant, spray-painted daisies – at my apartment. And you know, the thing is, after a while, it began to get to me. It was like he was playing with me. I mean he put pizza delivery boys in his movies and he wouldn't meet me for one drink and I let him live in my house for Chrissake.

The last straw was one day I was supposed to meet him at Max's Kansas City. You've read the bios, you don't need me to tell you about Max's. Listen, Angst said, he says he is coming this time and he has something important to tell you. Like what? I said to her, I was kind of pissed by this time. Just turn up, he's not gonna spoil it by letting me tell you what he's gonna tell you, is he? I went down to Max's at nine-thirty like Angst told me and they said, sorry, Andy's not here yet, can you wait in the front. They wouldn't even let me into the back room because it was reserved for Andy and guests and I wasn't on his damn list. I sat in the coat-check area with my raincoat on and one by one giggling kids and pop-eyed screwballs went by me headed for the back room. I sat there for two hours and then I got up and left and I never tried to meet Andy again. Two months later Angst rang and said could Andy go out to the island? I said sure. The guy was Andy Warhol for crying out loud.

After he'd been to the island I'd go out there and wander from room to room looking for evidence of Andy and the wild Factory kid ways. I never found any. I looked every-where. I thought maybe at least some graffiti on a wall maybe by the telephone, maybe just telephone numbers, the particular telephone numbers those people would have used. One thing. I found a stripey Breton fisherman's T in the derelict boathouse. To this day I wonder: what was Andy doing in the boathouse? And why did he take his T off?

But then, as I found out a couple years after he died, the Factory kids never knew about the island. He never went anywhere without a dozen people. But it turned out he did go somewhere alone. I guess people thought Andy was at Montauk or staying with C.Z. Guest or Mick Jagger or someone when he wasn't around. But he wasn't, he was at my grandmother's house out on the island.

I guess, looking back, I let Andy manipulate me the way he did the Factory kids and the newspaper photos. I suppose I let him do it because I was an artist too. I had gone to art school all fired up and ready to follow my dreams. It's a particularly American disease. Andy realised early on it wasn't about following any dreams, it was about fashion. You know his first drawings were copies of Maybelline ads? Mine were sketches of boys I knew, and seascapes. I was young and I was good. I just wasn't fash-ionable. I got zilch reaction to my paintings, and in the end, after quite a while, you know, of pure suffering and rejection, throwing myself like some bitch dog at the gate, I gave up and went to work in a restaurant. Now I have the organic French bakery and it's made a lot of money. We brought the stoneground, open-fire-baked sourdough to this country. Keep moving forward. Andy used to say that. It's in the bios.

Last year we sold my grandmother's house. This woman wanted to turn it into a boutique hotel. It was a wrench but then I thought, aw let it go, you never go up there any more and you and Pete could use that money to expand the bakery. After it was all through, the hotel woman called up and said, OK, we disposed of the furniture like you said but I just want to check, did you mean for us to get rid of the paintings as well? My grandmother had been fond of old sporting prints. Years ago I'd taken a couple down and tried to sell them in town. Turns out they were cheapo modern reproductions. Oh, you mean the sporting prints, I said. No, said the hotel woman, I'm not talking about those, I'm talking about the ones in the attic; and they're paintings not prints. Oh, I said. I really had to think. I hadn't been up in the attic for years. Whatever was up there was stuff I didn't need to think about any more. Baggage. She was hanging on the line and I had to make a decision. I decided, keep moving forward. It's OK, I said, just give them to the houseclearers like the other stuff.

It was raining in New York that day. I made some coffee and read the paper, then I ran over to the bakery to sort out some deliveries of flour from France. I was in the back office there, going through the invoices when it was like someone flipped a switch. I grabbed the phone. The paintings, I yelled at her, have you thrown out the paintings? We're just getting them down now, she said, I wasn't going to throw them away, they're too beautiful. Thank God, I said. Stack them in the music room and I'll be on the island tonight.

I got in the car and I headed out of the city. I was shaking, my mind racing. Driving constantly I was able to get across to the island on the last ferry and around ten I was driving up to the house. The hotel woman met me at the door and offered me a glass of wine. I said, wait, do you have any champagne? She looked surprised and I laughed. I should have brought champagne, I said, this is worthy of, at least, some amazing vintage of champagne. This is like when you've been looking for the *Titanic* for twenty years and suddenly you locate a hulk on the seafloor and you send down your robotic submarine and out of the deep it brings up these pieces of history. Wow, she said. She said she didn't have champagne but she had some prosecco in the icebox and we could share some. We went into my grandmother's kitchen and poured two long chill glasses and then she led me to the music room.

She switched on the light and there were the paintings stacked against the far wall, about twelve of them, covered in dust sheets. I put the prosecco on the floor and pulled off one of the sheets. It was a portrait of a woman, in oils. She was naked to the waist leaning forward on a chair. I tipped the painting forward. Behind it was a landscape abstracted into big brushstrokes of cloud and earth and sea. Next to it was another oil. A bed stands in an empty room. On the bed two naked men are lying asleep. By the foot of the bed there's a crumpled slipper. It was one of the bedrooms upstairs. There were lots of studies of the sea below the house. The paintings of human figures were particularly poignant, built up from layers of translucent glazes in the old style.

I dropped the dust sheet. You must be so happy to have found them again, the hotel woman was saying. You were an artist when you were younger, right? Yes, I said, no. What I mean is, yes, I was an artist when I was younger, but these are not my paintings. These are paintings by someone else. Someone close to you? she said. Someone famous, I said slowly. Someone that no one in the world would think ever painted like this. The hotel woman lifted the corner of a dust sheet to take a peek. Wow, she said, who could that be? Andy Warhol, I said. The soup-can guy? she said. You're telling me the soup-can guy painted these beautiful things? I know it sounds crazy, I said, but he used to rent this house and come up here alone. No one else ever came here. It can't be anyone else. This is historic, you know. Jeez, said the hotel woman, these must be worth a fortune, but wait a minute. She started flicking from one to the other back and forth, examining. Aw, it's too bad, she said, he hasn't signed them. I picked up my prosecco. That's the thing, I said, that guy was ready to sign soup-cans like he was signing cheques. In his case, not signing the paintings was like not tainting them. That's the gesture that speaks volumes. I raised my glass and proposed a toast. The hotel woman got her glass and we clinked. To Art, I said. Yeah, to Art, she said, to the real thing.

I have the paintings here at the apartment now. I have to decide what to do with them. Pete says we should contact Warhol's estate to authenticate them, but you know what? they wouldn't be very happy if their Warhol brand turned out to be a different brand altogether. It'd be like Pepsi actually turned out to have been Coke all along, or worse, Château Margaux. Better to let them come to us whenever. Word is getting around. People ring up and ask to come see the lost Warhols. I've let a few key people in. They were blown away. Journalists have started ringing. I have to be careful, I have to think how I'm going to reveal these beauties to the world. I remember the time Warhol made the arrangement to meet me at Max's Kansas City, how Angst said that Andy had something to tell me. And I wonder, was it this? But he chickened out. It was too personal, too dangerous. He must have known I'd discover them one day. He picked me to be the one who would reveal the truth. I guess he picked the right guy.

NOVEL

I had a brilliant idea. I headed down to the George and nursed it over a pint. Then I went up to the bar and got a bit of paper, found a pencil in a pocket and jotted down the basic structure. It took an hour in between chatting to the girl behind the bar, Cat. I've always fancied her in a so-what kind of a way. Black hair, built like a baguette. She's got some kind of eastern European accent. I started with a shape not dissimilar to hers. It looked like this:

But the structure continued to develop and ended up looking something more like this:

Luckily I've kept this germinal bit of paper in which you see the seed of an idea begin to sprout, mung-bean-like. Watered my brain some more. Found the structure led by the arcane process known as creation to a group of keywords:

emission vasodilation glaud prostrate
plasma prepuce duct
sac oxygen debt defæcation cloaca
frenulum labia minora vesicles
villi meatus tubule
sympathetic trunks ingestion fascia
labia majora sphincter
error signal homoeostasis

I just needed a title and I would be ready to start. I find it's always useful to have one, like an arrow pointing towards a mineral deposit. It came to me as I went up for another pint. *Somastream*. Growing out of stream of consciousness, a mode that was well played-out by the end of the twentieth-century. And soma. Soma is Greek for body. I wanted the novel to go beyond consciousness, beyond the unconscious and to exist at the level of the body processes through a twenty-four-hour timestream.

I also liked the play on sodastream and the word soma as used by Huxley for the name of the drug that kept everyone tractable and blissed-out in one of his novels. My title sounded like it could be a new kind of recreational drug. Cool.

Bart came in. He was working on an installation for an

exhibition in October, melamine boxes. The main box was to be almost as big as an average room and there were others, low oblongs, and narrow towers that went way up, and lots of shoulder-height uniform rectangles. He'd come in to think what colours he was going to have them made up in. He had the Pantone sample chart with him and we spent a good half hour picking colours. The concept was 'sunset'. He'd taken that great classic of landscape painters and Kodak snappers and was redoing it as sculpture. Cool.

He asked me what I was up to and I told him I was working on a new novel, *Somastream*. He loved the concept.

'I could leave it just at that, the body defining the total narrative but I want to embed it in the novelistic tradition at the same time. I mean, don't get me wrong' – I cadged a smoke off him – 'The organs and their like, functions, and then when they go through breakdowns – the breakdowns will be good – that all makes a carnivalesque structure in and of itself, but I think the body stuff will be brought into sharper focus if I counterpoint it with a basic story perceived from the perspective of the mind.'

'Like what story?'

'Well I was thinking of using one of the great novels, *Anna Karenina* or something. *Frankenstein* might be good. Or maybe one of those sanatorium novels, Thomas Mann.'

'Nah mate, too obscure,' Bart said. 'If I were you I'd use telly.'

Which pissed me off because I was thinking of that but I didn't want him to know. He always pretends he writes my fucking novels.

On my way home I ran through some telly programmes but the thing is, the thing that worries me as a modern writer is, I hate fucking telly. It's boring. I thought: sitcom? *Frasier*? *Friends*? I needed one fuck-off story. I thought for a bit about Jesus, but I needed a love story. *Gone With the Wind*. I'd never read it. I could check out the DVD.

But the problem with stories is that they're so fucking conventional. Much better, I realised, as I was lying in bed smoking, to use another form altogether. It came to me out of the dark. I'd take a medieval courtly love track. Courtly love was all about lofty love that was unrealised in the body. It would be good counterpoint for the somastream to grind against. Then I remembered Abelard and Heloise. Abelard was a monk or a priest or something and he fell in love with the scholarly Heloise, a virgin. They ran off, fucked. They were caught, she was put in a convent and he had his balls cut off. They stayed apart, still in love, learning Christian virtues and writing to each other. Bodily explosion followed by bodily renunciation.

Next day I ordered *The Letters of Heloise and Abelard* from Amazon and loads of medical textbooks, and anything else on-screen that took my fancy that was about bodies. I like that scientific language of medical textbooks. That was what I told Jim when I got through to him:

'Jim? got a job for you. I'm doing a new piece called *Somastream* . . . ' I explained how I wanted to tell the story of Abelard and Heloise from the point of view of their bodily functions and contrast it with sections on how their heads saw it as a high-flown love done in medieval courtly lyrics.

'I want the *Somastream* stuff done in a lingo that mixes medical textbooks – I'm having some sent to you – and a more visceral, flowing description of what happens in the body. I want all bodily functions, this is the point, right? Leave nothing out. Joyce already did the shit of everything going through the mind. I want shit literally going through the body. Literally. Or, like, imagine the chapters when they're having sex, seen from the point of view of the neurological pathways, the reproductive organs, the building blood pressure. Get me? Then alternate with shorter sections done as a modern take on the style of troubadours about the pure, like, more platonic love of Abe and Heloise – shit's also in the post. What do you think?'

Jim said he didn't know what I was on about and he didn't think he could do it. This was a highly skilled job, I'd have to go to New York for a big job like this. I said fuck that, Jim, you're the best and you had that six-month stint editing medical textbooks, it's a doddle for a fabulator like you. I knew what he was after. Dosh. Tons of it. They flay you, they really do. And all they have to do is construction. I offered him 25 per cent more than for *No-one*, and he hummed and hawed. He came back with 'thirty percent more and I'll need a one-off research fee on top.' It's all money, money, money. Makes you sick. I agreed. Thirty per cent more per word than for *No-one* and a whopping great research fee for taking in the relevant styles. Told him I had a deadline, six months hence, and he should deliver a section every two weeks. I was thinking 40,000 to 50,000 words depending on how the soma chapters worked out. The idea of all that cash got his juices flowing. He said he thought he could make the deadlines.

After the first week I rang him to see if he'd read the books. He was still reading them. Said he was really getting into *Maingot's Abdominal Operations*. He thought he would need the next week just for practising and working up the two styles and asked for some more, specific books on the two subjects and I ordered them from a medical bookshop and some academic place in Oxford.

I phoned my agent, Colin, and told him the gist of what I was working on. He was blown away.

'Christ, Phil,' he said, 'you're on to something major here. This will piss everyone off. Can you do me a synop?'

'Cool,' I said, 'Give me a week.'

I spent every evening that week at the George scribbling like a maniac on napkins, sleeves, tabletops, and finally took it all home one night and banged the synopsis out on the Mac. I had Jen, my graphic design bint, take it to the bridge with fuck-off graphics and realtime shorts of abdominal surgery and that really close-up slick 'n' slurp porn. I emailed it to Colin and went into an orgy of reading the *New Yorker* and watching *The Learning Zone*, the only thing on telly worth the watch.

Colin rang three days later.

'It's superb,' he said. 'You're a fucking nutter. How long before I get a sample chapter to put with it?'

I told him I would get something to him within the

next couple of weeks. Of course Jim, the bastard, was late. He's always fucking late. 'It'll be with you in a fortnight'. How many times have I somehow believed that? Fortnight comes, never fucking ready is it? I had to bug him and bug him – he left the answerphone on screening mode for another two weeks. Finally I blew it.

'Jim? It's fucking emergency break glass. I've got Colin breathing down my neck. Whole deal's off unless I get chapter one in the inbox tonight. Hear me now.'

An hour later I got a Word attachment with the first bit of text.

It was shite.

I picked up the phone.

'Jim?' I said. 'Jim, pick up. Listen, this is really interesting, but you haven't got the language right and Heloise is like a stereotype. I want her darker.'

He picked up.

'Oh hi. This thing has been a nightmare. Haven't slept more than four hours a night for weeks.' Whinge whinge whinge.

He was off, telling me it's all very well saying you want it like this, you want it like that, but it can't be done, moan moan moan. He always does this, thinking he can get away with something passable because I don't understand the mechanics of how it works on the page. On the page, that's his mantra.

'Look, Jim, I've red-penned this draft, plus I think you should come round here with all the books and I'll high-light the bits of medical writing I like and then I want the cuts to be more abrupt to the courtly love parts – but not highlighted by chapter breaks, OK? That's old. I never told you to do that.'

'You never told me to do any—'

'Jim. You're losing it. Calm down. Get your arse over here and we'll go through it.'

He came over and we spent a whole day in my studio with books all over the place – me getting carried away with marker pens, scissors and post-its rabbiting on about the extreme language in which we encode bodily processes. I really threw myself into it, gave it all my passion.

'"As the pressure builds in the seminiferous tubules the sperm are pushed out into the vas derens." No. No! I said use medical textbook lingo. Not write a medical textbook. Give me the the drama. "With each thrust, the Sertoli cells pump another squirt of fluid into the seminiferous tubules, carrying the sperm forward like matchsticks on the surging tide." Much better. Get it?'

Jim shrugged. 'Too melodramatic.'

'Jim – since when was that your division? Just put the shit down. I want sperm. I want cell division. I want the knife-edge drama of killer T-cells battling evil little cunts of viruses. I want the internal scream of the nerve-endings when Abe's balls are hacked off. Man, what a scene to do from the penis's perspective.'

Jim sagged forward on the floor.

I started bugging him a week later, because Colin was bugging me. Two weeks after that, I got a first section of

6,000 words and it was still all over the place. You'd be amazed, when I'm telling the idiot exactly what to do, how he can go right off and end up doing something else.

I got him round again.

'Look,' I said, 'I'm here, telling you exactly what I want, and you don't give it to me. Why?'

Jim ran his hand through his hair. It's thinning.

'Yeah right,' he started. 'It's fine you telling me you want it like this, but when you are actually on the job trying to make it come out like that, there are all kinds of like production issues that make it impossible.'

'What the fuck are they?' I asked.

'Look, for you the page is blank, a void. Well it isn't. It's full of these invisible molecules. When I write a sentence, these molecules exert a kind of pressure on the words that wants to push the text in a direction you couldn't have predicted before you put it down in black and white, right? It's like Brownian motion or something, all these words bumping up against each other and the resistance of the page as well, pushing each other around, refusing to stay in the relations you had planned. By definition, it's unpredictable.'

Again, typical. He gets above himself and thinks because I can't conjugate verbs or whatever, I'm a duh. Like spelling or whatever makes you a writer.

I got up and fetched him another Becks. I lit a tab.

'What are we talking about here, Jim? Words. If I can explain the concept to you in words, point you to exactly the kinds of nuts and bolts – words, sentence structures, verbs, adjectives – for each bit, tell you what each bit is about as well, what's to go wrong? Christ, architects don't have to build the fucking building.'

Jim shook his head, all doleful. 'Every word has its properties,' he murmured. 'Every little word has a different weight, form, tendancy. And when you fling them on the page, they kick off like chemicals. Shit happens.'

I ignored this smokescreen. 'Get it denser.'

'I'll have to use a different vocab.'

'No,' I said. 'You can get it denser with the medical vocab.'

After a lot more of this shit, Jim said OK, but he would need another fortnight to redo the first bit. Oh and the canny bastard wanted an extra payment of a thousand squid for what he'd suffered so far. Over and above. Sometimes I think I should do some sort of creative writing course so I can weld and mould the bits myself. But why go backwards?

I'll cut short your pain. It took eight more drafts over fourteen weeks to get that first section serviceable. I'm being grudging. It was more than serviceable. OK, it wasn't the Kabbalah of shining letters I'd given Jim the fucking sacred instruction booklet for. But what the fuck, it flowed. Out of the inertia of those medical textbooks he extruded this dense but kinetic layer of words that plopped and churned like a chyme from which cerebral choux of triolets and tornadas ascended like souls leaving the body. Jim is a good craftsman. A really good craftsman.

Colin pronounced just one sentence on that first section. 'You're a genius.' His plan was to send it off with the synopsis to three top publishers that week and instigate an auction.

He rang back the next day to tell me the packages had gone out. 'You're evolving your voice. You're creating new territory for the novel. Who's knocking it up for you?'

I told him Jim.

'Good little fabulator,' said Colin. 'No rough edges, precision-made. Who else uses him?'

I told him. None of the big writers know about Jim, they all use places with better research equipment and facilities. But Jim's like an old-fashioned artisan. Once he gets into it – that's what takes the pushing and shoving – he does the measurements, runs through the experiments, fusses over detail. He's a treasure.

Needless to say, Bart's show came up long before *Somastream* found a publisher. For him it's so easy. Still, let's not get grudgingly work ethicy about this. It looked good, the saturated colour blocks of glossy melamine dominating the usual huge, white former-industrial space. All the little people milling about with drinks in their hands in and out of this pixelated sunset or whatever. And so impenetrable. I heard Bart talking about it to some journalist and watched her catch all the balls.

'I wanted to drain the overblown idea of "sunset" like you drain a swamp,' he said. 'I've returned sunset to the twenty-first century, stripped.' He gives good head.

The after-show party was at the George and then we headed out to Boombox for a bit of a groove. Everyone was there. Bart is going places. At Boombox he came up to me and said he'd got the idea for his next thing already, watching Cat dance. There she was, bobbing from side to side at the edge of the crowd with some would-be artist wanker. They never want to fuck writers, by the way. Books – where do they end up? Bookshops. Not very sexy is it? Not very huge white industrial space. Books are missing something and I aim to find it.

Anyway, hangover. Like, hangover. But by the afternoon I was down on Jim like a pile-driver wanting to know where section three was. The day after that the auction started on the book. I was still ill. I had really caned it at Bart's. Beautiful people, out of control. I lay in bed with one of those masks you cool in the fridge over my eyes on a hotline to Colin. He was jamming. Juggling phones. He'd got them all sexed up over the book and how I was onto this new thing called somatic literature.

'They love it, they love it,' he kept telling me. 'You're beautiful.'

Fuck it, it's a brilliant idea.

It came down to two offering much the same and we both agreed I should go with Hoxton Paper Products as the more happening imprint. We signed the deal next morning and went out for a champagne breakfast. You could have wiped the floor with me.

I drove over, on several occasions, to Jim's place out in Crouch End. There he'd be, blinds half drawn, with his big goggles on, surrounded by piles of paper, anatomy text-books, dictionaries, histories of the body and with some tinky-linky troubadour music on the decks. I'd tell him he was brilliant and take him out to lunch every now and then at St John's.

Over the next six months, with endless mollycoddling, pep talks, expensive lunches and so on from me, he banged out the other chapters. I had to keep my finger on it. Had to read almost everything he sent, red pencil a shitload, get him back on track, tell him he was the best fabulator in the whole fucking universe. The day came when I had the final book in my hands. My greatest work to date. *Somastream*. I renamed it: *Poiesis/Somastream*.

I don't give a fuck what the critics say so I'll list a few of their words here:

Genius.

Pure genius.

An invaluable expansion of Morton's oeuvre.

A great leap forward.

We had a fuck-off party at Bethnal Green Working Men's Club and I finally got to shag Cat.

CHAPLET OF THE INFERNAL GODS

. . . the Artist's Way is a spiral path.

The Artist's Way by Julia Cameron, *p. 183*

After twenty-five years of procrastination I set my foot on the Artist's Way. I was forty-five. I weighed eleven stone. I had grey pubes. I was pre-perimenopausal. I was on God's dump. I said twenty-five years of procrastination, but the truth is I had wanted to be a writer since I was seven. I am a writer, because I say so and because I turn up at the page. Every day I turn up at the page the way other people turn up at the bus stop. It hasn't been easy. The Artist's Way is a spiral path. That means you keep coming round the mountain and experiencing the same old, same old, but what you have to realise is, each time you are doing it from a higher point on the mountain. You are moving on up. It's a climb.

It is at this point in the recovery process that we make what Robert Bly calls a 'descent to ashes'. We mourn the self we abandoned.

The Artist's Way, p. 6

For twenty-five years I have been a shadow artist. I work in PR writing press releases for prestige brand perfumes. It hasn't been the ideal training for seeking the truth. Deciding to be a writer at this age is like deciding now is the time to be:

a)   a pop star
b)   a quantum physicist
c)   a striker for Man. Utd.

Believe in the unbelievable. Howl at the moon. Descend unto ashes. I did that. I looked back at the last twenty-five years and I keened over Guerlain's 'Samsara' and Dior's 'J'Adore'. And, what's worse, I know how ridiculous that sounds.

Stop telling yourself, 'It's too late.'

The Artist's Way, p. 7

Julia points out that Raymond Chandler didn't publish anything till he was past forty and that *Jules et Jim* was written as a first novel by some dotard in his seventies. I look at the picture of you, Julia, on the back cover of my edition of *The Artist's Way*. You are wearing a sailor suit, Julia. You have decided as a style direction on frizzing your bangs. You peer out from under them like a rabbit from under a lettuce. Should I listen to someone who looks like this? Normally, no. I could ditch this whole project because you frizz your fringe.

As an artist, I may frizz my hair or wear weird clothes. I may spend too much money on perfume in pretty blue bottles even though the perfume stinks because the bottle lets me write about Paris in the thirties.

The Artist's Way, p. 180

She must be talking about Worth's 'Je Reviens' in its Klein-blue globe, launched in 1932. Five Worth perfumes link together to form a narrative. 'Dans la Nuit' (1924), 'Vers le Jour' (1925), 'Sans Adieu' (1929), 'Je Reviens' (1932), 'Vers Toi' (1934).

By the way, it does not stink. (One wouldn't expect Julia to get perfume.) 'Je Reviens' is built around absolute of *narcissus poeticus*. I remember Joan Juliet Buck, top maghag, writing how a few drops of *narcissus poeticus* on her wrists made her see silver running down the walls. Then she found out that it can make you go mad. Not for nothing did Socrates call it the Chaplet of the Infernal Gods.

Just hold on to one thing here for a minute. Absolute. It's a technical term in perfumery for the distilled essence of maybe thousands of narcissi thrown into a boiling vat. It's extreme, it's intense. It's – absolute. The absolute, in any form, can drive you mad.

There is another story about 'Je Reviens'. How it was inspired by a famous letter sent by Napoleon to Josephine from his first campaign in Italy. 'Je reviens en trois jours . . . ne te laves pas.' I return in three days. Don't wash.

Why not? You might think you know the answer to that. Napoleon was a man of the flesh and French to boot. He wanted Josephine ripe and runny as an old Camembert. One problem: did they wash even every thirty-three days anyway back then? But give it to him and you get a highly-sexed, olfactively-arousable skanky Napoleon who wants to dash home at the head of his victorious army and find Josephine emitting waves of vaginal effluvia from under her muslin court dress. He wanted to efface the stench of battle in the *odor sexualis*. Or maybe combine the two scents, the martial and the amorous. Promising.

But there is another explanation here. Years ago (bear with me), I had an on-off relationship with a highly unre-liable Jamaican who explained to me that the reason no Jamaican worth his salt would ever go down on a punani was because he might find himself licking off another man's come. I learned a lot from that. One, that he did not expect me to be faithful, that this unfaithful attitude was something he assumed was generic among women. Two, that it was a damn good excuse for making me go down on him instead. (Do not picture me with the grey pubes, etc., in this position, this was years ago.) At the same time he said: Do not ever sleep with another man because if I lick you punani I will know in an instant and woman I will make you fuckin pay. It is entirely possible that Napoleon's injunction to Josephine followed a similar line of reasoning.

'Inside you there's an artist you don't know about. . . . Say yes quickly, if you know, if you've known it from before the beginning of the universe.'

Rumi, quoted in *The Artist's Way*, p. 24

Yes! Yes! Yes! Yes! Yes!

Coming across *The Artist's Way* in the Angel Bookshop was like that moment they talk about in Zen. When the pupil is ready, the teacher appears. For years before that, I made intermittent attempts to birth my inner artist. I would write a bit, hit a block, and stop. I penned lyric poetry, genre fiction, gobbets of autobiography, radio plays, and eng lit. But I was busy with 'stuff'. I was sunk in the banal. I didn't make time for my self.

When Julia wrote that thing about artists wearing weird clothes, frizzy hair and stinky perfume, I did this kind of splurge in my Morning Pages about 'Je Reviens'. After eight months of coming round the mountain it was the first sign. My artist peeked out for a moment from behind some far-off clouds and waved at me.

★

In order to retrieve your creativity, you need to find it. I ask you to do this by an apparently pointless process I call the morning pages.

The Artist's Way, p. 9

Every morning before you do anything else you get your notebook out and you write three pages of all your gripes and moans and the general shit that's clogging your head. It's an artistic clearance sale. As you're sweeping out this detritus in order to purify the river of your creativity (see Clarissa Pinkola Estes, *Women Who Run With the Wolves*, 'La Llorona' in chapter 10), threads of gold are swept out with it. That was what my revelations about 'Je Reviens' amounted to. A little lost necklace of gold. One of those fine chain necklaces I had as a teen and then rejected as I grew older, more worldly. I rejected that fine chain of gold that was my True Self, my True Work. I turned from Beaux Arts to Faux Arts. When I realised this, I had another descent unto ashes.

The morning pages are the primary tool of creative recovery.

The Artist's Way, p. 11

For three months after that, Morning Pages were the only writing I did apart from my paeans of praise for the launch of 'Amor Fati' by Biabelli and D'Real's celeb perfume launch for Christmas, 'Ho' Ho' Ho". Once you set foot on the spiral path, it hurts when you swerve off. Writing those press releases I felt the vomit rising in my throat and choking my creative chakra. But D'Real and Biabelli kept me alive to do The Work. I have to honour that.

After this long period of splurging into my Morning Pages, I started to feel a bit better. I got out *The Artist's Way* again. The back cover caught my eye. There was Julia in that sailor suit. Heartbreaking. She has a long face with great, goopy eyes which she has mistakenly chosen to emphasise by lining her lower lids in black eyeliner. How could I empower such a style saddo as my writing guru?

We are victims of our own internalised perfectionist, a nasty internal and eternal critic, the Censor, who resides in our (left) brain and keeps up a constant stream of subversive remarks that are often disguised as the truth.

The Artist's Way, p. 11

It was my Censor who wanted me to doubt Julia, wanted me to judge her on her sailor collar and doleful eye make-up, not on her wise words and skilful task lists for beginner artists.

> More than one student has tacked up an unflattering picture of the parent responsible for the Censor's installation in his or her psyche and called that his or her Censor.
>
> *The Artist's Way, p. 12*

The picture I instinctively wanted to tack up was the picture of Julia in the sailor suit. She was blocking me! But then it hit me how that thought was just another of the Censor's Machiavellian tactics. That's how blocked I was as an artist. I was ready to string up my saviour.

I found a picture of my mother aged about thirty-five, caught on holiday in the act of swiping a hand across her nose to catch a dribble of snot. Most uncharacteristic. Her true self flashing through. Julia suggests maybe a big red cross through the Censor. I did it, even though it felt sacrilegeous crossing out my own mother. I blu-tacked the Mother-Censor to the wall in the laundry room, the only place in the house where I could pursue my secret life as an artist unknown to the family. I am an artist. I turn up every day at the page. I use the page to rest, to dream, to try.

> In order to work well, many artists find that their work spaces are best dealt with as play spaces.
>
> Dinosaur murals, toys from the five and dime, tiny miniature Christmas lights, papier-mâché monsters, hanging crystals, a sprig of flowers, a fish tank . . .
>
> *The Artist's Way, p. 154*

The shame of wanting to be an artist when you are actually a PR and a mother of two is no greater than the shame you feel as you paste dinosaur murals to the wall of your workspace. Censor, down!

Gloria, our cleaning lady, had already left me a note telling me one of the children had put 'a bad picher' in the laundry room, which she had taken down and placed on the ironing-board. I put my Mother-Censor back up. I am an artist. My note to Gloria: Please do not touch or change anything in the laundry room. Thank you.

I came back from Hamleys with a trove of treasures for my new play space. I pinned Christmas lights to the wall. I stuck a mural of a window in front of my little desk (there is no window in the laundry room). I placed a series of toys called Kute Kuddlee Kanines along the back of the desk. I got a Hello Kitty cushion. In a little pram under the desk I placed a doll that reminded me of Teeny Tiny Tears. I wrapped her in a tiny waffle blanket. She symbolised my emergent artistic child.

Five minutes of barefoot dancing to drum music can send our artist into its play-fray-day refreshed.
The Artist's Way, p. 22

Julia is American. (Censor, I hear you!) She can write things like that and not cringe. Maybe that is why she is writing creative writing handbooks and not Writing. OK, OK, apparently she has been a 'working artist', like some sort of old

Ginger drayhorse, for decades. (Mum! Back in your box.) Sorry, Julia, you'll understand. It's not me who is knocking all those episodes of *Miami Vice* you created. It's my Censor.

I got some drum music in the World Music section at the Virgin Megastore. I knocked back the best part of a bottle of Cabernet Sauvignon. It was two a.m. Upstairs, my husband, Brian (in finance), was snoring. Next door to him, Katie, eleven and Hannah, nine, were dreaming. I stood alone in the living room. I started on my play-fray-day. I took off my clothes and folded them on a chair. I tried not to think about my stomach. I put on the drum music and began to sway and move to the rhythm. At first I was a bit self-conscious, feeling a draught of air on my naked skin, aware that I hadn't really danced in years. But I persevered. I knocked back the rest of the Cabernet from the bottle and synched up the volume. I closed my eyes. Like an upswelling of the artistic inner river, words started to come through me. I did not censor them. I began to sing in a strange, spontaneous African language:

> Mbello mello cho ko
> hum bada, hum bada, hum-hum
> Meee no taklo bo bo
> Hum bada, hum bada, hum-hum

'What the hell are you doing?'

I was squatting in a kind of birthing position, swinging sensuously from hip to hip, and clutching the Cabernet. My husband. Like a bad dream, but he was really there.

'Go away!'

I stumbled into an upright position.

'Sally. What's wrong?'

'Why do you always have to invade my space?' It came out as a scream.

He came forward. I spat at him and ran into the hall, grabbed a coat. He tried to get hold of me but I managed to nip out barefoot into the night. I cried as I ran along, ducking behind people's garden walls in case he was following me. I was ashamed. Ashamed of what he had found me doing, ashamed of hiding behind people's dustbins aged forty-five. But it was he who should have felt the shame.

Be particularly alert to any suggestion that you have become selfish or different.

The Artist's Way, p. 43

'Sally, something's happened. You've changed.'

Silence.

'Sally.' Bugger started stroking my hand. 'About the laundry room.'

I closed my eyes and internally I said the words, Oh God.

'It's   it's like a nursery in there.'

'Shut up.'

'Hey. Hey listen. It's OK.' He passed me a tumbler of the whisky which had lurked in the drinks cupboard unused for six years. I knocked it back.

'You know, you're not alone in this.'

Oh yes I am, oh yes I am.

'I was talking to Ben and he said that Emily has gone on HRT recently and she's feeling much better. I know how you feel about pills but'

I opened my eyes. 'You and me are growing apart. You know nothing about me. Nothing. You think the laundry room is a nursery and you are right. But it's not a child I want to give birth to. Especially not yours.'

I got up and left the room. I stopped having sex with Brian. I told him if he ever went into the laundry room again it was divorce.

Those of us who get bogged down by fear before action are usually being sabotaged by an older enemy, shame.

The Artist's Way, p. 67

Why had I never told my husband that I want to be a writer? I suppose because I had nursed this secret so long, and my life had moved so far from making it the truth, that the shame was too deep. But it's worse. I did tell him once. One night a few weeks after we met we were walking along looking up at the stars. He asked me about my dreams and because it was dark and I was madly in love, I blurted I had always wanted to write. To be an artist. He turned towards me and held my face in his hands.

'We'll make it come true,' he said, 'and all our dreams.'

Then we were kissing. He never alluded to it again. I think he was drunk and forgot about it. But maybe he is a crazymaker?

The snowflake pattern of your soul is emerging.

The Artist's Way, p. 85

Every night, when the kids were in bed and Brian was watching telly, I went to the laundry room. I lit the Christmas lights and cuddled the doll. I had discovered that the doll – my own idea – was also part of Julia's plan: 'Choose an artistic totem. It might be a doll, a stuffed animal, a carved figurine, or a wind-up toy' (*The Artist's Way*, p. 161). Then I just turned up at the page, no matter how painful, no matter how dry the creative well. I sat there and I wrote for at least an hour. It was like slashing a vein and eking out a few gobbets of old dried blood.

What was emerging in a shaky, out-of-control way was just a first draft, no need to get judgemental, no need to read it over, just keep the hand moving (Natalie Goldberg, *Wild Mind*). It was a novel of sorts. A series of interlinking stories based on 'Je Reviens'. One strand was the story of Josephine and Napoleon during the Italian campaign. It had an innovative structure. It was done as a series of letters between them (this was at the height of his madness for her, he could send ten letters a day). What made it totally unique was that I realised that the culmination – their meeting, Josephine unwashed, Napoleon striding in in his spurs – would also be done as a series of letters. Even as they made love. Because they could never truly meet each other face to face. Only their bodies could connect. At the non-verbal level of smell.

'Je Reviens' became world-famous during the Second World War because it was the scent GIs gave their French sweethearts when they left Europe. 'Je Reviens' means 'I return'. How many of them did? Not the one in the second strand of my novel. He seduces his French sweetheart, gives her the perfume as a token of his faithfulness, and leaves her for ever. She never forgets him, dies unmarried.

The third strand was either to be:

a) my relationship with the Jamaican, disguised so none of my friends would recognise him (hard).
b) a series of meditations on love interspersed through the book, each titled after one of the perfumes that make up the Worth scent-narrative: In the Night . . . Towards the Day . . . Without Farewell . . . I Return . . . Towards You.

Every night before I began I took to picking up my copy of *The Artist's Way* and kissing the picture of Julia on the back. Not only was she guiding me through artistic recovery, she had directly inspired the plot of my novel. She really suited black eyeliner. It was defiance that drove her to don the sailor suit. It had panache. It was a potent symbol of the way Julia eschewed the arbitrary diktats of the lifestyle Nazis.

I was climbing the spiral path.

Green is the color of jealousy, but it is also the color of hope.

The Artist's Way, p. 124

And then it happened, and it went through me like the spike through one of Brian's carefully-pinioned receipts.

Someone turned to me at a dinner party and said, 'Have you heard about Carrie?'

Carrie used to work at the very same PR agency as me. She is about thirty-eight, thin, wizened really. Her press releases were terrible.

'She's writing a novel. Can you believe it?'

A stab of pain — the spike running me through. It's too late for me. She is younger. She is thinner. And she is out about herself as a writer.

Then it got worse.

'Get this. She's got a £90,000 advance.'

I put my knife and fork down.

'My God,' I said. 'That's amazing.'

I picked my fork up. I put it down again. I couldn't get food in because of the spike.

'What's it about?' asked someone at the other end of the table.

Then it got worse.

'It's about perfume, of course. Don't they say: write about what you know?'

I had never believed enough in my subject, thought it was a bit silly, thought perfume wasn't 'good enough', I didn't honour my artistic child, and as a result, the Great

Creator has taken my subject away from me and given it to – Carrie. I wheezed from a small, stabbed throat.

And then it got worse.

'*A Life in Twelve Perfumes*. It's a series of interlinked short stories.'

So, a non-conventional structure as well. Like mine. But she'll be first. Maybe it was a sign, her not being good at press releases. Maybe she wasn't good at press releases because she was a True Artist.

And then it got a lot worse.

'Sally?' It was Brian. 'Sally? Didn't you tell me once that that was your dream? To be a writer?'

Everyone at the table turned to look at me. I focused on Brian.

'I've never said that.'

'Years ago. When we first met.'

'I think what I said was, "I wish I could write more easily. I wish these damn press releases weren't so strangely hard to do."'

'Oh? Oh well. Maybe you should give it a go anyway. You always said Carrie's press releases were rubbish.'

I closed my eyes for a second.

'Yes, why don't you? You'd be brilliant, fantastic,' said our hostess, a woman called Janey.

'Because I have nothing to say,' I said to Janey. 'Do you?'

Zip the lip. Button up. Keep a lid on it. Don't give away the gold.

The Artist's Way, p. 199

In the car I said nothing.

He said, 'Look, there's no point hiding it. I know you must be writing a novel in the laundry room.'

'You've got no idea what I am doing in the laundry room.'

I kept all my notes and CDs locked away in a metal box in there so there was no evidence.

'Why be so weird about it? Why not just be honest about what you're doing and let the people who love you read it?'

I buttoned the lip.

'You've turned into a weird, buttoned-up bitch.'

'And selfish?'

'Yeah, and selfish.'

I rented a room above a pub. I went there every night at eight-thirty after I had shoved the dishes in the machine. Brian could make sure the damn children went to bed.

For some people, food is a creativity issue.

The Artist's Way, p. 163

In my room above the pub, I ate pub food. I ordered treacle tart, trifle, or sticky toffee pudding at the bar, with custard, and took it, with a pint, up to the room. I could hear the music coming faintly from downstairs. People having a banal time, letting time slip away from under them like tilted chair legs. OK, maybe not like tilted chair legs. Above their heads, I nurtured my artistic child with delicious nursery food and did my affirmations:

I am a brilliant and successful artist.
I am a brilliant and successful artist.
I am a brilliant and successful artist.
I am a brilliant and successful artist.
I am a brilliant and successful artist.
I am a brilliant and successful artist.
I am a brilliant and successful artist.
I am a brilliant and successful artist.
I am a brilliant and successful artist.
I am a brilliant and successful artist.
I am a brilliant and successful artist.
I am a brilliant and successful artist.
I am a brilliant and successful artist.
I am a brilliant and successful artist.
I am a brilliant and successful artist.
I am a brilliant and successful artist.
I am a brilliant and successful artist.
I am a brilliant and successful artist.
I am a brilliant and successful artist.
I am a brilliant and successful artist.
I am a brilliant and successful artist.
I am a brilliant and successful artist.

After three months of this I weighed twelve and a half stone.

Complete these phrases.

1. **As a kid I missed . . .** the chance to write my first novel
2. **As a kid I lacked . . .** parents who were artistic
3. **As a kid I could have used . . .** encouragement to be creative
4. **As a kid I dreamed of being . . .** a true artist
5. **As a kid I wanted . . .** to write
6. **In my house we never had enough . . .** sweets

The Artist's Way, p. 125

You pick up a magazine – or even your alumni news – and somebody, somebody you know, has gone further, faster toward your dream.

The Artist's Way, p. 172

Carrie!?

Instead of saying, 'That proves it can be done,' your fear will say, 'he or she will succeed instead of me.'

The Artist's Way, p. 172

That's all very well, Julia, but is there really room in the world for two middle-aged women writers from the same PR agency, who are writing near-identical novels, only one is thin and the other is fat?

Whose novel would you publish?

This choppy growth phase is followed by a strong urge to abandon the process and return to life as we know it.

The Artist's Way, p. 5

I gave up the room above the pub. I put *I Return* away in a drawer. After quite a long time I started having sex again with Brian.

If I don't create, I get crabby.

The Artist's Way, p. 181

I was now forty-seven. I was in despair. I couldn't live and not write. Even though writing was hell on earth. I got out *The Artist's Way* and told Julia I was sorry. I went out on an Artist's Date, the other thing you have to do alongside Morning Pages if you want to be a true artist. It was a trip to a bookshop. There, I saw a display table with Carrie's book: *A Life in Twelve Perfumes*. I confronted it. I bought a copy, took it home, and flicked through it rapidly while eating a packet of HobNobs. A surge of hope: it was nothing special. She had thrown the material away. I told myself: you can do better.

I burnt Carrie's book in the fake log fire. It felt good, wild, like dancing in the moonlight and running with the wolves.

Never, ever, judge a fledgling piece of work too quickly.

The Artist's Way, p. 174

Two a.m. that same night. I crept downstairs to the laundry room with a bottle of brandy. I opened *I Return* with a beating heart and started reading. As I sat there, swigging brandy, and smelling the sickly smell of fabric conditioner, it crept up on me with mounting certainty. It was not the twenty-five years of not writing I had thrown away. It was the last two.

I finished the brandy.

The next day I cried and cried and then I opened *The Artist's Way* and the first line I read was:

Remember that in order to recover as an artist, you must be willing to be a bad artist.

The Artist's Way, p. 30

With tremendous courage, I put my blistered foot on the spiral path. I picked up my pen. I opened my notebook. I bled.

The refusal to be creative is self-will and is counter to our true nature.

The Artist's Way, p. 3

I am forty-nine. Soon-ish, I will be dead. I am no longer pre-perimenopausal. I am menopausal. I am back on the Artist's Way. The Artist's Way is a spiral path. I have been climbing up it for the last four years, writing good stuff, writing bad stuff, not able, really, to tell what kind of stuff I'm writing. But my job is to do the work, not to judge the work. I wrestle with the Censor like a old-fashioned priest grappling with Satan. I view my inner artist as a skittish colt that I am bringing along. He's talented, but he's also young, nervous and highly-strung. I take him out for lovely runs on the psychic turf. I give him lots of little toys, horse-chews and the like. I am divorced from Brian. Our paths had diverged. One of the upsides is that I get the weekends and Monday free to write in when the kids are with him. One of the downsides is that I feel so guilty all the time. My darling girls have suffered through the divorce. Even when they are here, they don't get their mother's full attention, because part of me is always down there, in the creative underworld, riding my artistic colt.

And all because I want to write. But then:

As blocked creatives, we focus not on our responsibilities to ourselves, but on our responsibilities to others.

The Artist's Way, p. 43

I can't focus on my responsibilities to others if I want to be true to myself. And plus, if I don't make room for me,

I will only be resentful of them and hence a worse mother. Julia says, 'Our creative dreams and yearnings come from a divine source. As we move toward our dreams, we move toward our divinity.'

Giving up *I Return* was a typical Creative U-turn (see Week 9: 'Recovering a Sense of Compassion'). That's all. I must keep working on it. I must just get to the end of the first draft without judging and then I must muster the artistic courage to go back in for a second draft, and, eventually, summon the will to get it out there. To actually Show It To Someone. The Universe will deliver. Because I have committed. (Julia quotes Goethe here: 'the moment one definitely commits oneself, then Providence moves too'.)

But, for now, don't try to see too far ahead. Just do the work. Turn up at the page. Use the page to rest, to dream, to try. Climb the spiral path. As Julia would say, baby steps, baby steps.

CORPUS

FIRST DAY

The double doors swung shut behind me and it was darker than the tomb. I knew the Examination Hall was vast. There are always noises in a big room in the dark, and little plays of air. I took a step. The test is you have to ignore the over-active imagination. Another step. You have to think. Herr Doktor would never send us into a dangerous situation; it wouldn't be rational. I struck out into the middle. I held my hands out to ward off anything that might be in my way, a chair, a pillar. A draught was coming always from ahead and to the right. What if something touched me? I stopped. He hadn't told us anything about what was in here. Why not something alive? It could be alive. Maybe it was like that game kids play in the dark, except instead of someone being It and trying to find the others, It was trying to find you and you were trying to find It. I wished I'd looked at the others as each came out, to see how they'd looked, scared or triumphant. Any excuse Conor's face would have looked triumphant. I hadn't really checked. Maybe It was dead. That in itself would be quite scary. I breathed out and at the same time sent out antenna-like extensions of my senses to feel about in an extra-sensory way for extraordinary signals of life or death.

Nothing. Just the deadness of things that had never been alive. Walls, pillars, chairs maybe, and air, and It which, of course, was a Thing and not a Being. Though a Thing was in a way a Being even if it had never lived. Which was why Things could be a bit eery in themselves.

I reached out to the right but there was nothing there. Just the dark clamped over my eyes and the draught that came always from that side and crept on my cheek. I laughed. I had assumed so much! Once again I was all assumption and precondition. He hadn't even said if this thing had a physical body or not. I took a step. I had assumed it was either here, as a material object, or that there was nothing. But what if it was a thing that existed in the mind? That would be very like Herr Doktor. Another step. I knew very well that one of his methods was to show us by showing us how stupid we were. We weren't exact enough. We started with too much and rushed forward from there, expecting to see better that way. It would be very like the Doktor to send me in here for an encounter with myself. Another step. Or even with The Self. Or even with The Self as Other. That most of all. I'd already projected so much into the dark. I'd stepped forward when he said 'Your turn'. Whereas what I should have done was first of all to step backwards for at least a hundred steps back down the corridor outside the Examination Hall. Conor's face would have screwed up into a big Urh? as he watched me tracking away from the Hall. Then he'd have gone into one of those knowing gurns when he got it. My toe touched something. I opened my eyes wider in the dark. I retracted the toe smoothly. An object certainly. So he wasn't being as clever as I'd thought. In fact I had been cleverer.

Listened. A wordless noise coming and going. It was me. Panting. Gathered self. Reached out. A large resistant but slightly giving form of unknown extension. A Thing. I walked alongside tracing its surface. I counted my steps. Seven eight nine ten eleven twelve thirteen fourteen fiftee   hand fell away and I into the hole where the object should have been. I scuttled away on all fours fast. Safe distance. Stopped. Gathered self. I sucked teeth. Idiot. All it was was I'd reached the end of it in the dark and fallen into the space where it wasn't.

Then: something prickling me. One moment the touch seemed to be coming from inside rather than outside, the next prick-tracing my face a micromillimetre above the skin. The feeling faded. It didn't stop all at once. My face continued feeling minutely fiery after the feelers seemed to withdraw. It died itchily away. I rubbed at my cheeks to stop it. I went forward on hands and knees, moving my head from side to side so as to catch any frond or ticklish wisp. Ground falling away under me. Whooshing up on something, grabbing for a purchase with fingers, knees, soles. Opened my mouth to scream but no scream just gape swallowing the dark. Carried away the air rushing me. Couldn't tell if I was riding It or It was tossing me smallfry.

Flung helter-skelter. Falling headfirst with heart in mouth waiting for the floorsmack but going up up again. Pushed, lifted. Scrabbling on fats and glissading on muscle, skiting down the rumpus of its neck, scratched by lashes, horns; pawed, pushed, palpated. A thwump of a possible tail knocked me flying through the dark and right thwack through the double doors and out in the bright corridor sliding on my backside blinking to a stop in front of Herr Doktor.

FIRST NIGHT

In the canteen for supper. My head hurt. Voices nagged it.
   '. . . rupture . . .'
   '. . . unattributable . . .'
   '. . . actually speaking of its suffering through history . . .'
   '. . . She's pregnant!'
   I bit into an onion bhaji.

SECOND DAY

Nine sharp. We filed into the Examination Hall. Light came through the row of windows that yesterday had been covered with blackout blinds and curtains. Herr Doktor stood in front of a bristly grey hillock striped with sun.
   'Name it.'
   'A site.'
   'A mirror.'
   'A machine.'
   'A corpus.'

'Ineluctable modality.'

'A set of figures and its deconstruction.'

'The phallogos.'

'Burial chamber.'

'Trojan horse.'

'Cultural commodity.'

'Chimera.'

'Polyphony.'

'Giant hedgehog.'

'Out!' Herr Doktor pointed at the double doors.

'Please.' I looked at my feet. 'I don't know why I said that.'

He ignored me. 'Probe, prod, sample, check, dissect, resect, assume nothing. Clarify. Expose. Propound. Defend. Refer. Defer. Instigate the Method.'

'Which one, sir?'

'The UnMethoding yet Methodical Method that fore-grounds a counter-insurgency riddling the Overmethod. And by the way, if you capitalize that in your mind you've not understood. Also, I will permit an approach using your preferred method from amongst those alternative methods we have studied, so long as you include a rigorous account of your method together with annotations and references. Anticipate my challenge.'

We fell on the body.

Conor pulled measuring equipment from his kitbag and began to calculate.

Boomie chalked up the body with signs, squiggles, diagrams.

The Japanese girl who sucked on small candy revolvers snipped hairs with nail scissors and caught them in a perspex box.

Jean-Luc the French genius went out the opposite set of double doors that gave onto the lawn. He propped the doors open, lay down on the grass and lit a cigarette.

Manish Mehta got a leg-up from David Jelinek, took a crampon from his bag and thwacked it into flesh. The beast registered no pain. Manish swung up on a rope, jabbed in another crampon.

The Japanese girl sucked a candy revolver, shaved skin shreds into a second sample box.

Manish lobbed another crampon at the body, attached a rope, hauled.

Morag clipped together cylindrical sections to form a probe. She snapped a surgical mask over her mouth and strode towards the tail area.

Something flashed up on the summit. Manish, his glasses. He got something out of his kitbag. A flag. He tapped it into the body with a hammer.

I slipped round the other side.

Darker, different atmosphere. The beast lying in tons of matter to my left. Promontories that resolved themselves into legs folded at the knee. No sign of a head. Either it didn't have one or it was tucked under the legs from ears to snout.

But there was something. An outbreak of underarm hair. It clung tuftily between torso and upper leg, maybe with static. The more I looked the less it looked like underarm hair and the more like a hairy tent flap. Maybe a screen erected by some parasite sucking secret blood. A fat tick. I squatted, peeked. The girl who always sat at the back. Sleeping, cool as. A tiny pile of hairpins by her feet. She always wore her crazy hair pinned up. Now she was letting it frizz to the max to seclude her where she was tucked into a crevice of its flesh.

I heard my name called and ran round the front. David Jelinek and Boomie dragging a bunch of scaffolding-poles.

'Hop to it,' said Boomie.

He liked dusty English phrases. We got a move on erecting the scaffold. No one else noticed the fuzzy armpit. I said nothing. By mid-afternoon a structure complete with plank walkways and a network of ladders surrounded the beast on all sides. We hared up and down it signing body parts with chalk. Jean-Luc the French genius abstained. He sauntered in from the lawn and drew a chalk circle on the floor at the far side of the room then sat in it smoking (forbidden). The girl who always sat at the back stayed wedged away. The rest of us argued pithily over our staked corpus zone claims. Herr Doktor strode in.

'We adjourn. Calculate tactics. Forge your weapons. Rendezvous at dawn.'

SECOND NIGHT

Back in my room. Eyeballing instruction manuals. I sketched designs. Knocked up a couple of maquettes. Dismantled. Reconsulted. Reconstructed with minor but crafty modifications. I tried taking a bit of one weaponmaquette and reinforcing it with another. Either my putative weapons didn't hold together or I didn't have the necessary wield-skill. I would have to fall back on my trusty. I could ply my trusty shut-eyed but such a weapon, lacking fashion-forward features, would hardly impress Herr Doktor.

I decided to take a nightwalk.

The dorm corridor was deserted. I tiptoed past Morag's door and Jelinek's and Manish Mehta's. A lightstrip under Conor's. Swot. Music through Jean-Luc the French genius's. Continental melanchopop. Seriously uncool. I sped out of the dorm and across the lawn to the Examination Hall.

The moon was high. It came in the row of windows just enough to pick out the paler metal bars around the body. The structure seemed to loom. As I got closer I saw that the creature had rolled onto its side. The bottom of the scaffolding was crushed under it and the top stuck out precarious.

I hurried towards its vague lumpen tail but it wasn't vague or lumpen any more. It stretched out rigid and ended in a tassel of hair. I rounded it to the other side. Scufflings, snufflings. I clicked on my torch. A vast belly wavered in the light. It was completely lined in a double row of swollen teats. Clinging to them, Manish Mehta, David Jelinek, and Conor. When they sensed light on their closed lids they wriggled closer into the breasts without taking their mouths off the nipples. Suckling in a dream.

The light snapped off. I must have dropped the torch. I continued on to the front and saw not a head but a monster-snake reared up and silhouetted against the moonlight. I screamed. But then I saw it was a swan's head with a tiny figure astride its neck. She started to sing in some gibberish language. The girl from the back. I ran to the double doors, the ones that gave onto the lawn. I pushed them open and belted through.

THIRD DAY

The structure had been rectified overnight. The beast lay on her back with her spine clamped to the floor, erecting a pop-up belly armed with teats. They bristled flabbily.

Herr Doktor stood on the structure above us, his double-edged sword held drooping. He had disdained the mask and wore only the light padded breastplate.

'Take up your positions!'

We assumed them, fidgeting and clanking.

He tapped the point of his épée on a plank.

'Do I stand unopposed?'

I felt faint. Faint enough to be excused? The Doktor looked dapper and none too tall. I knew he was lethal in the insubstantial but vaporising way of a laser.

'I challenge you, sir.'

Conor, ever canon-fodder. A gurner but a midnight-oil lover of learning. Why knock that down? He crossed the floor and climbed up one of the ladders screeching and caterwauling. He hadn't oiled his armour. They sized one another up. Conor unsheathed not one, but two, blades. I sighed. As if. He charged braying from every joint, an iron donkey. Morag yelled something Celtic and doomed from the floor below. Then it was all over. Herr Doktor pressed his double-edged point against Conor's rib. Conor relinquished his gear, withdrew to the back of the room, played dead.

'Do I stand unopposed?'

I looked along the line. No movement. Then the shaking of a golden plume as someone stepped forward. David Jelinek in a Grecian helmet tarted up with modcons. I groaned. A few brute seconds of so-called combat and the darkness came down across Jelinek's eyes. The plumed helmet bounced across the planks to join Conor's kit in Herr Doktor's hoard.

'Do I stand unopposed?'

The voice warming to its task.

Gasps. The Japanese girl swarming up the scaffolding not bothering with the ladder. She chucked candy slasher weaponettes as she went, not at the Doktor but into the airspace around him, forming a shadowDoktor of flashing sugarblades. All at once they stopped spinning, collapsed in a not-insignificant heap. The Japanese girl ran up to the Doktor with her very thick ankles, stopped short, and committed verbal hara-kiri. Down below we clapped. Yet he was still standing, she not. She rolled off the walkway and we caught her and placed her play-dead body in a corner.

So it went on, each of us making our essays against the great man. Manish and Boomie, reasoning that there was no rule stipulating one-on-one gladatorial combat, did a double act. Morag, trying to approach through differently-gendered ground, slipped coming over the top from the other side through the welter of teats. She dangled by a nipplehair, then, rather than be rescued, let go before he reached. The trusty did not serve me well. It led me through all the known fernickety moves like a red-eyed white mouse down a /lab\yrinth. Snickersnack; mousemeat.

Jean-Luc the French genius refused to climb the structure claiming that it was a plank of the state apparatus. Volleys of arrows back and forth then Herr Doktor abseiled down and walked towards him.

'Enter the beast,' said Jean-Luc indicating the floor inside his chalk outline.

Herr Doktor walked right through 'It', got a light off the end of Jean-Luc's cigarette and returned to the structure. He whacked a few strategic poles with his double-edged. The structure half-collapsed. We clapped.

The girl who always sat at the back had sent a sick note.

THIRD NIGHT

I got up suddenly urgent and ran out of the room in my bare feet and across the lawn into the Examination Hall. In faint moonlight I made out half-scattered planks and poles. The beast had turned again. On its side but this time with its belly towards me. Tentative I approached and rubbed my nose against it. Biscuits and wax flowers. It had grown fur. The moon went back into cloud. I slipped into a reverie.

Vague movement caught my eye. A flick of shadow that semi-detached itself from shadow then re-attached, then detached, then re-attached. The moon strengthened.

'Morag?'

The shadow semi-detached then broke away completely, a polyp of the greater shadow. It wavered towards me from between gigantic thighs.

'What are you doing?'

She pushed past me zipping and headed for one of the sets of double doors.

FOURTH DAY

The doors on both sides of the Examination Hall were propped open. A breeze blew in from the lawn, crossed the Hall, and into the corridor where we had waited our turn for our first encounter with the beast. David Jelinek entered ahead of me carrying an outsize drill bit. He was talking to Boomie.

'We have to go deeper,' said Jelinek.

'There is no deeper,' said Boomie.

The beast lay on her back in the sunshine. Her upturned belly was stuck into an enormous block of what looked like jelly hanging on pulleys. Over by the far set of double doors the Japanese girl sucked on a small candy revolver and pressed buttons on a wall console. A whirring noise. The pulley-ropes tightened and with a series of suckpops the block unstuck itself from two dozen breasts and tracked across the ceiling to the far end of the Examination Hall.

Some backtracking and a medley of tricky maneouvres with the pulleys, and the resin edifice turned upside-down. The Japanese girl set a final lever in place. The resin came to rest on the parquet, virgin side down.

We crowded round. It was full of holes. What had been flesh was now nothing. What had been space had turned to solid resin. Through the thick clear substance I watched distortions of Morag and Jelinek move in a mesmerising way on the other side.

'Very good,' said Boomie.

The Japanese girl with rather thick socks rolled down over her very thick ankles propped a ladder on the resin and climbed up. She disappeared into the pockmarked bowl-shaped sculpture and began to take soundings.

We drifted away in the sunshine. I noticed the girl who always sat at the back wiping sticky stuff from the corners of the beast's eyes. Boomie got out a chamois and began to polish its claws. Morag got a mop and bucket out of the cleaner's cupboard and started giving it the once over. I made my way to the back thinking I'd comb out its tail. I came across Conor leaning against a thigh and chewing. He had a clasp knife in one hand and was cutting squares of blubber from the haunch and stuffing them into his mouth like chunks of Turkish Delight.

'You'll never get it all in.'

He stared at me with bulgy eyes. He was about to say something but instead he retched, quickly moving to catch the vomit in one of the buckets grouped round his knees.

'You think this is clever? It's not the same!'

I pointed at the lumpy green slag in the buckets. He belched weakly.

'That's the point.'

He stuffed another chunk in and flapped his hand at me to go away.

The plok–plok of someone running along the remains of the superstructure. Mehta. He appeared on the topmost walkway, now leaning at a crazy angle and well below the summit of the belly. As we watched he hoisted himself up using crampons and rope. The teats quivered as he pushed through them. He pulled a pair of lopers out of his back-pack and opened them wide round the base of a breast. Schnick sound of the two blades sliding together. The breast squidged out over the blades whitely. Morag yelled. The lopped breast fell. A firework of milk ringed with jets of blood shot into the air, danced, and died. The shears sliced through the soft flesh of the breast next to it. A second firework spouted. Mehta was already chopping off the next breast. The next. The breasts tumbled down the sides of the beast and rolled on the floor like two dozen heads of John the Baptist. The red and white fireworks hissed, spurted, died away. Mehta stood on the bloody stumps and wiped his head with a forearm.

Down below him Morag began to gather the fallen breasts, pressing them against her shirt.

'Don't touch what isn't yours!' yelled Mehta.

He started to climb down, slipped in blood, and fell off the semi-demolished structure. Something flitted past. The Japanese girl. She ran up to the beast's head, jammed the heels of her hands in its nostrils and shoved upwards with all her strength. The upper jaw creaked open a little way. She jumped up on the lower lip and looked in. The great jaw began to shut with the slow stiffness of a clam. She dived headfirst between the sets of teeth. They clicked shut, leaving her very thick legs protruding in a forked tongue.

Conor clapped.

FOURTH NIGHT

It was just off the full moon but the cloud cover was total. I listened while my eyes adjusted to the dark. Not a sound. I thought I could see the denser dark of the beast's body. Greenish light tracked dorsally in gnomic morse. I blinked. The morse tracked again, vanished. The darkness settled back so completely that I wondered if I'd imagined it. A flicker over the body like summer lightning. It vanished. So was it alive then? Bioluminescing. Or was this the afterglow of putrefaction?

I went near it. It was much smaller and lying once again on its belly. I checked its head. Mouth closed. But no sign of the legs with the very thick ankles. I felt sad. Either she'd been taken in completely or her bottom half had snapped off and been swept up by the cleaners. Or could she have crawled out?

A nervy glow dappled the body, died. It wasn't furred as it had been. Skin smooth and unctuous. Flukes folded onto the parquet. I touched it. A nerveshower of invisible but felt sparks on my fingers. I reached out my other hand in its direction. Electrical impulses jumped between us.

The double doors burst open and the girl who always sat at the back came in dragging Herr Doktor's boat trailer. Without a word, she threw me some rope and I wrapped it round the flukes and under the tail. We attached the ropes to the pulley system in the ceiling and hoisted the beast onto the trailer.

We took her outside across the lawn to the car park and clipped the trailer to Herr Doktor's four-wheel drive. Then we drove to the harbour. It was quite a long way down to the water. We rocked her body left and right to get all the ropes out from under it. The mutilated stumps where the breasts had been sliced off were all gone. She or he was smooth all over with a slit on the underside like the one dolphins of both sexes have to stash their sex organs.

She pressed a button on the trailer and it started to tip towards the sea. There was a pause while the weight of it fell through space. An almighty splash. Glugging. It was too dark to see down. Just the sound of the waves the slap they made on the quayside. I listened out for swimming sounds but there was nothing and after a while we got back in the jeep and drove away.

FIFTH DAY

Had I dreamt it?

Because there it was. As big as before, far too big to get out of the double doors, onto the lawn and away down to the water. A smell of crustaceans and smoke, wisps of which hung in the air above its snoozing face. It was covered in overlapping scales like roof tiles.

Wasting no time Herr Doktor entered with a pin between his teeth. Wordless we ran for it, hearing hand grenades roll onto parquet. I dived under one of the floor-length curtains at the far side just as the first munition exploded. Conor zoomed under next to me. Bom! Bom! Wrapped in curtain we turned to witness. He was unrolling yards of barbed wire off bales as big as haystacks. They spooled across the no-man's-land between the beast and the back wall of the Examination Hall where we cowered. All except Boomie. He'd been taken out. I tried to avoid looking at him brokenly-angled in the middle of the Hall. And soon it was hard to make out him or anything, since once he'd covered the floorspace Herr Doktor went on unrolling yard after yard of barbed wire so it piled up like foam in an Ibiza nightclub but one maybe run by neo-Nazis, great wobbling crests of barbed wire tumbling over each other, falling and rebuilding, filling the airspace with bubbles of steel instead of soap. Underneath, stealthily, Herr Doktor mined the area.

He stopped, a tiny figure blurred by a whirlwind of wire scribbles. He began to dance. Weird beyond the wilful weirdness of modern dance, the dance of the Doktor. Convoluted, highfalutin, preposterous in its figures, excessive in every direction, lost in ridiculousness, virtuoso, unfaltering. He darted and birled through jaggy swirls, he flowed through wire like a moaning breeze. He staccatoed on points. He launched breakneck grandes jetées. He landed just shy of a mine every time. Not a nick on his baby face, not a cut on his hands. One minute dry as steel dust, rigorous. The next flashy as a roller disco babe; putting out, pulling. He got away with murder not least his own.

We stared, nerve-racked.

'Is he right? Is he wrong?' whispered someone.

'Is he right? I she wrong?' said Conor, who was working on the allusiveness of typing errors.

'Who can say definitively. I just feel its power,' said someone else.

And in spite of all Herr Doktor had told us, that was what it was. Power enforced by an arcane, elitist, infuriating lingo of dancesteps from which he fretted and stropped falling edges of sheer beauty.

Aaaaah!

A shot of cerebral steam escaped us where we pressed up against the wall. We the penniless renouncers. The eschewers of jobs in finance, politics, the media. The ones who had refused to make a difference in Africa, or go up our own arses in art. As we tracked his figures we affirmed. This was why we had done it. For this we were willing to sort through the piles of pitchblende like the apprentices Marie Curie never had. Slaving through fairytale mountains of slag to separate out the minuscule microphone eeks of the radioactive element. For the chance of a dance with the corpus. Every now and then he seemed to beckon us to join him in the jig. Each of us wanted nothing more. How to take a single step without getting slashed to pieces? But then Conor ever canon-fodder made a brave sortie.

He unfolded his clasp knife and hacked, trying to cut a caper or two at the same time. Within minutes snared on barbs and stuck like a fly in a web.

Jelinek was next. He never lacked courage. Now he dived into entanglements with a certain amount of grace. Immediately stopped short. Frozen in forward dive position, he struggled till his hands and face were a sorry slush of nicks and slashes.

Morag had more nous. She tore down a floor-length curtain and attempted to roll over the wires in a textile wrap. She got quite far in, cheered on by the rest of us. But then she too came to a halt, laid up in mid-air like a sausage roll.

Herr Doktor had barely begun. Prancing through thorny thickets, just showing off now really, he unsheathed his rapier and stuck it in the beast full thrust, other hand on hip, front foot off the ground — Huzzah! And pulled out a plum, a prune-like object.

He stuck his sword into the ground — still pinning the prune — and quick as a wink swept the wire from the room, prised up the landmines, and cut down my marooned classmates. Soon we could see clear across the Examination Hall again to where the beast lay in the sunlight, emitting tiny puffs of smoke, smelling of sulphur and crustaceans.

We eyed the prune.

'What is it?'

'A nothing.'

'An appendix?'

'An unmentionable.'

All that he'd yet done had been but a preface to the actual work, which Herr Doktor now incomparably warmed to. He tossed the prune into a handy chalk circle – the very one vacated by Jean-Luc the French genius – and from this unpromising knob of material began to magick build or rebuild a body. And not just any old body. The whole corpus. Herr's Her.

Scaly, 3-D. A monolith of a creature that soon outgrew the chalk circle Jean-Luc the French genius had drawn round himself on that second day. And as this body grew more and more definite, so the beast, the other beast, the what? The double? The old beast? The first beast? The pre-beast? The 'real' beast? The   ? The pale imitation or precursor of this Herrbeast seemed to become paler and paler until there came a moment when we wrenched our eyes from Herr Doktor's corpus to compare and contrast and couldn't see the old beast any more.

FIFTH NIGHT

' . . . a mirage . . . '
  ' . . . murder . . . '
  ' . . . he's trying to rescue it? . . . '
  ' . . . must be done . . . '
  ' . . . why clone it? . . . '
  ' . . . but it's not the same . . . '
  ' . . . the method won't be discredited . . . '
  ' . . . it will die away, but it won't be discredited . . . '
I knocked back a vodka.

Late, very late.

I ran across the lawn quite drunkenly and slipped inside, back to the wall. There it was. The Simulacorpus, or the Revealed Corpus, or the Anti-Corpus, or the Mirror-Corpus, or the Doppelcorpus, or the Uncanny Corpus, or the Emperor's New Corpus, or even the Resurrection of the Corpus? But one thing for sure, the only corpus in the room, lying in its scales that reflected the moonlight.

Somehow I knew she'd be around, the girl who always sat at the back. She came up and put her hand in mine. Her hair was like something a cat had sicked up after eating a mouse, but huge and springy. More an ecological niche than a hairdo. Akin to those cities of multiple mud nests African birds build in thorn trees. She pulled me away from the wall and over to where the the old corpus had been. She squatted down and felt at the air in front of her. I got down next to her and she grabbed my hand and spread the fingers out and pushed my open hand forward by the wrist. I felt something. Just a faint resistance, a current of air maybe. Only not moving like a current but static, a difference between one part of the air and another part. Just a barely detectable sense of difference. Air is like that. Warm bodies of air lie above colder bodies. There must be a border between the two different types. I was feeling one such border. The air I was touching the border of was warm. Just maybe point one degree warmer.

She never seemed to answer questions so I didn't bother asking any. I sat back on my heels. But she pulled me forward again onto my knees, indicating that I should feel about in the air again the way she was doing. I closed my eyes so I could focus more precisely on the differential surface. The more I rubbed at it, the warmer it got and the better I could feel the shape of it. It curved away from me, then as I shuffled round on my knees to the side, it swelled up and fell away in a shape I couldn't visualise. I rubbed. I rubbed at the air so much my fingers started to itch then almost to burn. I opened my eyes. The air directly in front of me was moving or something was moving through it. Black flameshapes vaguely denser than almost black air. They disappeared so fast they could have been illusion. Then again, black ripples, a mane of air. Soundless, almost invisible black fire. Visible only because it was darker though not denser than air. I figured it. The beast was bioluminescing, only not light but darkness. Some kind of presence that might be marked by non-presence.

We got the trailer. We loaded on the 'anthyphophorical' or maybe 'nonexistent fantasised' or just 'feltsomehow' body and dragged it out to the car park. We got into the jeep and drove, not to the quay this time, but further along to the shore. She sang the whole way, her hair frizzing so much it filled the cab of the jeep and I had to keep pushing it off from tickling my nose and getting in my mouth and even down my throat and gagging me.

The jeep backed across the sand and right into the wash. Waves hissed under rubber tyres. She pressed the button, the trailer tipped, and the beast flumped into shallow water. We got out of the jeep and waded in, hauling it further out. I couldn't see the beast but I looked for the impression she made in the water. A gouge in the flood. Green lightning playing over.

SIXTH DAY

I stood in the Examination Hall. I thought back on how last night she had swum away. She actively swam. I'm not kidding myself. I saw the way the hollow moved through the water like something was sweeping its tail to propel. So someone must have gone out there and brought her back and dumped her here in the Examination Hall before breakfast. No one paid her any attention except me and the girl who always sat at the back. She kept moving her hand through the air as if feeling a ghost. The beast wasn't visible. There was a small puddle of water.

It was the other one everyone was gathered round. But not too near. That one's scales were blackish blue and shiny. Its back was ridged with waves of horn. Its tail looped through the air in coils. Its nostrils glowed red. Umbrellawings folded along its sides with venomed spurs at the end of each spoke. Its stillness was the stillness of a crocodile sleeping on the banks of a river. Thin smoke hazed the air.

'A magnificent site,' said Jean-Luc the French genius. He was draped in the trough of a horny wave, smoking.

'Get down!' roared Conor.

Jean-Luc ignored him. 'You may have your doubts. You may be wondering. But it is beautiful, isn't it? Who is to say? It would be easy to presume.'

'The future of the beast does not belong to Herr Doktor,' said Morag.

'This is what we have to work with now.'

Herr Doktor entered the Hall.

'Someone has been watching us. We have not been paying them attention,' added Jean-Luc. He stubbed out his cigarette on the horny wave.

'Excellent, Jean-Luc,' said Herr Doktor, adding, 'Battle stations.'

We scrambled.

They came in white rubber aprons with chainsaws. We fought back with everything we had. Carnage. Smoke, fire, buckets of blood, flying blubber, its tail sawn off but not before I saw its springy coils swat several of them against the wall. Triple splat. We cheered and rushed out from behind the beast with all our firepower.

They retreated back to their own campus. We hoisted Herr Doktor on our shoulders and staggered to the canteen and lay about unable to eat or drink. Birds flew in to the Examination Hall and pecked out the beast's eyes in our absence.

Darkness fell.

SIXTH NIGHT

Late. Bone-tired. I crept to the Examination Hall. The air a bloody reek. The visible beast, mutilated. Dead possibly, but he could do anything, that Doktor. I went past it to where there was nothing to see. I felt the air with my hands, all around, at foot level, above my head, from side to side. I walked up the length of the room, feeling. At the wall I turned and walked back down again but a bit to the right. Furrowing the air. I ploughed up and down and up and down, covering the whole room, right into the corners and even behind the curtains. One was still missing, the one Morag had rolled herself up in. I couldn't feel anything. Which could have been me, I thought, as I pushed the last curtain aside and swept the floor there with my foot. It registered something. I bent down and felt about the dusty space with my hand. There wasn't much of it. I held it under my nose. Biscuits and wax flowers. I tried to trace the shape of it with my other hand. An internal organ? Its body had shrunk a lot in the last couple of days. The heart maybe? A fluke? An eye? I pressed to test the texture but too weary.

A bang. The double doors that gave onto the corridor swinging shut. A shape running across the Hall. Her, I could tell by the big ball of hair. I shouted out. She paid no attention. She headed for the other set of double doors, the ones that gave onto the lawn. I sprinted, got there first. She reached a second later. Pushed me aside but I grabbed her shoulder and she bit my hand so I let go. She scarpered and in a minute was over by the row of windows, shinning up a curtain.

'Wait!'

She kept on going like a boy up a palm tree. I flitted across and tugged on the curtain.

'Come back. This is all that's left.'

She pushed the window sash open, got a leg over the sill.

'Wait. Take it with you. Please.'

She looked out the window then back down at me holding it up in both hands. She swung her leg back in, slid half down the curtain, grabbed it from my hand and shinned back up. I encouraged her endeavour.

'Yes, you can save it!'

She struggled up one-handed, holding the last piece to her chest in the other. Got a leg over the sill again and sitting astride, threw the leftover out of the window with all her might maybe as far as the bushes or at least onto the lawn. I couldn't see. By the time I'd clambered up the curtain and reached the open window she was running away out of the campus. Just before she disappeared from sight a flock of tiny birds or bats flew out of her hair and streamed away screaming. Though I searched for ever, I never saw her or its remains ever again.

SEA

She was at the age when you can sleep till noon if they
let you, half-dozing, half-dreaming, turning over to the fresh
side of the bed and stretching your leg and arm across the
cool bottom sheet and letting the top sheet ripple over the
arm and leg almost like a breeze. All those dreams you
could have morning after morning in the summer, when
you didn't have to go to school or you were waiting for
the day you started college. If the dreams had been books
they would have made a library of thousands, a dozen of
them generated every morning as easy as clouds being
generated out of the blue. Dreams so rich they flavoured
the rest of the day giving you an out-of-it look. Dreams
that defined those thousand or so days but which went like
clouds and you never remembered the shape of any of
them.

So when her father said to her that she would have to
get up early if she wanted to come, in the dark, because
they would have to be out there at dawn, she didn't know
if she could do it. She asked her mother if she would wake
her. Her mother said, you want me to wake up just to wake

you up? Her father said Come on, Cricket, set the alarm and when it rings, get up. That's all there is to it. You sure you want to come? She said she was sure.

She got into bed and set an alarm clock and a clock-radio on the bedside table. One for three-thirty, and one for three-forty. Three-thirty was the middle of the night. You probably haven't even started dreaming at three-thirty, she thought. She turned out the light and lay back looking up at the darkness until the ceiling appeared out of it and then she looked at the ceiling. She was aware that she felt kind of sad and she didn't know why. Think of the sea out there now. It would be much darker in the sea now than in the night above it.

She was watching the black surface of the sea a little below her when the clock-radio started beeping. The beeps got louder and louder till she reached out a hand and batted the button. She turned over under the comforter and nested her head into the pillow and a big dream began to generate out of nothing. She felt it begin to take her over, just for a minute, and then she wasn't looking at it, she was in it and the alarm clock burred and she reached a hand out and found the place on the back where you slid a knob up and the sound stopped. Now, she said. Up now. Right now. And the dream gathered force and came back at her and she felt herself sway back as it came over her and she ran to the window and saw a wave drawing itself up ready to crash down on the house.

'Hey, Cricket!'

His hand rough on her shoulder.

'Come on, we're late.'

He lifted the pillows from under her head and propped them vertically. 'Up. Five minutes.'

She heard him cross the room and made the decision that when he reached the door she would swing her legs out of the bed. Then he reached the door and she did it. She sat on the edge and saw the white cup on the bedside table in the dark. She touched it. He hadn't heated the water properly. She drank it anyway, her legs goosepimpling in the draught from the air-conditioning. While she was drinking it she thought about what it would be like to shrug her shoulders back against the pillows and pull her legs up under the covers to drink the last few mouthfuls.

They drove through the empty streets without talking. There was no one on the sidewalks and only a few other cars on the roads. After a while they turned off the highway and went between rows of lighted shop windows with no one to look in them. Then they turned off down side streets till they came to a gravel road. They bumped down it to the dock. There were boats pulled up in rows along the jetties, and electric lights, globes on top of short black poles, all along the dock. The lights were on. All the boats were lulling in the oily water and a windchime sound came from high up on the masts of the sailboats. Right away she saw Cougar doing something at the back of his boat. He stood up and waved at them. He was wearing a T-shirt with Suntan U written in blue letters on faded brown. The boat's motor was already ticking over.

'Morning, old timer,' he said to her father.

'Hope you know what you're doing there,' her father said.

'Why don't you come on and show me,' said Cougar. He looked at her standing beside her dad. 'Morning, young lady. Step aboard the *Yolanda*.'

They climbed across the gangway. When she felt the boat move up against the soles of her feet she tingled. She slipped off her flip-flops and pushed them towards some coolers tucked in where steps went down to the cabin. She was wearing a T-shirt and a pair of towel shorts. She was shivering.

'I didn't know it could be this cold in Miami.'

'Colder out there.' Cougar went down into the cabin and came up with a small tarp. He looked down at her legs. 'Hope it's not dirty.'

She wrapped the tarp round her shoulders and stepped from foot to foot.

Her dad said, 'Got a bit of rope, Coug?'

Cougar gave him some and he took the rope, pulled his knife out of his back pocket, and sliced some off. Then he poked a hole in one corner of the tarp and poked another hole further down the fabric on the other side. He threaded the rope through.

'What're you doing Dad?'

'Wait.'

He readjusted the tarp on her so it came over one shoulder, and under the other armpit like a toga. He used the rope to pull it tight across her chest, wrapping the rope once under one arm, through another slit he made in the back so the rope came under the other armpit under the tarp, then knotted it in front. It fit snugly, leaving one arm totally free and the other shielded but free to move.

'Calvin Klein's looking over his shoulder,' said Cougar.

'All the fashion folk are after me.'

'Thanks, Dad. Aren't you cold?'

'You don't feel it at my age.'

'What can you feel at your age?' said Cougar.

'Everything you can't feel at your age.'

'Can't wait,' said Cougar. He went over to ladder-like steps that went up to the small upper deck. Up there she could see the curve of a windshield, some dials set into a panel of wood, and whatever they called the steering-wheel on a boat. There were two swivel chairs side by side and that was all there was room for. Cougar was almost at the top. 'We'd better get going if we're gonna ketchum!'

Her father went back across the gangway, undid the rope fastening the boat to a mushroom-shaped thing on the jetty and, looping it over his arm, came back on board. He hauled the gangway up. The boat bumped against the boat next to it, squishing the rubber balloon-things that were slung over its side. She stood on the deck hugging the tarp toga and watched her dad push the other boats off. The smell of diesel came up off the water.

The *Yolanda* nosed out from between the other boats and swung her behind out like a horse frisking and fighting the bit. Cougar pushed the throttle out further and the boat straightened and they motored ahead. Little waves started to wash against the sides. She looked over the stern and saw the dock receding and heard the clinking of the windchimes in the masts come a little faster as their back-wash hit the boats. She watched the line of globe-lights along the dock reduce and saw the dull greyness in the sky as they opened up space between them and the dock. In a few seconds the windchimes were just whispers and the sound of the motor chugging and the slap of the waves grew louder. They headed out in a straight line from the coast.

Her father was leaning against the steps to the upper deck. He lit a cigarette.

'You all right?' he asked her.

There was another change in the engine noise as Cougar accelerated. The front of the boat lifted against the pressure of the water and the wake came out thick and foamy at the back.

'I think I'm gonna have a nap.'

She climbed onto the narrow walkway that went round the front of the boat, using the metal rail that went round the roof of the cabin to hold onto. She went as far forward as you could go and sat with her legs dangling over the edge on either side of the bow rail. She looked out.

There was a kind of light everywhere that wasn't light and didn't have a source. The darkness was decaying and what was left behind was a kind of limbo. Everything was grey; her arms jogging on the rope slung along the rail, the air in front of her face, and when she looked over her shoulder she could see Miami black and grey and pricked with lights under the draining grey of the sky. The sea was light grey nearby and dark grey at a distance.

After a while she slid back across the boards and went up onto the smooth hump of fibreglass which was the shape of the cabin underneath it. Looking over her shoulder, she could see the windshield of the upper deck and her father and Cougar behind it and the glow of her father's cigarette flaring and fading. Behind them she saw the tops of the four antenna-like things that bristled up round the lower deck of the boat like the whiskers on a catfish.

She lay down on the flattest part of the bulge and looked at the zenith. She saw a big star. She felt the bump bump bump of the waves under the boat and felt the vibration of the engine coming through the dome of the cabin. She pulled the tarp more tightly round her and curled on her side. The dreams burst out quickly like a flood that had been dammed and she caved in to them, feeling the movement of the water under the boat intermittently.

When it was over she felt empty. She leaned up on her elbows.

They were headed dead east. Ahead there was a white patch on the horizon. Above the patch a string of clouds stretched yellow-grey. She looked back and saw that Miami had shrunk down to a clotted line above the ocean. A low cloud band extended part way up the coast.

She fixed her eyes back on the seaward horizon. She couldn't remember when she had last seen the moment when the sun actually came up out of nowhere. It appeared now, a red chunk that seemed to eat out a strip of sea along the horizon line. She was able to see exactly how fast it moved, measuring how much of its circle came up each few seconds over the line. It looked as though it had a strange kind of life to it in all the grey and it came up much faster than she thought it should and balanced for a moment with its radius touching the flat of the sea.

Then it began to move up through space and if she kept staring at it without blinking it looked like a mass of burning worms. She looked down. The tufts of the waves were pink in splashes that extended across the sea on all sides. She looked back at the coast and saw Miami was purple rose and the cloud range above dark rose. The shadows on the lee sides of the waves were violet now and the side of the waves nearest the sun were pearly pink that as she watched was paling almost to white without her being able to pinpoint its changing.

She closed her eyes and let herself feel the wind on her face and the throb of the engine coming up through her legs and buttocks. When she opened her eyes the sea had turned a dark intense blue. If she craned her head to look down into the waves off the bow she could see the blue was deep almost to blackness but translucent like stained glass. She remembered what she'd learned about blue on their big trip when they had gone to Paris and she was jet-lagged and woke up at first light. She crept out of the hotel and walked through the streets to the river. There was the cathedral on its island. She walked over the bridge and went up to it and saw that a little door set in one of the big doors was open so she went in. It was full of shadows. Light was coming out of a chapel niche set into the stone wall at the far end. When she came up to it she saw there were people and a priest. They were praying by the light of a few candles. She slipped in and stood at the back, kneeling when they did and standing when they did. The priest was sing-songing in French and her attention wandered up to the stained glass windows. They were flat and grey. Then all at once the blue bits in the windows flared like they were coming alive. She watched the lit blue surrounded by greyness until after a while the other colours came alive too, green, yellow and rose. But the blue was way ahead of the others.

She went round to the back of the boat and looked over the water. Miami had gone, it was all just sea. Cougar waved down at her. He was leaning his butt against one of the pedestal chairs and resting one hand on the steering-wheel. Her dad was sitting on the other chair.

'When do we start fishing?' she shouted up.

'Few more miles.'

'A marlin?'

'If you bring us luck.'

She shifted her weight to one leg and held on to the side of the boat.

'How d'you like it?' said her father.

'I love it.'

'It's the life,' he yelled back down at her.

'You wanna Coke?' said Cougar.

He pointed to a cooler with his free hand. She shook her head, wiping back the hair that was whipping across her face. She faced the stern. All along it was a locker with two fliptop lids. You could sit on top of it like on a bench. Just in front of the locker was a low plastic chair on a pedestal. It was swivelling from side to side with the sway of the boat. A metal funnel projected up from the pedestal. If you sat in the chair, you'd have to put one leg either side of it.

When they'd come to live in Miami they'd gone to a restaurant in Coconut Grove called Snowy's Stone Crab. A cobalt fish was leaping across the wall next to the bar. It took up most of the wall with its body and the big blue crest rising all along its back and the long, pointy sword that came out of its upper jaw. She had never thought that there were fish with swords. She kept looking at it while they waited for a table. When her father went up to the bar she went with him. Up close the fish looked like a giant toy. There was a small brass plaque under it that read:

509 lbs. June 22nd, 1969 Capt. Roy Gomez

She waited till the barman was at the other end of the bar and rapped the fish with her knuckles. It felt like some hard kind of plastic.

She swung up onto the walkway and hung out over the ocean. The boat nodded as it dove through the water and bounced hard when it hit a big one, sending up spray. Now the sea was turning a young, strong green. As the sun got higher its rays slanted further down into the water and she could see shadows moving about down in it. They wavered as the waves wavered and she couldn't tell what shape they were. They were very far down.

The air was warm and she went back on the deck again and undid the rope and worked her way out of the tarp. She shaded her eyes and looked up at the sun. It was getting higher quickly. Maybe it's a myth, she thought, that it always moves at the same pace. Maybe it comes up quick and then slows down as it reaches the top like one of those big wheel rides at the funfair which shoots round the bottom and then slows and chugs up till it's hanging at the top, then shoots down again.

The engine noise changed. She felt the boat's nose drop and when she looked up she saw her father standing by the steering-wheel and Cougar coming down the steps.

'OK,' he said, rubbing his hands together.

He shoved a cooler across the deck with his leg and stood with his feet planted apart beside one of the whiskers coming up off the side of the boat. She saw how thickly the dark hairs grew straight down on his brown legs below the line of the shorts. He bent and prised the lid off the cooler and she saw his legs a paler brown covered in dark hair above the shorts-line. He fiddled with the whisker and she saw a length of line hanging straight down from it and when he took his hands away there was a hook on the end and she realised it was a fishing-rod. He reached into the cooler and came up with a silver fish in his hand. It was alive. He jabbed the hook in through its mouth and out through its eye and tossed the fish out into the sea. The reel at the base of the rod rolled as the line fed out.

'What's that?'

'Breakfast. You hungry?'

She shook her head.

He laughed. He moved the cooler along to the second rod and leaned down to get another fish out.

'This ain't marlin tackle, but I reckon it'll hold up if we hook one,' he said. 'That's what you want isn't it?'

'Yeah.' She thought about the cobalt fish with its sword leaping across the wall at Snowy's.

He worked the fish onto the hook and swung his arm back and threw it out as far as he could. It flew out into the air and was swallowed by a wave. The reel clicked over as the line fed out. He stood beside it till he figured the fish was at the right distance then he did something and the line stopped feeding out. Above their heads, the end of the rod curved slightly and the line ran away clean from it down into the water. Cougar slid the cooler across to the stern.

She glanced up at her father steering the boat.

'What do you call that?' she pointed to the upper deck and looked at Cougar.

'What do you call it?'

'I don't know.'

Cougar whistled. 'I thought you knew about boats.' He pulled another fish from the cooler and stuck the hook through its mouth, tugging it back and forth to work it through some bone or cartilidge.

'I've been on a few, but I don't know the names of anything.'

'Wanna learn?'

'Sure.'

'Up there is the fly-bridge.' He swung his other arm back. 'This here is a bait tank.' He flung the fish out over the sea. The line started to click over. 'Right now we're aft. Earlier you were forward.'

'I know that, it's the more specific things.'

'This here' – he snapped something onto the base of the rod – 'is a clicker. Don't use 'em much, but this one's for luck. If a fish bites, it will tell you.'

'How will it do that?'

He slid the bait tank across the deck. 'It'll scream.'

He pulled out another fish and gripped it while he talked.

'Down there is the head, though I usually piss over the side. That's it.'

'What about the walkway that goes round the edge of the boat to the bow?'

'You got me there.' He stabbed the fish through the roof of its mouth. Blood sprinkled on his instep. 'Don't have a name that I know of.' He threw the line out and she watched the fish hit and then sink down into sunlit water. He wiped his hands on his shorts.

'OK,' he said, 'let's see if there's any big mothers running around out here.'

'Marlin?'

'If you bring us luck. Fishing and gambling – gotta be lucky.'

He fixed the lid back on the bait tank and went down the steps into the cabin. She thought again how she was going to ask her dad to teach her one of the card games he played with Cougar and Sam Wilson and the other man with the beer belly whose name she didn't know. Montana Black Dog. It would be a good game to have up her sleeve, one of several good things she could do now, like dress a crab, which her dad had taught her, and play pool, which he had taught her when she was really small and she used to go with him and chalk his cues, and pass him the bridge when he had to take an awkward shot over the top of another ball.

He hadn't taught her how to swim. She thought about that time she was swimming in the pool at the club when a woman came out the clubhouse with a naked baby under her arm. As she walked towards the sun loungers the woman threw the baby in the pool. It disappeared under the water.

She had stopped dead in the middle of a lap, treading water. The baby's fat body popped to the surface. It started thrashing its fat-baby arms, its face underwater. The woman busied herself putting her things on a sun lounger with her back to the pool. She was about to shout something, swim over. There was a smooth boom. The woman had dived into the pool. She glided under the baby and came up on the other side. The baby kept thrashing its legs and arms and when it bumped against the woman's solar plexus she picked it up and held it high. It pistoned its legs in the air.

'Is she OK?'

'Sure,' said the woman, 'she loves it.'

She dropped the baby in again and walked backwards

across the shallow end with the baby beating along after her.

'How did she learn to do that?'

'They can all do it until they learn how to walk and then they forget. She won't.'

The woman put her hand on the baby's bottom and tipped it down so its head came up. It gave a shrill scream and then another one. Its mouth was open in a half-scream, half-smile so big you could see its pink gums.

The tarp had slid off the stern locker and was flapping over the deck, the rope twitching. She picked it up, flicked out the hooks that fastened one of the lids and looked in. Rope, a snorkel, and a pile of straps linked with double-D rings lying on some canvas. She pushed the tarp in on top of them and shut the lid and sat on top of it. She looked at the wake coming out white and pale green and the smooth hump it made behind the boat churning with white froth underneath, and the swirls of small eddies caught between the flat place and the push of the waves all around. The waves were a light-filled green and she felt a strong desire to dive down through them and burst into the air like a porpoise and dive down into the green again.

'Bastards.'

Cougar was behind her with his hands on his hips looking at one of the lines going out into the sea. She looked at it and couldn't see anything wrong. He reeled in and the end of the line started to dart in the water as it got near to the surface. Then it was whipping about in the wind and she saw there was nothing on the end of it. She got to her feet.

'Marlin?'

'Shark. Evil bastards keep snapping my old leaders.' He held the line out for her to see. It was sheared-off.

'Big teeth.'

'All the better to eat you with.'

Something caught his eye.

'Shit.'

He shook his head as he went over to the other side of the boat and started reeling in another line.

'Two down.'

The bit-through line came up out of the water and jerked about in the air.

'Fish misbehaving?' yelled her father.

'Never do as I tell em,' yelled Cougar. He started up the steps to the fly-bridge.

She let her eyes go from one to the other of the remaining two lines stretched out over the back of the boat. She wanted to see the moment when, way down, a big shark peeled back its jaws and snapped its teeth shut on the bait. The shark would twist its head against the sudden weight of the boat dragging it forward then bite clean through the line. She reckoned the rod would bend and the line would stretch out taut and then slacken and she'd see it. She watched for a long time but nothing happened. She leaned over the side and shaded her eyes so she could look down into the water. Through the green plenitude she saw shadows that wavered some distance below.

The engine changed again so it sounded like it was half-choked with water and the boat began to dip down and up. Instead of trying to hammer the waves down it stroked them all the way along with its underside as it moved slowly forward. She felt the sun hotter and heard the sound of the waves slapping against the sides of the boat.

Cougar was prising the lid off a plastic bucket. He grinned at her from where he was hunched over it.

'Your starter, ma'am,' he said and his arm swung across the stern, letting go of a bright fish that made a smack as it hit the surface and sank. The boat chugged forward and Cougar waited, one hand on his hip. Then he groped in the bucket and came up with a stringy red piece that flew out and into the water. The blood spread out slowly as the piece sank.

He looked up at her father. 'Maybe pick her up a tad?'

The engine growled and the pitch rose. The boat beat more surely through the water.

'Is this chumming?'

'Yeah, they smell the blood and their bellies start talking to them.' He flung another chunk out over the back. 'Smells travel more quickly in the water.'

She looked at the blood pooling on the wake. It didn't seem possible that smells could travel more quickly in water given that water was much thicker so there was more stuff for the smell to get through. She said nothing.

Cougar flung another lump of flesh into the sea. 'So any predators out there, marlin if you're lucky, smell bacon and grits and come on up to the breakfast table. Which we have laid out nicely for them' – he threw a fish overarm – 'with napkins, tablecloth and dainty little hooks.'

He stirred the mass in the bucket with his hand and pulled out a blood-streaked offcut.

'Wanna help out?'

'Sure.'

He pushed the bucket towards her and leaned over the side of the boat. He dipped his hands in the sea and started rubbing them together to get the blood off. She thought about the scene in *Jaws* where one of the men, she thought it was the policeman, the scaredest one, puts his hand in the water and at that moment the head of the Great White shark breaks through the surface right next to him. She threw a squidgy blob and it passed over Cougar's head and slopped down.

'Keep it more over the back,' he said from where his hands were wrist-deep in the water. 'Make it easy for them.'

She had never been good at softball. She stood sideways on to the stern so that if she swung her arm straight down across the front of her body it would continue up and out in a straight line pointing over the stern. When her arm was parallel to the stern she'd let go of the chunk. She tried it and the chunk went wide on the other side.

Her father's voice came down. 'How're you doing?'

'Doing good,' said Cougar. He stood up and dried his hands on his shorts. 'Is she still due east?'

'Looks that way.'

'Maybe take her a couple degrees south east.'

'Aye aye.'

She was getting close to the bottom of the bucket. Feeling around in the bloodswill her hand slipped on pulpy masses that swished between her fingers. She tipped the bucket to the side to see better what was in there. When she could feel with her hand that there was nothing left but mashed-up guts and shed scales she held the bucket over the side, filling it half with seawater, then swirled it for a moment and emptied the bloody water out into the sea.

She put the bucket down on the deck. The waves jumped up at the boat. She looked down through the full greenness and after a moment, saw the wavering outline of a shadow that massed, seemed to break up, coagulated again. She put her hands gingerly into the water, rubbed them once, then lifted them out and worked them together well above the waves. She dipped them in again to rinse them. She heard her father's voice.

'Cougar?'

Cougar's voice came from down in the cabin. 'Yup. I'm comin out.'

'Quick,' her father said from up top, 'a coming-out party for Cougar.'

'Aw you shouldn't have.'

Cougar appeared at the entrance to the cabin carrying a second bucket of slops. He raised an eyebrow at her and she nodded and bent to pull the bucket towards the stern. She prised off the lid and the smell of blood and the other, foul smell came up off the bucket. She started throwing the chunks over the back. She tried to pace herself the way he had done, leaving a gap between slings. When she had finished she did the same as before, rinsing out the bucket with seawater and then washing her hands quickly in the swell.

She straightened and looked at the water. As the sun had gotten higher the greenness had gotten deeper and more brilliant. She wanted nothing more than to dive down into the green light and feel how cold it would be all over her body.

She went over to the beer cooler and got out a Coke and popped the cap off with her teeth the way her mother had told her never to do and spit the cap back in the cooler. She glanced up and saw Cougar smiling at her. His teeth were very white in his beard. She moved over to the side of the boat, drinking the Coke and looking out at the waves, their east-facing sides flashing near the boat and glittering hard away in the distance.

The boat swung and she saw her father turning the wheel and the bow came round till they were facing in the direction they had come. It was moving very slowly, feeling over every wave. Cougar took the wheel and her father came down the steps and stopped to shield a cigarette in his hand at the bottom.

'What's that?' she said to him.

'What's what?' He craned his neck to look into the water where she was looking.

'Those shadows further down.'

He tilted his head.

'Are they fish?' she said.

'Could be.'

'Maybe sharks.'

'More like your marlin. Or just shadows.'

She watched the way some of the shadows seemed to be single things and others could be groups of shadows moving together. The way the light played through the water made it hard to tell.

'But shadows of what? There aren't any clouds.'

'Beats me,' he said. He took a drag on his cigarette. 'Just a trick of the light.'

He walked over to the stern and sat down in the chair. It was almost hot now and she felt the warmth coming up off the deckboards under her bare feet.

'Anything nibbling down there?' said Cougar.

'Not a sardine,' said her father.

'Do you think we'll get anything, Dad?'

She heard Cougar laugh above her head. 'You gotta trust me, ain't that right, Jeff?'

'Depends how far you can spit.'

She swung up onto the edge of the boat and walked round to the bow. If she could just swim in this water so far out from anywhere with only the sun and the warm diesel smell coming out of the back into the clean cold of the water and the slight creaking sound the boat made and the waves jumping at it. It would have been nice to smoke up here on the foredeck in the sun but her dad didn't know she smoked. Cougar had seen her doing it once in the Pantry Pride car park. She was loitering by the car waiting for her mom to come out of the supermarket and

Cougar drove up with his arm hanging out the window and his sunglasses on and said: 'Caught with your pants down.'

She whipped her hand behind her back and threw the cigarette on the ground. Curls of smoke came up off of it and blew round the front of her. She looked towards the supermarket and then back at Cougar.

'So, Cricket,' he said, 'I'll bet there's a lot your daddy doesn't know about you.' He drove off laughing and she saw him park outside the liquor store and go in. Then she saw him come out with a paper bag and drive away.

A squealing sound rose above the thrum of the engine. She heard her dad yell, 'Coug!' and the engine cut out and the squealing came over louder. The rocking of the boat increased and she smelt the salt evaporating off the deck boards. She slid off the fibreglass hump and ran round to the back. Cougar was bent over one of the rods.

'OK, Jeff, pick her up gently.'

The engine started up and the boat inched up and down the waves. The line was screaming as it reeled out into the ocean.

'OK now!'

The engine churned and the boat picked up speed. The screaming stopped.

'That's it!'

The engine sound dropped and her father came running down the steps. Cougar reached into the locker and got out a kind of harness with straps and handed it to him.

'Figure it out, Calvin.'

He unclipped the rod and leaned back slowly. Gripping it in both hands, he bent forward and turned the trigger fast. The line flexed at a sharp angle down into the water.

'Is it a marlin?' she asked.

He hauled back a little on the line then hunched forward and reeled. He exhaled. She looked into his face.

'Have we got one?'

He sat in the chair and dropped the base of the rod through the holder in front of the seat. It was shaking. He clamped his hand on the rod.

'Bitch is big. Wanna take her?'

'Sure,' said her father.

'In the fight chair?'

'On my feet.'

Cougar took the rod out of the holder. It jerked away sideways and he gripped and hauled it round. He slipped it into a holder over her father's groin and clipped it to the side of the harness. The rod jerked.

'Wow,' said her father.

She saw how the line bent down at an oblique angle towards the water. The waves jumped up at the boat. The rod pulled hard and dragged her father forward a couple of steps.

Cougar yipped like a cowboy.

'Hold her there, old timer.'

He went next to her father and placed his hands ahead of his on the rod showing him how to play the fish, talking about how she would fight to the death, and he had to keep fighting back every second and never let her get the upper hand. Her dad looked out at the water while he listened. He lurched forward as the rod lunged.

'Jesus Christ, the kraken.'

Their arms tensed as they gripped the rod and she could see the veins standing out all along her father's forearms. She willed him to hold on. She wanted him to have a beautiful big fish.

Cougar ran back shouting, 'Pump the line! Pump the line!'

The rod buzzed and her father leant forward and tried to reel against the weight of the fish. The line veered off across the stern and out over the side of the boat. Her father braced then took a few quick steps closer to the side leaning back all the time.

The engine rumbled. Cougar brought the boat round so it lined up more or less straight again with the line going into the water over the stern.

'Keep her over the back, Jeff!'

Her father breathed out audibly through his mouth, fighting the fish in a way she couldn't see. His arms were jerking about from side to side and every now and then he pitched forward before he was able to pull back on the line again. All the time it looked as though the rod might jump out of his hands and she willed his hands to stay on it.

She walked away from his side and scanned the sea. Then she looked back at him where he was bracing with his legs bent. The rod coming out from the harness was a spindly thing and for a moment she wanted to laugh seeing how much effort it took to hold onto a thing like that. She walked to the cabin steps so she wouldn't have to see and looked out at the water from there. Then she came forward and looked up at Cougar. She saw his brown forearms and the dark hair on them. His arms moved slightly as he nosed the boat round every now and then.

'You got her, Jeff.'

He kept looking over his shoulder at her dad, his eyebrows pulled together in a frown.

'Keep her coming. Keep her coming.'

Her father didn't say anything. His feet were sucked onto the boards of the deck. She saw how his arms were a pale pink and how the flesh was drooping a bit off the bone. She ran forward and put her arms round him.

'Come on, Dad, you've got it.'

He staggered like someone coming awake and his back hit against her head. She could smell the stuff he put in his hair.

'Now!' yelled Cougar.

Her father leaned forward and turned the trigger on the rod, reeling the fish in and then pulling back and up with the rod in a smooth long movement. He was drenched in sweat.

She heard the engine cut out and then Cougar thumping down the ladder.

'Cricket,' said her father, his eyes on the water, 'dyou wanna take over?'

She looked at the line trembling where it ran down taut. Drops of water kept jumping off of it in pulses.

'You can take her in the chair.'

She wanted nothing more than to sit in the fighting-chair and put her hands on the rod and feel what the big fish felt like at the end of it. She wanted to bring in the marlin with its sword and fight skilfully and at the end the two men would pat her on the back and tell her she was one helluva girl.

'No, Dad, it's OK.'

'It's a lot of fun.' He looked at her for a second then back at the water.

She backed away, shaking her head.

'It's your fish, Dad, you take it.'

As she said it she felt unhappy. She held back and then she opened her mouth to say OK, she'd do it, and then she held back again.

Something appeared above the sea. It hung in the air in a shower of bright drops. It hung there longer than seemed possible and then it crashed back into the water. She stared at the space where it had been. It had been cobalt blue above and white underneath and there was a blue wing stretching out from its head to its tail, running in line with its body, not side to side like a bird's wing. There was no sword coming out of its nose. She heard the men whupping.

'What was that?'

'Dolphinfish,' said Cougar. 'Biggest I've ever seen.'

'But   that wasn't a dolphin.'

'Dolphin*fish*. Dorado.'

'It's not a marlin?'

She had come out here to see a marlin, the great fighting fish.

'It's not a marlin. But dolphin's a fucking good fighter.'

She slid her eyes to her father. She wondered if he realised Cougar had said fuck. He wasn't paying them any attention. He was sweating as he held the line.

'It's a beauty, Dad.'

'Just keep pumping the line old-timer,' said Cougar.

Like the Virgin Mary rising in a beatific vision out of the earth, the fish came up out of the sea and hung, sparkling blue. As it reached the peak of its parabola, it bucked and twisted. It smashed down in a show of foam. Cougar whooped and her Dad leaned forward and tried to reel.

'Dad, your fish is a beauty! It's a beauty!'

He ground his teeth.

Cougar ran back up the steps and she heard the engine kick and the boat swung round again. The line from the rod straightened up perpendicular to the stern. She leaned her thigh against the side of the chair, itching now to put her hands on the rod and feel the fish gathering to make a jump on the end of it. She couldn't ask to do it now, not now. They looked out at the water and the fish burst up out of the ocean and sailed. It tossed its head like it was crazed.

'What a fighter,' said Cougar.

It was so beautiful, she thought, such a rare colour. It was the kind of living thing she hadn't known or imagined existed. She stared at the water and saw herself diving into it and the fish down in the green light looking up at her. She wished it could get away. Now it appeared again and stood vertical, jerking across the surface of the waves and beating the water with its tail. She could feel the strength of the fish as it beat down with its tail on the waves. She willed the line to snap.

'She's tailwalking!' said Cougar. 'What a mother.'

The surface of the sea broke into spurs of foam now as the fish planed across the surface from left to right and back again, raging its head. Spray and foam shot into the air.

That's enough now, she thought, watching the fish and hearing Cougar yell. She wanted her father to bring the fish in and know he'd done it and Cougar to slap him on the back and say he was an old son of a gun. Then they would bring it back to her mom and her mom would see that he'd caught this big fish. But she wanted the fish to break free.

She saw by the angle of the line that the fish wasn't very deep down. Her father was reeling and hauling and the fish was only about fifteen yards from the boat when he burst out again, not so high, heavier-looking now, the sun glinting on the blue of his side barred irregularly with gold and his raised wing. She saw how solid he was and then he went down again with a crash. She saw the shape of him just under the surface, and lying a little over on his side.

'Let's bring her in,' said Cougar.

Her dad walked round to the side of the boat and Cougar started pulling the line in hand over hand. The fish slid up to the boat's side and lay there in the green deep water. She could see his big gills working.

'Cricket, the gaff.'

She looked around the deck.

'Right there.'

There was a pole with a hook on the end of it. She handed it to him.

She imagined herself saying, 'Can we let it go?' She stood back and she imagined herself saying it again while Cougar leaned over with the line in one hand and the gaff in the other and made a sudden movement. There was a mashing, churning sound. Then her father bent over the side next to Cougar and they hauled him dripping out of the sea. He thrashed out of their arms. For a moment everyone stood and watched the fish jack-knifing on the deck then Cougar was beating him over the head with a bat. The fish lay with his mouth open staring up at the sky. There was blood coming out of his back dark red. Cougar cut the line.

'Open the box, Cricket.'

She followed his eyes and then flipped up the lids on the stern locker and pushed down the tarp and felt the fish rush past her. His wet skin brushed her forearm and she stood back, feeling the place where he had touched her like an electric shock. Cougar banged the lids shut and fastened the hooks. He slammed his hand down on the top of the box.

'You got her, you old son of a gun.'

Her father stood with his arms slack. She ran over and hugged him.

'You did it, Dad, you did it.'

He was damp with sweat.

'Huge,' said Cougar. 'A monster.'

'I can't believe it's not as big as the boat.' Her dad laughed. He pushed his hair off his forehead and scratched it.

'What a fighter. What a fish,' said Cougar.

'How did it feel, Dad?'

'Like ten rounds.'

They laughed.

'You deserve a beer.'

'All right. Cricket, you want one?'

It wasn't every day her dad offered her a beer.

'Yes please.'

Behind her the fish pounded suddenly on the side of the box.

'Thought you knew how to fish, Coug. She's still fighting in there.'

'Hell of a fighter.'

'But is he OK in there?' she asked.

Cougar bent to get beers out of the cooler. She saw again the paler brown of his legs above the shorts-line.

'All tucked up.' He handed round the bottles. 'To your first fish, old timer.' They drank. 'The first of many,' he added.

The fish pounded against the locker so hard she thought he might break out.

'Here's to the fish,' said her dad.

She thought, maybe I'll get a chance next time when it won't matter so much. We might get a marlin. They're bigger and fiercer, the king of fighting fish. I'll fight him well and then I'll let him go.

'It's gonna be the best lunch you ever ate,' said Cougar, knocking back his beer.

'We're going to eat him?' she said.

'You bet. Soon as we get back we'll light the barbecue. You've gotta eat them within hours and then they're the sweetest fish in the sea.'

'To the sweetest fish in the sea,' said her dad.

She lifted the bottle to her lips and felt bubbles hurt her throat. Cougar cracked open another couple of bottles and held them in one hand and went down into the cabin. Her dad followed. She saw him lie down on one of the benches that could turn into a bed. Cougar sat back on the other one with his legs sprawled apart. He put the radio on low.

Cool deep water to the horizon. It was elastic and full of light. The fish had stopped pounding. She looked over her shoulder. She could see into the top of the cabin, but her father and Cougar were just out of sight down on the benches. She let out the hooks and opened a lid. He was lying on the tarp. His mouth was open and his gills were opening and closing like a heart beating. His skin was satin with water and cobalt blue above and white underneath with faint gold marks tigering the sides. He swivelled his gold and black eye and looked at her. She looked into his eye then she closed the lid and fastened the hooks. A second later he threw his body on the lid so hard it lifted against the tug of the hooks.

The water dreamy green, deep and clear. It was just a

couple of feet away on the other side of the fibreglass. All she wanted to do was get the fish out of the locker, maybe haul him up onto her knees, from where she could push him over the side. He would lie there in the water for a moment taking in oxygen in quick gulps. Then almost before she could see the movement he'd shoot away.

Her father and Cougar would come clattering up the steps wondering what the splash was.

'What happened?'

She'd stand up. 'I threw him back in.'

'What?'

The two men would look at each other. Her father would be angry later because she'd let Cougar down when he'd invited them onto his boat. Everyone was going to get together in Cougar's yard for the barbecue and now there wasn't going to be any barbecue. They'd have to tell everyone she put the fish back in.

She leaned down and opened the locker. There he was. He rolled his eye up, watching her. She saw how long the spines along his sailfin were, and folded in pleats. Pointed teeth showed between his curved lips. He wasn't moving. She slid one arm round his body and felt a current vibrating all through him. She slid the other arm round. He smelt of the breeze. There was a punch to her abdomen. Flashes of blue and gold blurred in front of her and she retched at the air, staring. The fish bucked in her arms and she retched and got her arms away somehow and fell back on the deck. She couldn't breathe. The fish thrashed in the locker. She gasped. He thrashed so hard he came half out of the box. She drew a shallow breath. It hurt. Another breath. She looked over her shoulder. There was no sign of the men. Radio voices came up from the cabin. She looked back at the locker. He had stopped moving. She dropped the lids and sat on them to slip the hooks through. She wasn't strong enough to lift him out anyway. He'd throw himself all over the deck and damage himself, then she'd seem like an idiot standing there with the fish going berserk across the deck. She took a painful breath. A bloodied line showed on her forearm where his wing or his tail had raked it. She sat on the lid and licked at the blood as it swelled out and looked at the green light jumping and falling all the way to the horizon.

'Can I go for a swim?'

They said nothing.

She looked at Cougar. 'Coming in?'

'You mean' – he did a double-take – 'get wet?'

She laughed. 'Come on, Cougar.'

'Someone's gotta drink this beer.'

She hooked one foot around the other ankle.

'Is it OK to swim?'

'Course it's OK,' said her dad.

'Is it safe?'

'You'll be all right,' said her dad.

'I know,' she said. 'I just wondered.'

She stood by the cooler and took off her T-shirt and shorts and tucked them down behind it. She adjusted the little triangles of the bikini top and went up the ladder to the fly-bridge. She swung her leg out over the side and stepped onto a narrow lip on the outside of the fibreglass. Then she swung the other leg out and stood there on tiptoe with her heels up against the side, leaning back so as not to fall and looking down at the walkway and beyond that the sea. The furthest-away waves were prickled with sparkles that stuttered across the surface. She felt the energy of the waves rocking the boat more strongly up here. She looked at the blood oozing out along her arm then she shaded her eyes and looked down into the water. The sun was high now and the light went deep down into it and she could see shadows that changed their outline as the prism of the water moved and stretched.

She took a deep breath and bent her knees, taking her arms behind her and then flinging them overhead, pushing her heels back against the boat so she was propelled right out and away from it and she was rushing down, feeling the air comb her body and seeing blurs shoot by then a soft boom and all the sounds changed and she had penetrated into the water and was soaring down through it. She was rushing down through the water but she felt that she was flying up light as a bird, and her eyes were open and all around her the water was full of light and she felt that she was breathing easily in her element through a substance light and empty as air, flying with no sense of her body's edges. All she was was sharp happiness and the desire to keep going further and further down into the expanding green light as she beat the water back and up with her arms to keep going down and down which felt like up and up into the green light but now she could feel pressure in her ears and something across her chest and she turned without willing it in a big curve and she could see the surface of the waves far above her and the underside of the boat rocking. It looked very far up and she thought maybe she wouldn't be able to get all the way up there without breathing and she skimmed her arms through the water and kicked so she would go up faster, feeling a stream of bubbles escaping from the corner of her mouth. All the time she felt the green light expanding and she was kicking up as hard as she could. She was desperate to breathe but she knew she mustn't do that and she kept her eyes on the surface, which looked like a separate thing, like clingfilm adhering to the water, and she pushed up hard through the heaviness feeling the tension screwing tighter in her chest. She stared at the surface. She burst through with her mouth open.

An explosion into another world of clear sounds and strangeness. All around her the waves were a flock of green birds riding a current of air and she felt herself held up and down on the same current. She saw the white boat rocking and the lit green of the waves and how the sunlight dove down into them. She could feel the cells of her body trilling like a live current. She started to swim, striking away from the boat so all she could see were the waves. She loved the waves as they came at her, loomed over her and then lifted her quickly up and down the other side. It was easy to swim with them.

She swam fast, feeling the freshness of the water, tasting it, looking down into it every few strokes, seeing it sinking away fathomless down under her and the darker green and then grey of shadows. She dove down into it again, her eyes open, watching the shadows moving further down in the green depths, and she turned the dive into a somersault and came up facing the boat. It was a few hundred yards away and she felt herself thrumming with happiness at the same time as she followed the shadows in her mind and swam without thinking as fast as she could towards the boat, a way off with no one in sight on it. No one on the boat can see what's happening out here in the sea she thought and she swam fast and as smoothly as she could and the boat looked a long way away. Then suddenly she made it up to the boat and looked for a ladder and remembered there wasn't one and felt a panic before she thought to swim round to the stern and climb up on the footboard there, water sloshing into her mouth, and hauled herself up and over the side, banging her knee in her rush to get the last leg up that seemed to dangle alone into the water for a moment too long.

She stood dripping onto the deck and looked back at the sea moving constantly with its magnetic rhythm. She could climb back up to the diving-spot and have it all over again but while she was telling herself that she knew she wouldn't. She wiped off her nose and lifted the lid of the box. The fish had turned the same living green as the sea and a blue-tinged white underneath. He swivelled his big eye to look at her. She looked away. She went and got one of the chum buckets and dipped it several times in the sea, then lifted it half full and poured the cool water slowly all over the fish. When it felt the water it started to shudder. She shut the lid.

'Hey there.'

Cougar sauntered up out of the cabin.

'Hi.'

His eyes travelled down her body. 'I see you got wet.'

'Yeah.' She laughed thinking how it had felt.

'Good?'

'Yeah.'

Her dad appeared. He looked better now. 'Shall we head home?'

'Let's do that thing,' said Cougar. 'Dolphinfish has to be real fresh.'

He climbed up to the fly-bridge and her father went up after him. She saw the two damp patches in the pockets of his shorts where the beer bottles were. A minute later the engine kicked off and the sea began to mash behind the boat. She tried to think which way Miami would be but when Cougar headed the boat round it wasn't exactly where she'd thought he'd head.

She looked back at the sea where she'd swum. She could still feel her body vibrating but the whirr of the engine coming up through her feet was changing her body away from the vibration of the sea. After a while she went over to the box and looked in. The fish was lying still. Its gills opened and closed slowly. All along its length it had turned permanganate purple marked with fainter spurts of yellow. Underneath it was white. They looked at each other. It moved its tail a little.

She closed the lid and after a moment she sat on it, pulling her knees up. She saw the salt crystals lining each blonde hair on her calves the way frost lines every blade of grass on a winter lawn. She licked some off her leg. Then she looked at the thin line of blood along her forearm. She hoped it would leave a scar. Every now and then she looked ahead to see if Miami had appeared. She must have forgotten to look for a while because when she did see it it was already quite dense along the horizon.

She slid off the locker and opened the lid. The fish had changed. It was pure white all over with just a few blue freckles here and there and a dark blue edge to the folded sail down its back. She could see the gill fluttering. But when she leaned over further to try and meet its eye she knew it couldn't see her.

She sat down on the deck with her back against the locker and propped the lid open on her shoulder. She was facing the coast now and she watched Miami getting bigger and bigger without thinking about anything until Cougar cut the engine speed just out of the jetties. He let the boat drift in so its stern came round and she heard the wind-chime sound coming in snatches off the masts of the sail-boats. Then she let the lid fall gently off her shoulder and stood up and went forward to put the rubber things out down the sides so the boat wouldn't be damaged by other boats as it went in to its moorings.

When they opened the box to get the fish out he was just the way he was when they'd laid him in there, deep cobalt blue above and white underneath and barred with light yellow. He was dead. Cougar had to help her father lift him out, though she noticed how much smaller he was than she'd thought. They took a picture of her father standing on the jetty, his chest curled forward and his teeth gritted with the effort of lifting the fish with his two arms high so the head swung for a moment above the dock.

PIERROT AND PINOCCHIO

Look what the little Pierrot is doing. She drags her cart
across the square. She looks a bit scared. Looks a bit sad
as well. Pierrots don't smile ever. Sad Pierrot and her little
dog Patch. It's not light properly yet. The olde worlde
lamps are still on in the square. Trundle trundle the noise
a cart's wheels make on cobbles. Trundle trundle across
the square with Spot or Patch and her cart which has a
big clock in it like the one in a railway station. All her
earthly possessions. She's not well. She's got black patches
round her eyes like Patch has on the one eye. To hell in
a handcart. That's what this is. This is what a handcart is.
You pull it by
   – What you doing here?
He's here. I look at the side of his face. Look away.
   – Nothing.
   – What's that?
I shove it back in the plastic bag.
   – Nothing.
   – Budge up.
He's actually going to sit down on my bench. Sprawls.

I have to move right over to the end so as not to touch him. I don't know what to say to him. I lean forward. Pull up my socks one by one. See his arm snatch the plastic bag from beside my leg.

— Give it!

He jumps off the bench. I've got his jumper. It stretches. He slaps my hand off.

— Aow.

— Well behave yourself then.

He stands there and reaches into the plastic bag, gets it out.

— Give it back.

I grab at it. He swats me off.

— Give it.

— Shhh.

— It's my mum's.

— Not yours either then, is it?

— She knows I've got it.

— Yeah yeah.

He sits back down. He gets gum out.

— Here.

I take some. I watch him put his in.

— Stupid name.

He spells it out.

— Vaw goo way.

— That's not how you say it.

— How dyou know.

— It's Vaw goo. You don't say Es at the end. You still don't know that? I shake my head.

He laughs big and loud.

– It's foreign, stupid. They say them.

He flicks through. I watch. He reaches Pierrot. I make a snatch. He pulls away. Pierrot rips a bit.

– Don't!

– That was you.

– It was not.

– No skin off my nose. It's your mum's.

I slump back against the bench. It's not my mum's but. She's got to give it back to the coffee morning lady. I look across the park. I hear the pages. He's flicking them any old how.

– For God's sake.

He acts like he doesn't hear. I hear his teeth squidging saliva into the chewing gum. I wrinkle up my nose. He doesn't see. I look away across the park. A woman is throwing a ball for a pig-faced dog. Those dogs bite. I hate them. The same old men who are always here drinking wine are doing it and going doo-lally. I look over his shoulder. The Pierrot and the little dog are in a café having some tea. Pierrot's face close up is sad and magic. And really not well. He turns a page. Pierrot looks out the window. She's thinking to herself, I've got to get away. On the other page she's playing a tiny instrument. He turns a page. Pierrot dancing on a bridge all by herself. No there's Patch. The other page. Pierrot looks at the moon. He turns a page. A girl lying on a bed staring into space. It's in colour. Pale pink panties. Satin panties more like little shorts. And not well. Dark patches on her cheeks. Her eyes are fine but they're staring away sad.

– This is rubbish.

Bright red lipstick.

– No it isn't.

Red curly hair. What I always wanted.

– It's shit.

Funny cheeks like going-bad apples.

– Well give it back.

He makes a snorting noise.

– You can see her titties.

It's true. Weirdy pointy like witches' hats. I feel a blush.

– Shut up.

He turns. The bed empty with the covers back. A maid is hoovering. She sees something sticking out from the floor on the other side of the bed. Legs with shoes on. He turns. The maid is looking at the girl with the lipstick on the floor. Blood. Murder. She's got high heels on and different panties made of lace.

– Tits.

He laughs loud. I look away across the park. The old men are leaving. The pig dog chases the ball.

– They're too small. Rubbish.

I move against the armrest of the bench.

– I bet yours are about that size.

– Shut up.

He looks at my school jumper.

– Let's have a look then.

– Shut up I said.

He pulls the jumper down at the bottom. I shove him.

– Get off!

– There's nothing there. You're not even in a trainer bra yet.

– Piss off.

– Oo-oo-ooh.

What he thinks is a girl voice. I look away red. The old men have gone. Another dog after pig dog's ball. I imagine a trainer bra, what it might look like. I hear him flicking.

– This is rubbish.

I follow the ball with my eyes to show I'm not listening. Pig dog snaps his teeth at the other dog while they run. The other dog's got the ball.

– Dolls and shit. What's that all about?

I glance.

– She's not a doll, she's a Pierrot.

I point to where it says on the page Hi Pierrot Hi Pantaloon. That's what the baggy white trousers she's wearing are.

– Pier rot? What's that when it's at home?

– A Pierrot. Ha ha ha.

His leg is touching. I go still. Pig dog jumps and pushes his front legs against the other owner. Trying to shove her over. I look back at the page.

– Haven't you ever seen a Pierrot before?

He gives me a friendly look.

– Maybe. Have you?

– Yeah. Lots of people have them.

– Girls you mean?

– Yes girls. They're meant to be sad. Sometimes they're poorly.

I point at the circles round her eyes.

— What's wrong with her?

— She's wasting away. She comes from Victorian times.

I think back on the Victorian film with the well-off girl wasting away. On her deathbed. He's flicking. He reaches the girl in the pale pink panties. Now I see. That's what this is, a deathbed. I slide my eyes away to the grass. I feel his leg pushing.

— I like her better.

It's just my imagination. He wouldn't do that not to me.

— So?

— So who cares about stupid Pier rots and shit.

— Stop calling her that. You don't say the tih. I thought you did French.

I make mine a dead leg.

— You're making it up anyway. You don't know anything.

— So don't ask me anything then.

— I won't.

He gets up and walks across the grass. He runs for the ball where it's rolling past and throws it for the pig dog who barks.

I pick it up. The girl on the front is smiling right at me under the VOGUE. I could run out the park with it while he's doing that. I rub the place on my leg and open it up. I find the place with the Pierrot story. The one of her with the moon is the best. She'd like to fly up there. I look across. He's holding the ball high up and the pig dog can't get it. I turn the page. The girl with the panties. Blood coming out her mouth and going down as far as the high heels. It makes me feel a bit weird. I turn the page. Another page. It's black and white again. Two nice girls in jeans and lovely smock tops. One girl is going over a gate into a field. The other girl is laughing and holding a bunch of flowers. And they're not even normal flowers they're smudgy and pure white and fizzy at the edges. I look up. He's going through the bins. I look at the woman with pig dog. I look at the other woman who is calling her dog. They don't shout at him. I look up at the trees which are boring. I look over. He's coming back over the grass. I turn the page. It's brilliant. The girls are running down a path in a wood hand in hand. They are wearing bobbly hats and big long dresses and boots. Skipping. The trees are special there, thin and close together, not like trees round here. He slides onto the bench beside me. He sprawls. His leg goes against mine. Don't be stupid. It's not on purpose. I turn the page. The girls sit on a fence and a white horse gallops by in front across both pages. A white horse all fuzzy and smudgy like it's on fire like the flowers. A magic horse. I look over. He's got a magazine. The pages are all wavy and there's stuff on them. Ash, stains, maybe even dog pooh.

    – Yuch.

    – Want a look?

    – No.

    – Come on. Mine's better.

He holds it open in front of mine.

    – Check it out.

It's a woman not wearing anything. She's sticking her tongue out.

– Look at her tits.

I feel his leg. I shrink the insides of my leg further in.

– Look.

He turns a page. The woman is on her front now and her bottom's bare. There's a worse bit you can see. I feel not well.

– Don't.

– No look.

He turns pages. I look at the two women on the grass with the dogs. I look at my knees.

– I don't really like it.

– Grow up.

I hear the pages. I watch pig dog looking for his ball in the bushes. He's wagging his tail.

– Do you know what these pictures do to my willy?

He said willy. I make myself laugh.

– Pictures don't do things. They're pictures stupid.

– My willy stands on end.

– Do you think I'm stupid?

– It stands on end and it gets longer and longer.

I look at him to show I'm not stupid.

– Like Pinocchio's nose? Ha ha that's just a fairy story.

He turns a page. Another page. I look down for a second. I see two women without any clothes on. Their bosoms are very big. They are doing things.

– I'm telling you. I can't stop it. It's getting longer.

– Bits of your body don't get longer just like that. It's not scientific.

I look down without meaning to. She's lying back showing

between her legs. It looks sore. I move so as to get my magazine near my face. The girls hold their hands out to the white horse. He looks for sugar in their hands. I turn the page. The girls have fallen asleep during the day. They are under a tree. I see apples in their laps. I let my eyes roam all over the pages to take it all in. They're wearing patterned dresses and shoes that tie with ribbons. This must be what an apple tree looks like. This one's got her head on the other girl's shoulder. They are best friends who've fallen asleep in the forest.

— It hurts.

— What?

— My willy.

I face him.

— Stop it! Stop making things up like you're Pinocchio.

He keeps staring at his magazine. He moves his hand in his pocket a lot. I turn a page of mine. Colour again. Lovely black trousers and top and a straw hat. The buildings are all white. It's somewhere hot.

— Is anything happening to you?

I turn the page. She's next to a foreign church. His leg is jiggling. I feel he's looking at me.

— When you look at the pictures does anything happen to you?

She's on a balcony and you can see blue sky. She's wearing a white loose dress like an angel. I think of something good.

— My baby toe gets longer.

I laugh out loud. I feel better.

He shoves me.

– Shut up. I said. Does anything happen to you?

She lets doves fly out her hands into the sky. It says on the page Shadows of Your Future Self.

– No.

– Nothing?

– Nothing's supposed to happen.

– But what if you look at mine?

– No.

– Look.

He moves his magazine away so as I can see. His trousers are up in a tent shape. He takes his gum out and sticks it under the bench.

– Give me your hand.

I look across the park. The women are talking in the middle. The dogs are sniffing the grass. He holds my hand. I feel it for a minute. What that feels like. Warm and like I'm inside the insides of his hand. He starts to take my hand over to where he is.

– What for!

I get my hand away. I hold it in on my chest in the other hand.

– I want to show you something.

– No.

– It's something nice. I promise.

I look at him. He gives me a nice look back.

– I won't hurt you.

He keeps looking in my eyes. He puts his hand on my hand. It's really warm. I let him hold it which is weird.

– What are you going to do?

– It's OK. I'm not going to do anything.

He slides a bit closer. His whole leg is next to my leg. A funny feeling.

– Don't do anything.

– It's OK.

He keeps looking in my eyes.

– Is this a trick?

– No. I promise.

He pulls my hand off my chest. I let it go slowly. He turns it upside down so you can see the palm. His head comes closer looking down at my palm. I look down at it as well. He's really close. A gob of spit lands in my hand. I try and pull away but he's too strong. He gets his other hand and forces my hand to stay open so as he can rub his hand flat in the spit.

– This is what you do when you really like someone.

Our hands are pressed together with the wet spit in them. He rubs them to make the spit spread out. He looks at me close.

ORANGE GIRLS OF ESSEX

I man the Space desk. I pick up the phone.

'Hello, stud*io*!'

I have to say studio very fast with an upward-swinging oh at the end because Space Studios is a happy, happening place to work. I book photographers in, I meet and greet at Reception. Space Studios is run on a tight budget. I also help stock the fridges and kitchen cupboards, wash up when everyone's gone, fetch stuff for the smudgers like paper rolls, tripods, reflectors, filters, lights. I also have to flirt with them. Be nice to them, it's called. They are our clients, we want them to rebook. 'Trish, you are not being nice enough to our clients.' I get that from Matt from time to time. I am nice. Nice, efficient and actually, I'm an artist. I have a degree from the Royal College of Art. First, with distinction. That's the nail in the coffin apparently. If you get the distinction it means you're Too Good for This World. You can't relate, you're too highflown. You flew in, meaning to land, but you miscalculated. You've overflown it.

'So, Trish, you went to the Royal College?' Gavin Moody accosting me in the kitchenette off Reception. 'Funnily enough, I went to the Royal College. Photography. I dropped out. Wankers. They know nothing about pictures. Old Picasso, he didn't give a fuck about the function of the form or what have you. He liked a bit of'

'Do you want milk in this?'

'Yeah, one sugar please. A bit of all right. No time for artsy fartsy tossers. A proper'

'Oh there's the bell.'

I run out and press the intercom button. 'Hello, stud*io*!'

'Yeah. I've got a photoshoot with Gavin Moody.'

'Come up, top floor.'

Gavin comes out the kitchenette and waves as he strolls up to Studio 5. We're not really supposed to have scum-smudgers like Gavin in the studio but every now and then he rings and Matt comes up to me, says – as though I care – we're on a tight budget. Keep him away from Fabio and the *Vogue* shoot, that's your number one. Stick him in the back at the top, Studio 5. Keep him out of reception, off the stairs. And those models.

But how do you keep them off the stairs? Today it's some glamour girl who shagged a footballer and he dumped her and their kid, and now she's selling her story to some tabloid. We've had plenty of them here, the famous ones and the nothing ones, with their fake tits and their fake tans and their stories, usually sob stories. Coming up the stairs in fur and hotpants and tiny ripped Ts with Playboy bunnies toting handguns on the front. Orange girls of Essex, every one of them this all-over tantastic colour, this modern sexual battle-maiden's version of the old Briton's woad.

Sour with chemicals. A bit stripey over the calves. God they would have frightened the centurions. *Marcus Agrippa, the line will not hold. Over yonder, the British flameskins!* Sliver bodies cantilevered out at the twentieth floor. Baby-blue eyeshadow, streaky bacon hair.

I stand at the door of the studios to greet the one making her way up the stairs now. I hear her long before I see her, panting and blowing over the metallic tunk tunk of her heels. She stops two flights down.

'Christ.' Her voice echoes in the stairwell.

She starts up again.

A minute or so later she comes round the corner and I'm looking at the Grendel's mother of glamour models. At this angle, I can see straight down her pink knitted top. She's not had them done.

'Christ.' She grabs both hand rails and hoists herself on kitten heels. She's a heifer with mad cow disease trying to haul herself out into the yard for the morning milking, splaying on mincing hoofs, wild-eyed, desperate, udders slapping. She draws level, yells over her shoulder: 'Shanelle, can you urry up please? Someone's waitin.'

I step back. She swings round on the doorjamb and struts through stiff-legged to the reception desk on which she props a tense arm, the other hand to her chest.

'Where do I go?'

I wince as I say, 'It's two more flights up.'

'Christ.'

'I'm Trish, by the way. I run the studio, so if there's anything I can get for you?'

She presses the hand harder against her chest.

'Would you like a glass of water?'

'No thanks.'

She lifts her upper lip briefly in the symbol of a smile. Squealing comes up the stairwell. She bellows, 'Darren!'

I look down the stairs. A girl in a pink miniskirt and white boots is coming slowly up dragging a little boy by the hand. When he sees me he yanks back on her hand.

'Darren, shurrup. Shanelle, give him something, will you?'

'A'right.' Shanelle fishes a bag of crisps out of her bag and shoves them at Darren.

When they've gone up, I phone Studio 5.

'Gavin, can you come down a minute, please. I have to talk to you.'

He comes down. 'Trish, Trish, my one true wish.'

'Matt doesn't allow kids in the studio.'

Gavin spreads his hands. 'I told you the story. He bonked her, scrammed, left her holding the baby.'

'First of all, that's no baby, he must be what, three? four? And you didn't say she was being photographed with the kid.'

'Come on Trish you're not just a pretty face. What else would I be doing for an Abandoned Mother story?'

'You never told me.'

'What've you got against it? I thought you were a feminist. She's been dumped in it by some footballer, thinks he's Jack the Lad, don't wanna know.'

'I never said I was a feminist.'

'OK have it your own way, Miss Conceptuelle Artiste.

So maybe you're not a feminist. I'm a feminist. I'm helping her get her own back.'

'That's big of you. Dragging her kid all over the papers.'

'Oh it's like that, is it? You may have your degree in advanced origami but you don't know a whole lot about the human condition, do you?' The pacifying grin. 'I cover the human condition. No comment. Let others judge. See ya.'

He nips back up the stairs in his cowboy boots.

I wait till I know he's up there then I dial.

'Gavin?'

He's too mean for pay for an assistant, it's just him and them.

'Hi, sweetheart.'

'Don't let that child touch anything. If he breaks anything, you'll have to pay.'

'No probs. He's an angel. You should come up and give him a cuddle. Good practice.' The scuzzy laugh.

I decide not to ring Matt. It's too late now. I get back to work confirming bookings and ordering some HMI lights for Studio 3 where *Vogue* are shooting a story called Posh Punk. The doorbell goes.

'Hello, stud*io*!'

'Delivery for Gavin Moody.'

'Third floor.'

When I hear voices in the stairwell I come round and open the door. It's two burly men carrying binbags stuffed with props.

'Straight up, Studio 5.' I indicate with a hand.

I start looking over the accounts, a new job Matt's got me onto. I get quite absorbed in it, balancing the different columns. The internal goes.

'Trish, tender and slender?'

I press Save.

'I need some jazzy colorama, you've only got white and black up here.'

'What do you want?'

'Let's see now, something classy, how about aqua, and we'll have a roll of your best pink marbled effect as well.'

'Coming up.'

I go into the store, find the nine-foot paper rolls right at the back and lug them upstairs. Gavin is crouched over his camera crooning. 'That's it, love. Loooovely. Bit more thrust, that's it. To camera. Lick your lips. Good girl.'

The abandoned mother is kneeling on all fours on a shagpile rug. Her knees are apart as far as they will go, her arms bent slightly, only slightly, so her nipples can toy with the shag. She is wearing a scoop-necked purple top and a pair of purple knickers. As I stand there, she wriggles further back into the rug and grazes a palm across the end of a breast that's hanging like an almighty gobbet of snot from a string of straining skin.

'Wooh babe.'

Gavin's shutter chatters like mad.

Darren runs into shot and stands in front of his mother.

'Muuum, I gotta do a number two.'

'Go with Shanelle, love, Mum's busy.'

'I don't wanna go wiv Sha-neeeelle.' He sits down heavily

and slaps at the breasts with the flat of his hands. They start the slow swing of battered punchbags.

Look, I say to myself as I watch Darren dragged down the stairs ahead of me clutching the back of his trousers, why be so uppity? She's got to live. She must have a horrible time with that poor little kid. But God, I think, going over to the percolator, she has designed herself as a sex toy, why shouldn't men treat her like one? She looks like an orange satin pillow set with a nice pink frill in the middle and big bobbly bits on the top. Why wouldn't he see it as stuff? Just stuff. Luvverly stuff. And so he boinged on her bouncy castles, both of them knocking back champagne and snorting coke, and if she got pregnant, well it *was* a fucking bore and a stupid thing to happen, and probably a trap as well because she's no innocent. Imagine how he feels now.

I stir some milk into the coffee and go back to the desk. The phone is ringing.

'Hello stud*io*!'

GQ wanting to do some new actress. I flip through the diary with the phone jammed into my shoulder.

He just wanted to have a good time and she was up for it. He didn't ask to be trapped, hampered, chained into any kind of *relationship* where he'd be forced to think about what stood behind those semi-deflated orange footballs and cogitate 'it's a person'. 'Person' was not how she presented, she presented as yet another game involving footballs, then once she'd got him dribbling up the pitch, bam! off with the mask and it's the Big Bad Wolf, but no one else can see it, they all believe in Little Orange Riding Hood with a baby stuffed in her basket.

A little hand creeps across my desk. It grabs two rubbers.

I look up, mouth *No* and say, 'I can only give you second option on a daylight studio for the Friday.'

Darren puts one of the rubbers in his mouth and runs off, munching. He's heading for Studio 3. *Vogue*.

'Uh, Jake, can I ring you back? Two minutes. Yeah. Hey, Darren!'

I snatch at him but he slips round me leaving a brown streak across the door of Studio 3. Shanelle strolls out of the toilet snapping her handbag shut. I can see she's been doing her face.

'You'd better take him back in. Look at his hand.'

She grabs Darren's hand and turns it palm up.

'You're a shitty little boy, you know that?'

He starts bawling.

'Can you keep him quiet, please?'

She smiles at me and yanks him into the Ladies.

I sit down at the desk and check to see if he's left any of it on me. I dial *GQ*. With the other hand I prod at the remaining rubber with a pencil. I flick it with the pencil into the wastepaper basket. Shanelle comes out of the toilet leading Darren, pulling his arm up high so he has to prance on tippy toes to keep up with her. As she passes she rolls her eyes. I widen mine in a sort of sympathy. Shitty little boy. But hold on a minute, poor little shit. He's got to go back up there and watch his mother flubber about on shag-pile while Gavin corrs.

The buzzer.

'Hello stud*i*o!'

'Yo. Dino's Deli.'

'Hi, Si.'

I buzz him in and get out the sheet with everyone's lunch orders on it. I mean why can't that male thing of just wanting to have some squelch be accepted for what it is? Nature. We're supposed to worship nature for God's sake, always saving whales and pandas. We're out there on the moors night and day filming the rutting season of the mad-for-it male deer. Why do we have to pretend humans aren't the same? Sex is life-affirming, blinding, a belly-laugh, a deep, irrepressible impulse of the species, any species. Oh yeah, he could have taken precautions. In Neverneverland you'll always find Peter Pan flittering about in a condom. But the man's a striker for Arsenal, for God's sake. What did she expect? Its all about goal kick not standing there like Hamlet thinking to be or not to be.

Si comes in with two big boxes.

'Hey, Trish. How's it going?'

'Bearing up. How about you?'

'Yeah, you know.'

He runs back down to get the other three. I check one of the boxes. Quinoa salads, sushi, and roasted organic vegetables on non-wheat bread. It's for *Vogue*. Si appears and dumps the others by the desk.

'So Saturday. Are you gonna come down?'

He wipes his hands on his jeans.

'I dunno. Where are you meeting up?'

'Dreambags. Around ten. You should come, it'll be good.'

'Yeah.' I bite my lip.

'Come ooon. Gotta kick back.'

Si's nice. He's got sad little eyes. He sells sandwiches.

'Yeah, might do that. Gotta take these in.'

I go into Studio 3 with two of the boxes. It's dark except on a podium where the tungsten fresnel lights shine on Rene Karstein and Oksana Shepetsova both dressed as Sid Vicious morphing into the Duchess of Devonshire. Nasty gobshites yelling on the stereo. Fabio's assistant, Danno, comes up to me.

'*Ah*lo, darlin, y'all right?'

'Yeah, yeah. How's it going.'

'Not baaaad. Not baaaad.'

I hold the brown boxes against my stomach.

'She's something isn't she?' I'm looking at Rene Karstein, fresh out of Nowheresville, Ohio. She is entirely made out of tines. Her stilettoes have sunk into the wood. If you grabbed her by the waist and pulled, her pointy ends would tear off a mouthful of podium. Probably all she eats. Apparently even wood lice have trouble living on it. Fabio stands up behind the camera.

'This isn't working. Rene you're not giving me anything.'

Rene sways on her tines. She looks at Oksana.

'Rene come on.'

He shakes his head, goes back behind the lens. 'Friggin' in the Riggin'' comes on.

From behind the camera Fabio's falsetto: 'Frigging in the rigging! Frigging in the rigging!'

Rene clutches at a chain on Oksana's ripped leather jacket to keep her balance. Her lip trembles. Fabio high-pitched from behind the camera.

'Frigging in the rigging. Frigging in the rigging. Oksana bébébébébébé!'

Oksana winds her body, leans from the waist, grimaces with teeth the size of big toes. Twists, gobs, gurns, jams hands in platinum spikes, tugs, pouts, swoons, pogos, shimmies, thrusts, gyrates, bites her lip, closes her eyes, yanks open her jacket so tulle froths out, smoulders, sniggers, licks, bats, winks, screams, rips tulle, rips tulle again, flays it, stamps on it, smears lipstick on her face, howls, bites tulle, snaps zips, slinks hips, squats, thrusts, cocks, tosses, leers, ices-over, melts slo-mo, refreezes, gives Fabio the finger and oozes scuzzy elegance over a shoulder. Fabio yells yes, yes, yes, yes, yes, yes, yes, and expertly abuses the camera shutter. Rene starts to cry. I take the big boxes over to the kitchen and get out the lunchboxes with each order typed onto a label on the top. I open the fridge, get out water, juice and lemon tea. There's an espresso machine in this studio. I check it for ground coffee and get the little white cups out of the cupboard ready. I walk back past the podium. Fabio's clicking away.

'Cry-beauty,' he shouts sarkily. Rene cries and mascara runs down her face. Oksana sneers, sicks, smoulders, stretches and tweaks Rene's nipple then bites her ear. 'Cry! Cry!' She cries. She opens black lips in a wide clown and bawls her heart out at the ceiling.

★

I get back out in time to answer the phone.

'Hello, stud*io*!'

Ed Griffin, the portrait smudger, a *Sunday Times* shoot. It takes a while to discuss his order for special lights and filters, then I do the boxes for Studios 1 and 2. I do Studio 5 last.

Grendel's mother is sitting in the round perspex chair that hangs from the studio ceiling. She leans forward, arches her back, and lifts her mohair jumper and bra part way up her boobs.

'Freeze, love. Brilliant. Top!'

Gavin's shutter gnashes away. I can't help staring at her, legs dangled in midair, top yanked up over wallops that swag from under bra elastic. Doing sex, even now, to sort the mistake of that other sex, sanctified by the name of child. I Have To Think of My Little Boy.

I carry on to the kitchen, sidestepping Darren who runs helter-skelter round the studio, tripping over leads and grabbing at things with Shanelle behind him.

'Come on, darlin',' she says, 'what about some of this?'

She shakes a bottle of Diet Coke at him. He grabs it and runs into the corner.

Well, I think to myself, putting the brown box down on the kitchen counter, she should have thought of My Little Boy before she put her knickers on her head and yelled, Goooooooaaaaaaal, shouldn't she? I feel for that footballer, I really do, about to be hounded by the redtop mob into spending his Sundays with her and that kid, dragging himself away from a bit of fancy footwork to some flat in Forest Gate, her sitting there laughing like a drain with her orange legs apart and her top pulled up over these supposed inducements. A woman who loves her mum, her soaps, her bubbly, her baby, all waterlogged emotions and dripping fluids, whacked-out on God's sexist drugs, oestrogen, progesterone, back-milk endorphins, and he's supposed to do the right thing and exalt her as the Mother of My Child.

I lay the lunchboxes out on the melamine countertop, fetch water, juice and lemon tea from the fridge and check the percolator. No, I know I should defend my sex and all that shit, but what I really feel like doing is running in to that flat in Forest Gate, snatching the footballer's hand and screaming, quick! and we run away out into the forest of Epping, running, running, batting away the branches as we head down the forest paths, away from that flat with the baby crying, the telly on at the same time as the stereo, milky tea, Friday nights in with curry and chips, baby snivelling, hauling itself round the furniture in its nappy and dummy tit.

I rinse the metal filter and tuck the fresh filter paper into it. As I'm pouring the ground coffee in I hear a crash followed by another crash. Everyone shouts Darren! I stick my head out the kitchen. Darren wailing by the stereo. One speaker has smashed over on its side and it has yanked the amp off the table onto the floor with it. Diet Coke is glugging out all over the amp.

I grab a cloth and run over. Shanelle lifts Darren up by one arm where he hangs, revolving slightly, while she high-steps over everything carrying him towards his mum. I mop the floor.

'Oh I'm sorry, I'm really sorry.' She struggles to get out of the hanging chair. 'Bad boy, Darren. Has he broken anything?'

Darren flips about at the end of Shanelle's arm half-choked with rage.

'It's OK, as long as the stereo works.'

Gavin appears beside me. 'No harm done, darlin. Just a knock.'

He puts the speaker back upright. There's a puncture in the fuzzy fabric on the front of it.

'Can you check it's still working please?'

I go back into the kitchen for a dustpan, I've noticed a broken glass as well. I get a Diet Coke from the fridge and hand it to Shanelle.

'No probs,' says Gavin, plugging in the amp. 'It'll be fine. Boys will be boys.'

Boys will be boys. I thump back downstairs. If I were a superheroine I'd come down to earth on a mission for womankind: free them of kids. No more moaning. Imagine that, boys, they'd stop tugging on pc heartstrings so you felt you had to give up your Sundays to take the little sod out to the football pitch/swings/zoo. Kids are supposed to be what Real Life is about, maturing, joyous, worth it, when what it's really like is having to wheel some gabby old lady and her bedpan around with you until you can hand them back to their mums and run out the door, run, really run down the road, punching the air, howling at the sky, thanking God for the miracle of other barren wombs, which, let's face it, are a boon for the environment, etc.

I open the accounts file on the computer and start clicking the mouse over last week's entries. The internal goes. Studio 3 light flashing.

'Trish here. Yeah. No problem. I'll send her in when she gets here.'

I type week 22 into the window on the computer and wait for the file to load. If there wasn't a God I'd put that little boy out of his mother's misery, smother him in the postbag the postman left downstairs. It wouldn't take long, the little lad jumping a bit like Betty Blue and afterwards it would be all over and I could stagger out of the hospital ward where his mother had been sectioned for having excessively injectible holes, and zigzag through the streets in my high heels and drag, knowing that I did it for love.

'Hello, stud*io*!'

It's the journalist already, come to interview up-and-coming Rene Karstein. I buzz her in downstairs, then wait for a bit before I get up to open the door. It's always been a trap, a con, a net to catch birds in. And little wild things, little Stringfellows birds, chirping their hearts out under glitterballs, they fall and are caught, and next thing you know they are squatting on the nest for twenty years saying, 'I live for my kid, for wiping his nose, his arse, his first word, his first step, his first day at school, the first day he turns on me and screams, "why were you never anyone? why did you turn my dad off me? why aren't we going to Barbados this year instead of Margate?"'

The *Vogue* journalist is coming up the stairs with this

big smile on her face. Amazing suit but then she's got privileged access to the Balenciaga sample sale.

'Hi, are you Lucy?'

'Yah.' She tucks her hair behind her ear. Thinks she's cool and street because she's got some Banksy Fuck the Pigs T-shirt on with pigs in police helmets having it off with other pigs, what does she know? Bet she never had the pigs round her door. Bet she's never had to spend years tunnelling out of some suburban hell either.

'They're in here.' I lead the way to Studio 3.

'Is Rene here?'

Er, *yes*. That's why you're *here*. 'Yeah.'

The journo tucks her hair behind her ear even though it's already behind her ear.

'And how is she getting on?'

'Uh. She's having a bawl.'

I'm standing by the Studio 3 door with my hand on the doorknob waiting for her to come forward. She dithers near the reception desk.

'What's she like?'

I puff out my cheeks. 'Really nice.'

She applies eyes like diamond drills. Chips out a gobbet.

'And like she's been born with plastic surgery.'

Another gobbet.

'And without an oesophagus.'

She stares.

'And just really tall.'

'Oh yah,' she says, relaxing. 'They're like Somali tribesmen, you know, where they look like they have two sets of legs

216

stacked one on top of the other?' She clutches her throat. 'Makes you feel like this   this   *squat* little toad.'

I examine her. She's about five feet eleven, natural tan and probably got an oligarch who loves her.

'Yup,' I say. 'Know just how you feel.' I open the door and she goes through.

I go back to the desk and drain the cold cup of coffee.

I rummage around in the wastepaper basket and find the rubber. I grab some pencils and felt pens and a few sheets of paper and go up to Studio 5.

The abandoned mother is sitting on a barstool placed in the centre of the shagpile carpet. She's in a bra and pants set and a babydoll nightie, sheer pink nylon with black edging. Darren is slumped on her knee. He's busy playing with something, my pink rubber.

'Can you get him to look over here, love?' Gavin has his face squashed flat against the camera.

'Dar-ren, Dar-ren.' She makes her voice sing-song. 'What's that funny man doing, then?'

I go over to Shanelle on the sofa. 'Uh, I thought these might keep Darren out of trouble.'

She looks up, her mouth hanging open. I see a grey gnarl of gum on her tongue.

'He was playing with this stuff on my desk.' I put it all down next to her. Shanelle seems to come to.

'Aw. Nice one.' She raises her voice. 'Int it, Nat?'

'Wo'?'

'That nice girl from downstairs has brought Darren something.'

Nat is looking at the camera with her mouth slightly open. 'Thanks,' she says without moving her lips. Darren spits out bits of rubber.

'Hello, stud*io*!'

Pop wanting to cancel the Studio 4 booking for Wednesday week. I rub out the entry under Wednesday and click the mouse on the pad. Spreadsheet 22 comes up. I sigh. OK so kids are all some Hallmark card kind of a con but the fact is he's here now, he's born, and Freddie the Footballer has run off and she's left, yes, holding the baby. But there's life in the old bitch yet. Now that she knows she'll never be a pop tart, thanks to The Kid, she's going to mutate her expectations, short-circuit resentment, and back The Kid, like betting on a horse, night at the dogs, koom on Engerrland. Her kid, the contender, offspring of England's finest, only the best for my kid. After all, he's her Own Flesh and Blood. Isn't that the eery expression? Just another bodily outgrowth, a gland that swelled, took shape and withered off.

I look up from my screen. Gavin running his hand through thin grey hair.

'Nearly done?'

'Couple more,' he says. 'I've got your stereo working again. Sort of.'

'Sort of? Have you left them up there alone?'

'They're having a cup of tea. I just need a break and a fag. You know Trish'

He waits for a prompt, a yeah or a what. I look at him.

'It's not an easy line of work. One minute they've got their tits out, the next they're moaning about you using them. What's a bloke to do?'

I shrug my shoulders. 'Gay porn? Huge market.'

'Very funny. You know, fashion is my first love. But it's a young man's game. Back in the day, I never touched this line of work. Did quite a bit of fashion and a lot of kiddies fashion. Catalogues, mostly. We'd go on location, Turkey, Mauritius. All the kids splashing about in the water having the time of their lives. And the mums' – he looks over his shoulder – 'the moment they left Heathrow they lost it. Night after night, tuck the kid up, get out and party.' He sweeps a hand through the grey hair. 'We had some wild times I can tell you. *Mums.*'

'They must have been desperate. For some fun.'

'I know what you're thinking. But they're only human.'

'Scuse me a minute, Gavin.'

I slip into Studio 3. Three enormous tungsten studio lights glare up at Oksana Shepetsova. She's bouncing on a trampette wearing a couture ballgown and full biker gear. She stomps down into the trampette, springs up, and in mid-flight, legs wide, tears at the gauzy skirts in a frenzy. I go right to the back of the studio where it's almost totally dark and pretend to sort through some polystyrene panels stacked there. I hear voices from the other side of the panels. I peek round. Two pairs of freak-length shanks poking out, both sets crossed, one set wearing bondage trousers.

'That's *so* interesting. So she discovered you at the airport. Where were you flying to?'

219

'Uh. I wasn't flying?' Rene gives a preteen laugh. 'I was, like, working in J.C.'s Juicees?'

'Was that a summer job?'

'No, it was more like, you know, my regular job?'

'So back then you were at the airport, but you weren't going anywhere.'

'Riiight.'

'Whereas now, you are always at the airport and always going places. Two days in London, three in Paris, back to New York. What's that *like*?'

'Oh man,' I hear Rene sighing. 'It's like insane, you know? I get really umm like tired of all those retard in-flight movies?' The little girl laugh.

'Is there anywhere you've travelled as a model that you've especially loved?'

'Uh. Greenland was *wild*. Like, they drink a *lot*. Uh. Africa? I'm not exactly sure what the exact country was?'

'Were you in a city? Out in the bush?'

'We went on like safari?'

'Ooh. Safari. Did you see any exciting animals?'

'Uh lions? And uh deer? Or something?'

'Wow. And what about how you feel about yourself?'

'Excuse me?'

'Are you happy?'

'Oh uh it's amazing. I wake up every day and think I must be dreaming.'

'Fabulous. And have you always known that you're beautiful?'

I close my eyes. Stupid inbred. As if she doesn't know what the girl's going to say.

'Are you kidding me? They used to call me Stickfinger in High School. I couldn't even get a date for the Prom? I could cry just thinking about the shame.'

I go back out to Reception. Gavin's cigarette is still burning in a torn-off fag packet lid on my desk. I scrunch it, swipe it into the bin, sit down and pick up a bottle of Evian. The screen's gone dark. I look at it for a minute and press a couple of keys on the keyboard. I take a swig of the Evian and wait for the spreadsheet to light up on the screen.

FAHSION

On a dark blustery wet and windy night at a stadium far from the centre of Paris, Alexander McQueen presented his collection inspired by the murder of a distant relative. The one related to Alexander was Elizabeth How who was convicted of being a witch in Salem in 1692. If you were beautiful, red headed, a midwife, a female healer or simply an individual this would be enough to receive copious amounts of torture and then to be burnt alive on a stake in front of all of your family, neighbours and towns people. In this case the stunning make up artist Charlotte Tilbury with a mass of flaming red hair would have not stud a chance and would with out a doubt gone up in smoke. Luckily for red heads 'the grate hunt' for witches is now over.

Hi, your hot ;-) do you have a face pic? Nice cock hope you like my attachment, Bobo

This sinister show was held in a humongous space, hung upside down from the vast ceiling was a gigantic glass pyramid showing haunting images of millions of cock-roaches crawling over each other and horrific tortured flaming faces, bearing there sculls. According to popular mythology Mount Osore in the north of Japan marks the entrance of hell. All soles on their way to the underworld must cross this active volcanic charred landscape of blasted rock filled with bubbling pits of unearthly hues and noxious fumes. Get the picture? McQueen often gives us a shady glimpse with his shows of forbidden life and death. All over, the glob in every sector of religion in all region of the planet the belief in witches was ripe and is still alive today.

Nice one Superman lets get a look at your cheeky chops Mr Jinormous, cherry-picked kisses, Bobo

'Hello?　　　　Yes it's me, Bobo.　　　　I'm writing it now Mooshymoosh.　　　Who? Tomboy. White cheeks, amazing élan, falling down powdered hair. Stars in your eyes!'

In ancient Egypt the legendary Queen Cleopatra used mica violet as metallic shadow with back coal heavily outlining her remarkable pupils caused by eye drops made from 'Belladonna' a shady plant. She was the kind of sorceress, who would have easily won your hart over with her big eyes. Charlotte Tilbury took her inspiration form the film 'Anthony and Cleopatra' the one with Elizabeth Taylor. Backstage I met up with Charlotte, who passionately said to me" Alexander actually called me on the way to the show and said;" I want electric green eyes". Looking into a crystal ball for next season, I see metallic eyes flashing at me. I cannot wait to see if my professy is accurate.

Hello Mr Postman, wanna post your French letter in my box ;-) how about a lunchtime delivery? Bobo

'Hello, Bobo here.   Hello daaarling.   Well, I'm at my desk writing up the collections. Hear that rustling? It's my hands reaching for the keyboard through a jungle of Casablanca lilies.   Karl Lagerfeld, sweetie.   I'm bare buck-naked except I've slipped into an exquisite pair of silk satin couture panties in cuisse de nymphe émue.   Almost the same colour as my skin when aroused. But I'm just that shade paler, darling, even when you move me. You know when the sky just slightly blushes before *l'aurore*, because it's the hour all the best bedrooms of superluxe hotels, and the naughty country haystacks feature lovers doing it madly, and raunchy buttocks are popping up in the hay and the sky gets a teensy bit of a surprise? Oops, the line's beeping, can I call you back?'

'Hello, Mooshymoosh?   I've done my piece on the McQueen show, it's pinging through space to you now, sweetness.   Gelled, teared, fucked, sprayed, backcombed, with fox tails, chinchilla, loads of bits of claw and paw coming out of it, big Mohicans of fur, sauvage, fab fab.   OK.'

Happy Monday 2 hot 2 handle! wanna gobble you up how about a tea time creamy snack chez mwa mwa? Wigel wigel, Bobo

'Hello Bobo here, Mooshy,　　　how can I write if you keep ringing me up, moomoo?　　Mm hnn.　　Mmm hnnn.　　No, definitely Viktor & Rolf.　　Ultra. In the basement of a palais with these cracking old stone tiles, no music, high drama, faint distant bells, millions of bells, coming nearer and nearer through the dry ice, you never saw the end of the dry ice, tiny, old ancient bells, brass, copper, bells from Mongolia, China, models stumbling over broken tiles, you saw nothing, fog, mist, you only heard bells spilling out of hemlines like hives of bees, unpolished dusty bell troves stuffed in huge scooped cowl of a cropped jacket, then trains of bells going far away down the catwalk, tinkling alpine cow herds lost in a cloud, organza dressing-gowns with maribou lining ombréd into bells, huge crusty dinging and danging, and sitting right next to Anna Wintour in the fog these two fabulous couture creatures with bubble lips and beagle's ears of diamonds coughing into their hankies. Can I put you on hold?　　I have to!'

'Hello?　　Daaaarling. Where was I?　　Oh, not just silk, charmeuse, with mother-of-pearl buttons and my schlong just peeking out all pink and clean as a baby's gums and just slightly bobbing against these ultra-chi-chi *volants* hand-tucked by sweated couture labour using heartbreak-ingly small stitches and if they don't make each stitch one half of a millimetre long and no longer it's into the toile garde-robe for them and no supper, no, not even a vol-au-vent, they just have to chew on calico or maybe their bleeding nails. Darling I'm terribly hung and on deadline can I call you back toot allure? The other line!'

'Moosh?   Navy court shoes with gold, butter-milk clothes, staggering on old flagstones, loose, breaking and see-sawing under their feet and one would slide and her bells would go Hey-ulp! Hey-ulp! and she'd recover and stagger on ringing and dinging in the fog, the mist, the Director of Experimental Retail at Barneys having a spasm in the corner and someone fell off a ledge at the back and fainted, and then layers of bruised pink tulle over gold with huge garland of bells clinking, so much intrigue, hair very swept away at all the shows, so direc-tional yet approachable, hair to study, the girls peach of innocence, pioneers of selfishness.   YSL.
I'll do Fashion Canapes now, Moosh.   Yes, right now.'

How do you want me studpup :-P hope you like my attachment, Bobo

FAHSION CANAPES
HAPPY VALENTINES

February 14th found me waking up with several silly Valentines text messages like' Cupids arrow cumming your way just feel the prick' but the best gift ever was by Allura Phillips (Condé Nasts' grey eminence of beauty) a certifi-cate of one hector of lush mexican rain forest with several Jaguar families living amongst the exotic vegetations. A jewellery designer I love very much is the beautiful Marie-Helene de Tieyak who gave her local leper colony in Rajastan a small heard of goats.

Hello Superdude well as above so below it wood seem wanna swing by? Bobo

RIO A-PAREEO

What's hot at Colette next season? I ask Sarah main buyer who are the lucky ones to be included into the directional elite group of designers? 'We bought Isabella Capeto because it's a fresh friendly collection with sun from Brazil. This new collection for A/W was inspired by the world of princess in Disney and by the book on this American artist who was doing lots of drawings that we found in his place when he was dead'.

'Hello? Daaarling. Well I've got a choker lashed round my neck, 1950s Schiaparelli jeuj.

Ver ver tight, really too tight and my neck is even whiter than usual and my throat's all sore and tiny like a little bird's, oh it's hurting! Black leather with these cruel lumps of amber dangling down and striking my throat so I'll get strawberry patches and my neck's all bent up like a swan's, I can't breathe! I'm turning the most mystical shade of blue. Keep going, back in a tinkle.'

'Hello, what? What you really can't find an Anchor Low? Well check the Chambre Syndicale on the worldy web, Mooshymoosh. Well get a trog to do it. I don't do spelling. Very feminist. Swimsuits worn the wrong way. No make-up. I'm writing!'

Charmed Mr Postman, cant wait for you to deliver your package ;-O and remember the postman always comes twice, antissipating Bobo

The Brazilian party was also memorable at the Crion Hotel on Place de Concord witch was covered with snow like a seen from Dr. Zivago. Inside the hot rhythmic beats were supplied by Olympia la tan hypnotizing the guests in a latino trance. Most were lashed by the abundance amount of baby Moet bottles with little tits to extract one's addiction by suckling. Michela Roberts was on the look out for male modles, Eric Brege looked the part with his suave water waves. The legendary Loulu de la Falaise could hardly stop smile ling.

PITTER PAT

Vlad Piper decided to keep Rochelle's four-month-old baby, having aborted all previous efforts. It will be a boy named Piers: [italic] such [unitalic] a Sloane name for a designer who revels in decay and macho-ness. The baby-safe catwalk had a rubberised astroturf runway.

You got me pink n poppin ;-★ come and do me now, Bobo

LONDON CALLING

A false mussel of gossip was that Edward Enninful fell out with Stephen Meisel so he was now looking for another stylist. I confronted Edward about this bit of info whiles giving him rides to different shows. One of the shows we went to was frost French in a heavenly church lit up by millions of candles. This is where Pat Mac Grath and Edward grew up, he showed me there opposing balconies in the touching estate nearby. As I was leaving the downstairs crib at frost French going up the medeville winding stairs You Know Who came down the oposite direction and her skirt fell down to revile a tiny purple polka dotted string hocking up her unkempt pink fleshy lettuce. In a bit of a fashion state I wondered back to my driver being harassed by local yobs shouting lady boy we doing to mug you. Edward was telling me back in the car that three seasons

'Hello!   Not now daaaarling I'm ultra busy.   Oh, darling, of course I am.   Darling of course heels. Scarlet leather hobble sprites, nasty vicious five inch with little rockabye platforms.   Balenciaga. They've got mirrored panels over the instep so if anyone needs to powder their nose they have to prostrate themselves at my feet. Byee.'

ago the skanderless You Know Who came up to him at a Vogue party and kisses him dubiously on the mouth then only to revile that she had just given her boyfriend a

'Hello?   Oh, sweetbird.   No, all the time in the world.   So did it hurt?   So now you're going to be a   Are you sure?   But does bleeding have to mean that it's   But maybe it's just your body making   But have you seen the   Oh.   Don't say that.   But you will.   Oh, please don't I can't bear it. Why don't you come over and I'll put a hot water bottle on your darling little tummy?

Very little tummy! Teensy weensy tummy, especially now.   Oh, darling, don't, please don't because I adore you so much and   OK, run and get a tissue, I'll hold.'

blowjob previously and that he came in her mouth. We then, went off to have a sushi lunch, which was not easy to deal with after the discombobulating sights.

'No, Sweetbird that was just me tapping my nails.   It was!   Do I hear you smiling?   Can I come over and make it better?   Can I cover you in bird of paradise feathers? Because you are a bird of paradise, you know.

Oh but I do have some, Sweetwings.

But I just adore anything illegal.   No, don't be cross. I went on a mission with Sultan – Thingummy's best friend, you know? He's going to be major. He has a dinky mews house next to the Heath and he puts mirrors up all round the room at night and wanks on the bed watching himself and all the munchkins crawl out from the Heath and put their faces against the windows and wank too. Isn't it sweet?   No, straight.   No, he's definitely straight just bad. Are you lying down, my precious jewel?   Good I'll call you back, the other line.'

'Hello?   Which one, Mooshy? I'm writing!   Hold on. I need my notes. *Première passage*. Ms Moneypenny, sexual frustration, scared of life. Hair held up with paperclips and office paraphernelia. Black dresses, red lips. *Deuxième passage.* Motherhood – pain – shock – damage. Anti-pregnancy demonstration. All mothers who had believed in men and as soon as they got pregnant the men left them and the women got bitter and twisted. Vicious triangular red lips, patch pocket maternity dresses, carrying plastic babies with fabric middles, the kind that can pee in their pants and suck their thumbs. Peter Pan collars. *Troisième passage.* Rock 'n' roll. Day-glo plastic early Madonna. I hate my mother and father. Goth/catwoman/groupie/lace/chiffon/velvet/compli-cated. *Quatrième passage.* Goddess, womanhood, beyond woman, true strength. Bronze body paint, head bronze, neck bronze, chest bronze, ears bronze, everything bronze, eyelashes, eyes. I talked to Liv Tyler. I'll send it in a minute.

Yes in a real minute!'

'Are you lying down, my Sweetest bird?   Well it was dreary without you but you missed YSL, the swan-song.   Two hours with catnaps. Screaming with prestige, all his collections from 64, there was a two to four minute pause between each one. Naomi amazing, Jerry Hall sublime. All the girls could handle the gloves, no button would faze them, they have handbags of their own at home, these girls were picked up by chauffeurs.   I can hear you smiling, darling.   Well, run and make some and I'll call you back. Snowdrop kisses.'

My manquest is over Silver Daddy Bear :-1 who's gonna be sleeping in <u>my</u> bed? Bobo

SPANISH HIGHS

At Versailles John Galliano dressed as a matador reigned supreme for the house of Christian Dior. The show embellished with super models was a feast to the eye and giant pie 'Eyah' cooked by Spanish pirates was a feast too. Under a night sky, exploding with fireworks the show video was projected onto a 60 meter fountain. All this opulence and yet back stage there was a slight melancholic feeling due to the passing away from John's right hand Stephen he will be greatly missed. The after part was lavish and the star studded guests dance to flamenco guitarists, like the ravishing Charlize Theron in a beautiful black tulle Dior dress who danced with John till dawn. Ole.

'Hello?   Daaarling, they're going to kill me.   No seriously I'm busy busy busy.   Fresh glove leather rising into the air with lungfuls of lilies. I'm also fainting and unable to breathe due to the choker but one must suffer to be beautiful. And now I'm sweeping over to the mirror and sliding next season's gauze chemise from Lanvin over my torso in palest charcoal with a crystal underlayer so you can just see my skin through it like milk under ice. Darling don't give up on me, the other line.'

'What now?   Don't be like that it doesn't suit you.   Well get a slavey to do that I'm not a sub.   I don't know how you spell her, Moosh, but her collarbones stick out so far that when it rains puddles collect and you can see tadpoles swimming in them. Toodle.'

'You're still there, little bird?   Are you alone?   Do you want me to come over and look after you?   Of course, my darling Sweetness the smoking *passage*. The girls did a very very old school walk. Everyone melancholic hoping a tear will crawl out of the fake lashes. Catherine Deneuve stood up and sang a melancholic song, trying to cry. Big arse but stunning. Paloma Picasso cried crocodile tears, all the plastic creatures, all the editors flapping. Lots of shoulder pads, everyone in YSL. Sophie Dahl, raunchy milkmaid. Gwyneth Paltrow, serene black smoking. The Tweety Pie Girl who's married to Johnny Depp. Lauren Bacall, snapdragon, she's had nothing done, a mean crack for a lip. Jeanne Moreau, eyes sad, the most beautiful. Amira Cesar. French actress. Natural beauty. Every night she wears Midnight Secret. She says it's the most nutritious cream ever invented. I'm going to get you the uber bottle.   No, don't even dream of it, Botox fucks up the third eye.   I can hear you giggling, sweet-ness.   Yes I do.   Yes, go and take the kettle off. Ciao and remember I love you very much.'

Need you to do me now scary monster man door on latch! Bobo

'Hello?   Who?   Mimosa. Jade. Pearl. Poached salmon. Nubian. Cream. 100 per cent silk faille.
I'm writing as fast as I can. Toodle-oo.'

NIGHT TO REMEMBER
Later on that evening I when to a marvellous party and believe me I went to nearly all of them. Held in the stamp

size studio of stunning avongard actress Tilda Swindon and art photographer Katerina Jepp who deals with her domestic chores in a white bikini made of towelling. That evening had a relaxed atmosphere with buckets of champagnes, platters of crudity and a pile of roast chickens rather than the predictible refined canapes. Stella Mucartney was calm as a cucumber after her well received show and also calm was the beautiful Nina Young in a white Boudicca mariboo dress whose boyfriend Simon helped set up Pop Idol and has just finished a fasinating documentary on the fabulous Alice Martineau suffering from MS. The music was perfectly spun by Jefferson Hack doing a bit of easy mellow then every body went bezerk when he played Age of aquarius by Hair. Dita von Tees was reclining on a antique dentist chair humming Marlene Dietrich tunes then at five thirty Tilda in navy drain pips and sever heels served up early grey to the hard core Katerina still wearing a grey and blue naval comme T shirt with combats and Jefferson who out spun himself dizzily.

'Yes?   Yemeni Bag Ladies meets Edwardian Doll. Cellophane, flowers, luggage, Coke cans and Fanta in the hair. Lacing the girls into tight-corsetted crinolines as huge as this house, Bill screaming "take two inches off her, take three inches off her!" One girl fainted. Screaming, feeding them sugar, alcohol, this girl swooning on my shoulder and everyone shrieking Bobo! Running, Mooshy, other line.'

'Hilloo?   Daaarling, you're being naughty.
Weeeell, can you hear that sound of a fine-toothed zipper
sheathing me in a black slither satin pencil skirt by Olivier
Theyskens with an evil slit up the back so high that if you
slid your hand up the back of my leg through the slit you'd
be   wait! Because I'm falling back onto the
ottoman now and guess what's lying on the rose-coloured
dupion seat? Oops, got to go.'

'Hello-oh!   Ahhh. And are you sipping from bone
china   But it's got to be bone china, Sweetest,
you're very delicate right now.   No, darling, I'm
not.   Why would I? I'm not sad.   But there
was something that made me think of you. At Dries.
Backstage. This artist in her smock grinding semi-precious
stones to make the colours for their eyelids   No,
I couldn't interview her because she was like something that
shouldn't be touched and me with my corney fingers.   The
usual spinster chic but a little twisted. Someone keeps beeping
it must be Moosh.   No, I want to talk to you, to feed
you. I'll be right back. Pink rose-cut diamond kisses of love!'

'Hello.   On the what?   Oh yes, on the
ottoman like the legs of Vivian Leigh's ghost is a pair of
jeuj couture stockings from Fogal in seven denier silk with
a tinge of Lycra shade "Aryan" and I'm snuggling the phone
into my shoulder now daaarling, and I'm holding one naked
foot high, high in the air with Chanel's Rose Tourbillon
nail polish on every perfectly-manicured toenail and I'm

unrolling the silk stocking up my leg, up and up, up my leg and smoothing it onto pastelle flesh as I go right up and clip! Did you hear that, daarling? Keep going, I'll call you back.'

'Hello?   Hell. Backstage was far too small and the girls kept clashing their antlers together like mating deer. Sort of medieval warehouse. People pissed off. All about Bambi. Girls late, stressed, crawling into the make-up tent because they couldn't get their horns through the top part of the triangular tent door. Very commercial.   Which show?   Robotic lit-up women, huge hump-backed things with lights inside, all the Americans loathed it. Mickey Roberts jumping up and down like Rumpelstiltskin he was so furious.   I'll do it in a mo.'

Quel gobstopper ;-) got a face pic? 24 kt gold kisses, Bobo

'Sweetbird? Are you cooing just a tiny bit?   I forgot to tell you about this one woman at the YSL show who had this thin nose so munched at it was like it was pickled in coke from the outside, all of the journalists were staring at her obsessively, eyes tightly scraped back and her upper lip so big it looked like her whole head had popped inside out, and her under-chin so highly scraped it's like bats live up there. Oh and Mr Fashion President was eyeing me up at every show.   No, don't ask.   No, it hurts me not to tell you his name but I can't. Every time he shags someone Marie-Hélène says he calls the shop and

says "*je veux une bague grande pour ma femme*".   I
hear you smiling. You will have one, sweetwings! Triplets!
Quadraplets!   I'm putting you on hold for three sips.'

'Daaarling not now!   Well, hurry up, I can
do you one minute. I'm wearing both silk stockings now,
blonde-nude, one cell thick, they would rip if you just
panted on them and I'm scared you will right down the
phone, Daaarling, guipère hand-made by Lemarie in bitter
chocolate heavy silk under a torrent of Valentino volumi-
nous petticoats of fine dentelle swishing round my legs
under an eau de   damn.'

'Hello?   I've just pressed go.   No, past tense.
       Yes.   Yes, all the Fashion Canapés.
       Well you figure it out. World-weary. Forked
chin holders. White trash hair.'

Hi Heavy n Horny, out for tea how about cockytails? :-) Bobo

'Hilloo?   Oh you sound much better.   And your
boy?   Well no, I suppose he didn't but he would
make the best daddy.   He will, they all come round,
sweetbird.   But you will, I know you will, you just
need to rest now and not get stressed and   Well,
I hung out with Pat "granny on acid" Fields. John had her
flown over first class for the show. Four or five manky foxes
wrapped round her neck really tatty she didn't care. John
said bring a friend so she arrived with a housewife in her

fifties who wrapped her Burberry scarf around her head to look wild. Surrounded by big trannies. A big black thing with the biggest wobbliest tits you ever did see. She had a string of black sexballs clanking round her neck like pearls.   You know, those Chinese balls people slip into their fannies? Been taking hormones since she was three. Huge mound of black wobble. Quite frightening but very exciting. Patricia's minions were reduced to seat-snatching because they all got standing. They were at every show.   Who? Oh yes, I spent two nights of mad passionate love with him. That's when I discovered my fourth chamber.   Well, you'll find out in a trice, Sweetness. Keep sipping! Back in a twinkle.'

'Moosh?   Classy very, very rich, very debauched women with candle wax on their nipples. You know, just good-time girls. And then at Lacroix they sprayed paper doilies and stuck them in the hair and opened big tins of caviar, it was delish. Hold on.'

'Hello?   Daaarling!   Pink, paillettes, panties, mousseline, flesh, leather, lilies, yes, drowning in layers and layers of fine Alençon yes petticoats frothing between my scissor thighs in foaming yes poverty de luxe cataracts of frenzied diaphanosity yes *major* magenta bustier embroidered by Lesage with Napoleonic yes frogging punctuated by foamy cutaways and organza pompoms yes the dupion yes the grosgrain yes the architecture the darts the line the technique the appliqué the elegance the fearless foundation

garments the Bavarian full-skirted dirndl worn with the Samurai biker blouson yes! yes! yes!   All done?
          Oh, daaarling I'm so happy for you.   Oh, fabulous.   Any time, Daaarling. Toodle.'

'I'm back, Sweetbird.   With Sultan?   Oh yes, to this woman who sells all the feathers to the Moulin Rouge, a little French hag with poodles running round her ankles and stacks of dusty boxes piled up to the ceiling. I said I'd come because I'd heard about *les oiseaux de paradis*. "*Euh, les paradis, les paradis!*" She had a fit, hands flapping, poodles yapping. "*Il veut les paradis! Ooh-la-la!*" She just kept flapping and yapping so we turned to go and she put her finger to her lips sssh! and climbed up a ladder and got down these long narrow boxes from the top. She laid them on the counter and lifted their lids. Whole birds of paradise, their little bodies dried, their faces frozen in expressions of avian terror. I pointed to the ones I wanted and she reached into the boxes and snapped the wings off. Bear with me, my sweetest thing.'

'Hi.   Well it was a pink lettuce so why not say so? Oh come on, she'll just laugh.   Oh blah blah, the readers the advertisers.   Oh honestly.'

'Hello?   Mr Postman or Pat?   Mr Postman!
          Turn left at the end of the street then right into the mews.   I'm putting my head under the pillow. Yes.   Kneeling.   Yes, they're down. Oh hurry, hurry!'

Hello your hot ;-P nice cock do you have a face pic? how do you like my attachment, Bobo

'I'm back, Sweetbird. How're you feeling?   Don't think about it because I know it's all going to work out. Do you know how much I missed you? That smell behind your ears like you're baking muffins under your hair.   Well after the party at the Crillon, you know, the Brazilian one?

I felt a little bit naughty so I went down to this new plumbing club everyone's talking about. I was a teensy bit scared because it's a boots plumbing thing and you have to put all your clothes in this horrible old Carrefour bag they give you and just keep on your boots, or in my case stilettoes   the silver   Yes. I had to tuck my money into a little hankie under an instep, so inconvenient, and you have to grope your way there's no light and you can hear people talking on other floors all spooky and echoey coming down the pipes and the sound of running water and things gurgling and plopping in pipes eurgh!   Because it's a plumbing thing.   Oh, I don't know, little lava-tory cells. Some have operating tables with instruments.

          Oh, very hygienic, the whole place reeked of Dettol. And then I felt myself being lifted up on dozens of manly hands and passed over the heads of the crowd like an idol, it was simply divine, Sweetness, when suddenly this vicious spotlight flashed on and then off again. I was completely dazzled for a second then it went dark and I could see this after-image. It was all these men. Bronzed, buff, ripped, fat, bald, saggy, puffy, paunchy, reaching their arms up towards me with this one expression of pure, pure well, blindness.   Do I hear you smiling, Sweetbird?   How's your baby tummy?   Oh the door. I'll call you back OK? There's more, there's more. Remember how much I love you.'

BRAIN

'I've got another idea. But it's a bit more leftfield.'

'*Take* is a leftfield magazine. It's subversive. Raw.'

'Well, I've been thinking about differential equations, quantum mechanics, Lacanian psychoanalysis, keyhole surgery and that synthesiser band, Matrixial Sonosphere.'

'Yes?'

She walks so fast I have to jog every three steps to keep up with her.

'Intelligence. It's all about intelligence.'

Pearl keeps striding. Then I see her far hand is making a rolling motion.

I go on. 'And you said it was an accessories shoot, right?'

'Right.'

'And it had to be something brilliant, a whole new take on accessories as a genre.'

'Yeah, yeah?'

'Well, intelligence.' I'm panting. 'It's the missing fashion accessory. Too much fashion is predicated on letting others think for you.'

'OK. But how is this, like, a story?'

Her New York accent, that rasp.

'Intelligence is the new accessory. That's the title for our shoot.'

I look down. I see her trademark shoes with the three inch pointy snouts speeding over the pavement blurred.

'Right. And? Give me something visual, Jen.'

'Well, it's an accessories shoot so I thought   put the missing item into the picture. Brains. We'll get some calf brains and   and we'll put them in bags. Expensive bags. Hermès. Fendi. Dior. Vuitton.'

'Mmm hmmm.'

'And maybe   maybe those Hello Kitty rip-offs of the Vuitton bags with Kitty's head instead of the LV logo.'

Pearl continues to propel herself forward. Her face with its warrior slashes of day-glo orange on the cheeks is fixed ahead.

'Brilliant. It's so *Take*.'

'You like it?'

She stops. 'It's funny. I wasn't sure you'd be right for this. But you rock. Start checking out the butchers.'

Next day the phone is ringing as I come in the door.

'Have you got everything?'

'I've got great bags. I've got unbelievable bags.'

'And the brains?'

'I went to Reg Tucker, the posh butcher's. I thought calves' brains would be about the right size but they were all mushy so'

'So, so? What have you got?'

'Well then I went to some halal butchers. They had lambs' brains. Tiny.'

'They've got to look human!'

'I know. So I got up this morning at four a.m. and went to Smithfield. One man had pigs' brains. He said the pig is the closest animal to the hu'

'So you got them?'

'Well I just couldn't believe this. They were pointy in front.' I thought of Pearl's shoes. 'And old-looking. A rusty colour.'

Pearl says shit, fuck and Jesus Christ, she's coming over.

She comes bombing in with a bottle of vodka and we sit hunched on my only two chairs. We smoke her Camels, drink from the bottle and talk about our story. After about twenty minutes we come to an important realisation. I'm the one who says it.

'We've got to get the real thing or this is not going to work.'

Pearl's eyes widen. 'So we behead Rich, right?'

We laugh.

'Yeah, but will we find anything in there we can use?'

We laugh again.

'Think of something, you're the stylist.'

My brain flatlines. 'Shit, well, mummys' tombs? British Museum?'

'No, no, come on.'

'Old medical museums – Wellcome Institute?'

'Like pickled in jars? Come on.'

'Teaching hospitals? Anatomy departments must have brains for'

Pearl jumps out of her chair. 'That's it!'

'But hold on, isn't it illegal? You can't just borrow a real human brain to shoot some fashion picture.'

Pearl whips round. 'This is where you keep fucking up!'

I go cold.

'Hey, I don't mean that.' She lowers her voice. 'It's just that you still have the mindset of someone working for *Marie-Claire*.' She goes over to the mantelpiece and leans her hands on it. 'This is not some corporate commercial magazine, Jen. We are not borrowing human brains to shoot fashion. That's the point of our story, right? It's not fucking ladies with their handbags. We are questioning, subverting that, right?'

She starts walking round the room in her destroy jumper and tunnel love hipsters with the tunnel of fabric sewn in at the back so your boyfriend can slip his hands in like into a muff. She's not beautiful but she looks amazing. The day-glo orange stripes where blusher would go. The orange streak in her hair. She can carry off tunnel love trousers as though they were any old jeans.

'Are you willing to push the boundaries? Or are you just working to pay the rent?'

I look at my hands. She squats down in front of me.

'Fashion is how we get out there, get exposed. Fashion is just the tool. You can be used by it like a pawn or you can use it like an artist. I want to strike. Strike at fashion by using fashion.' She touches my hand. 'Otherwise, what's the point?'

I get up and go into the kitchen with the bottle. I pour

the vodka into glasses and get some ice out of the freezer section of the fridge. I think about photographers I admire. Nick Knight, he started out shooting skinheads. Inez van Lambsweird. OK so you spell it Lamsweerde but still. Avedon even. I crack open a lucky bottle of tonic back of the mop cupboard. Avedon did that shoot in *The New Yorker* once of Nadja Auermann in stilettoes – taken with an X-ray machine. It was sick. It was brilliant. The one lemon is too dead to use. I pick up the glasses and take them back into the other room.

'I'm sorry. I need to break out of the box.'

'Sure. They got to you but you've found a weapon now.'

She gives that choking crow laugh she does. We sip the vodka and start to cook up a plan.

An hour later I ring Directory Enquiries and get the names of London's major medical schools. I tap in the digits and take a deep breath.

'South London University Faculty of Medicine.'

'Dissecting room please.' I wait for her to say, dissecting *room*? We don't say dissecting *room*. You're an imposter!

'I'm sorry, the faculty of medicine is closed for the summer.'

'There must be someone there.' I make my voice crisp, surgical. 'Can you put me through to anyone on that floor please?'

'May I ask who's calling?'

'I'm calling from *National Geographic*'s Mapping the Human Body Project. The name is Miss Wilson.'

There's a hold tone. Pearl hisses, what are they saying? I try to ignore her. I try to feel my way into the head of a boring but dedicated academic journalist from the Mapping the Human Body Project.

'Hello?' A flat, nasal tone.

'Hello. To whom am I speaking please?'

'Mr Phelps, but there's no one here at the moment.'

'Mr Phelps, perhaps you can help.'

'None of the professors are here at the moment. You're talking to the caretaker.' Emotionless, drab.

'Who is it?' hisses Pearl. I push her off with one arm.

'Actually perhaps you can help, Mr Phelps.' I give it to him. 'My colleague and I are shooting a series of images for *National Geographic* magazine of the entire human body: its systems – nervous, phlebotomic, lymphatic and so on – and the various individual organs. The project is known as the Mapping the Human Body Project and is being part-funded by the Smithsonian. It has been featuring in consecutive issues of the magazine. Perhaps you have seen them?'

'I'm sorry, Miss Wilson, I'm the caretaker.'

'Just a second, Mr Phelps. I think you can help. We have just finished our final shoot in Paris, just as the Faculté de Biologie et de Médecine at the Université de Paris-Sorbonne shut down for the summer and we've come here to process our film. But something terrible's happened. The lab has ruined the rolls showing the human brain. We are right on deadline. If we don't shoot a human brain tomorrow at the latest, the magazine will have to appear with two blank spreads.'

I deliver the whole thing with my eyes closed, emoting Miss Wilson, her Marks & Spencer 'cotton rich' cardi, her PhD in the Philosophy of Medicine, her slightly greasy hair.

'We can't let any body parts leave the medical school. It's against the law. I'm sorry.'

'Mr Phelps, I'm speaking to you as one academic institution to another. This is an emergency.' I flail around. 'Maybe we could shoot under your supervision in the dissecting room itself?'

'I can't do that without permission. I'm sorry.'

The receiver is snatched out of my hand.

'Mr Phelps?' Throaty, crooning. 'I'm Megan Bishop. The chief medical photographer at Lumbard Witherspoon Centre for Health Informatics at Harvard University?' I stare at her. 'How are you doing today? Good. Good. Now I know this is an exceptional request . . . '

I scribble *he is caretaker* on the message pad. Pearl's eyes flick over it. She is blathering on about being a single mother. She says it defines her life and repositions her goals. It's hard being a single mother, but it's the single most important job she's ever had to do. I waggle my hands at her and mouth no. She's off on one. She turns her back to me.

'Do you have any children Mr Phelps? A girl? How old? Hey, that's a coincidence, so's Lee-Anne. But you see, you are lucky enough to live with her, to fully   no? No, truly? Divorced? Uh-huh. Uh-huh. How long?   Oh that's hard, that's really tough. So you know what it's like to be parted from your child. You see, I've been away from home now for . . . '

When Pearl puts down the phone we have an appointment at 8:30 a.m. at the South London University Faculty of Medicine with Mr Phelps. He remembers there is a model of the human brain in the lecturing-hall cupboard. We can't remove it from the premises. But well, if it's only going to take an hour, we can come and take some photographs of it tomorrow.

'A cheap plastic brain? It's not the same.' I am struck low.

'It's an in,' says Pearl.

Next morning at 8:25 a.m. we walk up the white stone steps of the medical school, cross a portico spanned by Corinthian columns and enter the lobby. I am twitchy. Mr Phelps will have thought better of his offer overnight. One of the professors will have returned and rung up *National Geographic*. Two constables will be waiting to arrest us. We go up to the reception desk and ask for Phelps. She tells us to wait.

'Oh God, we're going to be in for it.'

'A night in gaol?' Pearl bursts into the choking crow. I look over my shoulder but the reception woman is on the phone.

Five minutes later we see the small figure of a man coming down a Scarlett O'Hara staircase. He is an underwater white with pale blue eyes and wisps of ginger hair. Pearl rushes forward and takes his hand.

'Mr Phelps!' Her voice is low but insistent. 'Megan Bishop. It's so good to meet you in person.'

We go up the stairs and along wide, empty corridors. Pearl walks ahead working on Phelps. The corridors smell of linoleum and disinfectant. Flies buzz along the bottom of half-drawn blinds. Somewhere, footsteps echo, turning down a corridor. They sound as if they are coming towards us. Phelps stops outside a door and gets out a bunch of keys.

'We'll have to go through here,' he says in his monotone.

We follow him into a lofty, twilit hall. The air makes my eyes smart like it's full of vinegar. I blink. Extending away into the shadows are steel gurneys arranged in rows. Each gurney has a thick, semi-opaque sheet of plastic thrown over it. Under each sheet there's a dark bulk. Bodies. Their feet are sticking out. There's a metal bowl between each pair of feet. On a gurney in the third row the plastic has been flicked back. I see a pair of skinny legs and a groin, pickled brown. It's a man. I blink my eyes rapidly.

'Through here please.'

Phelps goes down the side of the room where a stainless steel countertop inset with sinks joins the wall. Under one of the sinks I see two metal buckets. One is piled with meat torn from the bone, probably with the giant set of tongs that are resting on the draining-board. In the other, human skin excised in neat squares is piled up like remnants in someone's sewing-basket. On the countertop, a shallow steel dish with obscene slops. I look up at the wall, white and slightly shiny.

Ahead of me Phelps stops, looks round.

'Miss Bishop? Where are you going, Miss Bishop?'

I turn and see Pearl drifting between the gurneys, her hand trailing over the surface of a plastic sheet covering a corpse. She smiles and comes back towards us.

'Sorry, I just get carried away at the thought of medicine, science in action. It's supremely moving.' She tosses Phelps a smile. 'Oh, and please call me Megan.'

We walk on. I try to catch her eye but she's absorbed in something. Phelps unlocks the far door and leads us out into a narrow corridor. We go into an office and there on the desk is the model of the brain. Written all over it in flowing script are words like *hypothalamus*, *parietal lobe* and *cerebellum*.

'Oh Mr Phelps.' Pearl's smile has gone, she is shaking her head. 'What were you thinking?'

Phelps stands slackly. 'It's an exact replica.'

'Look at the writing, Mr Phelps.' She points to it with a long, day-glo orange fingernail. She's forgotten to take off her polish. 'Did you really think we could put that in the *National Geographic*?'

Phelps squints his ginger eyelashes.

My voice pipes up. 'Is there somewhere we can smoke?'

We follow Phelps into a small staffroom with brown nubbly armchairs and a low coffee table with medical journals on it. There's a single copy of *Hello*. Pearl picks it up and starts talking about Madonna and Catherine Zeta-Jones. Then she gets a picture of some little girl out of her handbag and starts showing it to Phelps. A professional. I get coffee from a machine. I pick up some little packets of sugar. I concentrate on pouring the white crystals of sugar in a steady stream into the dark brown coffee. Then I stir it for a while with the plastic strip.

'A cigarette out the fire escape, Mr Phelps?' Pearl is saying. 'Oh come on, we need to put our thinking caps on!'

Ten minutes later Phelps is leading us back along the narrow corridor, his bunch of keys jangling. Behind his back Pearl grabs my arm.

'Can you believe this place?' she whispers.

I shake my head. I hear footsteps walking rapidly along the corridor again. One minute they sound far away, the next minute, they're getting nearer. I hurry on.

We enter the shuttered twilight of the dissecting hall. Pearl strides along the steel countertop, running her hand along its length as she goes. She's talking to Phelps. ' . . . just a peek . . . '

He goes up to a row of grey metal cupboards, unlocks one, and swings the doors open. He gestures with one hand.

'The brain cupboard.'

It's full of metal shelves stacked with semi-see-through white plastic tubs. Inside the tubs shadowy lumps lie submerged in liquid. There must be about sixty tubs.

'My,' says Pearl. 'This is a far more extensive holding than the Sorbonne has.'

Phelps starts to close the doors.

'Wait. Let's see a sample of your collection. What do you think, Jen?'

'Yes, let's take a look.'

'Which one?'

I look at her sideways, trying to figure what she's thinking. Her eyes are serious.

'Uh. I think the third row. That one.'

'Yes that one, Mr Phelps, please.'

Phelps hangs his keys back on his belt and reaches up for the tub. Behind his back Pearl widens her eyes at me. I widen my eyes back.

Phelps carries the tub over to the countertop. There's worn gold lettering on the lid. ' anil a   sk m ed mil   wder'   May contain trac   nut '. He pops off the lid and there's the brain.

It's not the human brain as I'd imagined it, a bright, white cauliflower. This brain is covered in a fawn-coloured gelatinous membrane intersected by engorged purple veins. Pearl bends over it. She has tucked her black hair with the day-glo orange streak behind her ears.

'What do you think, Jen?'

'I'm not sure.' I'm looking at her face but just out of focus behind her I can see the rows of dead bodies under their plastic sheets.

She shakes her head. 'Can you show me another brain?'

Phelps goes over to the cupboard, fetches another tub and prises off the lid.

'Hmmm.' Pearl looks from one brain to the other. 'It's OK. It's a little old, I would say. We want upbeat, fresh. We need a role-model brain.'

I look down at the brain. Bits of yellow-red stringy stuff are hanging off it and swaying in the liquid. Another tub thumps down next to it. Phelps takes off the lid.

'This is a nice one,' he says.

'Hmm, it's a little veiny. Do you have anything without the purple?'

'That's how they come,' he says. 'If you don't like them'

'But I do. This is an incredible archive.'

I feel I have to say something.

'It's just that we're professional. We have to get it right.'

My voice sounds squeaky.

Pearl paces up and down in front of the shelves examining them. 'I'm looking for something new, something that's hard to put your finger on. How about this one   And maybe this one'

'How about this one?' I add, pointing.

One by one Phelps gets them off the shelves and places them on the table. Pearl flicks off the lids with a nail. We lean over the tubs. I feel a stoniness pressing on me through the air.

'That's the one,' I say. I point at any brain. We have to get out of here. Pearl nudges me.

'Too big. Think how that would work in the picture. It won't   go into anything.'

I grit my teeth at her. 'You're right, of course, it's wrong for the Mapping the Human Body Project.'

Phelps moves restlessly. 'We have to go.'

Pearl snaps her fingers.

'I've got it. We need a female brain. Something on the small side, maybe a teenager. You know, like, model age?'

I put my hand over my mouth. She is frowning, staring

straight ahead. Phelps trudges over to the cupboard. The stoniness presses from behind.

'Top shelf,' says Pearl. 'Look. That smaller-looking one on the left.'

He has to go on tiptoes to get it down. He brings it over to the countertop. Inside the tub is a smaller brain, still in its web of jellified blood but – 'more compact, more perfect,' says Pearl. I nod. My stomach is cramping. 'Wouldn't it be forward-thinking to use a female brain as the definitive symbol of human intelligence?' She laughs lightly, not her usual outburst.

Phelps puts the tub in a plastic bag from Europa Food Stores and hands it to Pearl. There's a sloshing sound as we go out the door. I look left and right along the stretches of linoleum. Pearl carries the bag back along the booming corridor and down the stairs gabbing to Phelps. I walk just behind.

'Tomorrow morning. On the dot of eight – thank you, Mr Phelps. American science thanks you!'

We go past the woman behind the desk in the lobby and out into the London daylight. I feel like a diver surfacing and drawing in oxygen.

Pearl runs towards my car with one arm held up in victory. 'Didn't he look like the Undead?'

I get in the car and light up a cigarette to get the smarting chemicals out of my nostrils. I can feel shiny livers in my throat. Pearl sticks the box in the back.

'We did it,' I say it to myself as much as to her. 'We really did it.'

We clutch each other's hands.

'We pulled it off!'

We burst out laughing.

'He was so creepy!'

'You were magnificent,' I say.

'Straight to the studio,' commands Pearl. 'Go. Go. Go.'

She's so hyper she's bouncing on the seat.

At the studio, Rich is hooking up the camera and taking readings with the light meter with the stereo tuned to Goa trance. There are smart paper carrier bags lying all over the floor bursting with tissue paper and glimpses of handbags. A smell of new leather fills the air.

'Get the brain ready,' calls Pearl, advancing towards her 5 × 4 plate camera. 'I want to shoot while we feel the energy.'

I go into the kitchen and put the bag on a melamine surface. I place the chopping board flat and open the ice-cream tub. The brain lies sunk in discoloured liquid. Right, I say to myself, let's do this thing. I put my hands in and slide them under the brain. I feel crevices and complex nodules underneath. I swallow. It's surprisingly heavy.

'Jen?' Pearl's face appears round the kitchen door. 'Get that ugly membrane off.'

'But he'll notice. He might get in trouble.'

'We'll just stick the membrane back on again afterwards somehow.'

'Pearl, we can't mess with the brain.'

'It's too late to chicken now. This has to be right!'

I get a pair of tweezers out of my stylist's bag. The brain sits there, its preservative liquid pooling on the board. I extend the tweezers towards it. I touch the jelly membrane with them. It dimples. I swallow. I start to tear off patches of membrane and globby lengths of veins. I look for something to lay them on and find a dinner plate. They stick together on the plate like wet pastry. Every now and then I look up and stare at the white cups on the shelf in front of me.

Now the dome of the brain is revealed, that creamy cloud that's supposedly the seat of the soul. In the fissures between each curly clump, dark red matter is wedged in tight.

I bend over the brain with the tweezers in my hand, examining the red matter. Pearl's voice hollers through from the studio.

'Hurry up, Jen. We mustn't lose it.'

I take a breath. I reach into a fissure with the tweezers. I have to tug hard. The tweezers slip and I pull off a gobbet of brain matter. It has the consistency of hard-boiled eggs. I reach deeper into the brain and fasten the tweezers tight on the red stuff. I pull. A tatter of congealed blood comes out. I lay it on the chopping-board. I reach in again, tug out another tatter. It takes a while to get it all out. When it's done, I try to smooth over the damaged portions of the brain with my fingers. Then I lift the brain up and cradle it against my T-shirt. It's heavy, heavier than a head seems to be when it's alive.

I walk into the studio and see the lights set up and a pastel-tinted Hello Kitty shopper propped open on a perspex box. And for some reason I also see her, and my mother and me sitting by her bed. We're each holding one of her hands. My mother leans to kiss her still-warm forehead and brushes back the hair. She keeps saying, 'Mammy, mammy' in a small voice I've never heard, and brushing back the hair from the bony forehead.

'Coo-ell,' says Rich. 'Can I touch it?'

'Back off.'

Pearl is on her folding steps, looking down onto the 5 × 4's ground glass, her hands blocking out the light at either side of her face. I slide the brain into the gaping handbag, careful not to catch it on the zip. It's too heavy and the shopper starts to crumple. I take it out again using both hands. I sit it on an Hermès carrier bag so it won't get dirty, balancing it on its front so the more delicate, gill-like portion at the lower back won't get damaged. I grab some tissue paper to use as wadding inside the Hello Kitty bag.

'Come on, Jen. I'm pumping to shoot this baby!'

I stuff more tissue into the bag. More tissue. I pick it up and place it gently into the top of the Hello Kitty shopper.

'Brilliant,' murmurs Pearl. She crouches over the camera. She draws the black cloth over her head. 'This is brilliant. This is hardcore. Fuck fashion!'

I walk out of shot and look down at my hands. White bits of brain have lodged under my fingernails.

SUMMER TREES

First plain branches against grey. Then new green against blue. The leaves hang in small downward bunches. They tremble on their stalks, try to stand up. Each leaf-bunch shoots up a spongy pyramid studded with knobs. The pyramids stiffen. The leaves spread out underneath, yellow-green engorged with sun. The knobs pop in twos and threes. The tree sways and faints, covered with pyramids of small foamy flowers. Each flower-clump held up out of the green like a candle. The tree blazing with candles in the light of day. Each candle tucked into a cone of leaves like a paper drip-catcher.

At noon nine hundred cream horns bellowing into the sky. At dusk pale candles against the dark mass of leaves. Flickering as a breeze goes through the tree. Full of promise as they wheel us back in on those lucky nights we've been left out this long. Nights when someone has a visitor and asks to be left out a bit longer. Then they don't bother to take in the rest of us, unless you make a noise. I don't make a noise. I lie under the tree and feel it stirring in the wind. The visitor stands up. She says, It's getting awful cold out here. Are you feeling the cold? She wheels in the inmate she's visiting by herself. There is a pause. The carers come out the front doors in their blue tracksuits. They spread out, each one heading for a wheelchair or a wheelie-bed. They slip the brakes and wheel us back in across the lawn.

To stay out here all night. For what must be years and maybe years and years I've thought about it. I can't ask for it. I'm at the mercy of fate. I can not make a noise. I don't make a noise. I wish myself invisible. I am almost invisible and it is darker under the horse chestnut than on the lawn and the branches droop down towards the ground on the outside and even brush the grass so I am inside a house of leaves. My walls rustle in the breeze. My candles go up and up in spirals above my head a hundred feet into the air and dapple the air with flowery smell mixed with damp.

They could almost not see me under here in the dark but they do. They come and wheel me in and the one who has put me under a tree to start with gets told not to put me there again. Gets told to put me by the wall of the main building where the others go and where they ask to be put anyway. One or two ask to be put by the trees sometimes. Ones that can still speak. Sometimes I can indicate in my own way that I want a tree. Sometimes I can't or the one pushing doesn't care. I always want a tree. I never want the wall. Back to the wall is good in summer, I understand that, the wall gives out warmth and you feel protected. I don't want to be warm. Inside it's always too warm, with the smell of mince and urine, mine as well so I can't say anything. But out here under the hundred-foot dome of the horse chestnut, a house fit for a god or a squirrel, I feel the cold and smell the blossom in a dappling of smell like a dappling of light, coming and going.

Then I am so happy I don't think I have ever been happier. I stop to think can that be true? Does it mean my life was the poorer? And how to remember the actual strength of the different happinesses? All the memories I still have and the greater quantity of memories that are laid away on membranes in the cool of the brain. Waiting calmly for me to reach into the cool of the brain and unfold them.

If they could forget where they've put me just one time. They'd wheel the others in across the lawn and lock the door. Later I'd hear some of them coming out and getting into their cars and driving away. Then the dark would settle. That summer dark that this far north is not that dark. The sky would go greenish. I'd glimpse it in chinks through the leaves. The wind would rise, stir the leaves, die away. I'd lie behind soft walls that shuffle and sigh. The way the wind lifts the sheaves that hang at the tips of the branches and shakes them and drops them and lifts them again. Drops them with a sigh. A bird might start up in the dark. Thin spurts of water out of a pipe. The wind stays. The leaves hang down. Then I hear it coming, rushing from far away, and then it reaches and swells through the tree and ruffles my hair and I'm carried away with it. I get cold. It gets cold at night even in summer this far north. I get colder and colder. Really cold, outside-cold when it goes on for a long time. I let it come into me. I listen to the tree breathe. It breathes through its leaves. In the morning they go into my room to give me my meds and see me not there.

I heard my niece say it when she brought me in. To please put me under a tree. Not against the wall and not just on the lawn, but right out under one of the trees. I hadn't realised she knew. I had said to my sister once or twice long ago how I loved the trees I could see out the kitchen window. I had said I would never move to a Sheltered House because of not wanting to leave the trees. Now I hear my niece saying to please put me out under a tree. I hear the big one answering her, the one who smells of crammed bra fabric. Uh-huh. Oh is that right? Uh-huh. Under a tree, right you are. But when she was on duty the big one never once put me anywhere but the wall.

Nearly all of them prefer the wall and most of them don't like to get out at all. When we're first let out after six or seven months inside, they shout and swear to be let back in. People that go in and out all the time, they don't realise what it's like outside, they've become inured. They just go in and out, in and out all the time, they don't really notice the difference. It's different for us who are always in. When they let us out the first time some cry so as their hearts would break to be let back in. The way the sky batters you. The light coming out of it striking your eyes like snakes.

We are in all autumn and winter. All day in winter it's strip lights and the sound of the tellies. Those same telly voices and the same ads on the telly day in and day out. The same people asking for the same things in the same tone of voice or complaining about the same things or telling the same stories in the exact same way. Then it's cups of milky tea and them changing pads and changing people's bags and then bed. They put the lights out early so as they can go home. I want them not to draw my curtains and my blinds but I can't say. I try to do it another way. They don't understand. They give me my meds and I get the heady feeling but I don't fall over to sleep. In summer, even with the curtains and the blinds drawn, you can see in the room after a few minutes. Sometimes a bar of pure light comes in under the blind and moves across the floor. The meds make me spinny. I concentrate on the ceiling tiles. I go over the grey squiggles on them that are meant to make them look like stone. I know each squiggle. I see an ugly face and a four-legged animal with big ears. I remember things whether I want to or not. In winter, nights are pitch black and you don't see anything in the room once the lights go out. In winter, nights go on for hours and hours. They go on way into the morning. When they come in to wash you and change your bag in the morning they have to put the strip light on.

The time they shoved the bed a bit over to the right for the annual cleaning-behind-the-bed and left it so it was a bit under the window. And how one night some nights later it was windy outside and a draught came in strong enough to blow the blind out under the curtains and if I rolled my eyes back I could see out, just. Mostly I saw the dark then small white points shaking. Stars. I hadn't seen them in years. I watched them on and off all night.

When we're first let out I'm like a cow that's been kept in the byre all winter. Let out into the field, mooing and galloping about. Just in my head though. I can only do it in my head, gallop right in under the trees and out the other side dragging low branches off in my hair, mooing. The smell of the cold air and the earth which is not a smell I can describe to myself or anyone but which my nose takes in the way your ear takes in music. And if they wheel me past the big rhododendrons a stink like an old tramp that they don't seem to notice. A fox that's been through. Maybe if they left me out all night the fox would jump up on the wheelie-bed and look at me with burning eyes and a lolling tongue. Maybe he'd lick the side of my face to sample it, then eat it off.

My niece told them to put me out under a tree. Then she never came back. Or did she? I can't remember. They nodded. Under a tree, uh-huh, right you are. Thinking, aye, dream on. Think I've got the time to put this one here, that one there, yessir, nosir, three bags full sir? They don't pay us right, it's a scandal. This is shadowlands, no a luxury hotel.

Uh-huh. Oh yes. Right you are. No bother. Under a tree. Uh-huh.

Grey when we first get out. I look up. If I'm put under a tree on that first day my happiness is more than complete, it keeps bursting out of complete to a new more complete place just beyond it. The branches bare, but with buds. On some trees the buds are brown like the branches. On other trees reddish like they're nipped by the wind. Old rotted conkers dangle, left from the year before. The branches move in a jangly way against the grey. The breeze fresh, my mother's word for freezing cold. We're not out long. People calling, Nurse nurse, even though they're not nurses. Nurse nurse, can I get back in please? I'm that cold.

The day I was under a beech tree for more than an hour when a chill came up from the ground and it started to rain. A drop came down through the leaves and landed on my face. I felt concentric circles of cold ringing through my head. Then drop after drop smashing on my cheeks and in my eyes and running down me and getting in under the blanket. The sound of the drops on the leaves and the ground. A pause, and then a full rush of rain. The air into grey static with it. I heard groaning and I realised it was me. I was crying. Of course they ran to get me in. They worried I'd caught a cold. They kept me in for days, worried.

Put me out please. Please put me out under a tree and not by the wall. They stack us side by side along the wall. It's easier for them. But it's not just that. They don't like the trees away out on the lawn like that. They are reluctant to go over there and it's not just because it's far. So they stack us side by side along the wall. I look up. I see the wall going up and the underside of the roof jutting out and sky.

But then Sheila comes and says Are you OK there? You like it by the trees, eh? Sheila that I throw love out my eyes at. She wheels me away across the lawn and under and I'm shrouded by the tree. It's the height of summer. The trees droop their thinner branches and trail showers of leaves towards the grass. The wind shuffles them. The sun comes through the leaves soft yellow and flashes in the chinks. A dove coos high up. Sheila tucks the blanket round me and goes away and leaves me with the tree. The wind comes up. Pollen thrown down on the pillow in fits and starts.

Half an hour, if you could be a hundred years. It's not that I'm not weary. I'm bone weary. The meds give me headaches and a dry mouth. The bedsores burn. I can't move my body myself. I'm off my food and my bladder's a hopeless case. But I can't be bothered with all that. Even if I die tomorrow, which must be more likely than not, today I'm under this tree and it's soughing in the breeze and a cushy doo is cooing up on a branch. I see it and another dove half-hidden in the leaves. The brown bark flushed with green and the brightness of the leaves and the way they shift. The dove coos. The sun comes warm through the leaves and touches my skin more felt than human fingers, and a hundred more years of lying here would not be enough, a thousand years. If they could leave me under the tree night and day. Language would dwindle away from me. My mind would become as fresh as sheets drying on a line. My head would fill up with the rustling of leaves. My light-filled head, my shadowy head. My head full of the sound of the wind in the leaves, that sound I can't get enough of, that full yet expectant sound always on the brink, then sighing back and dropping into deep greenness.

To be transparent and near-weightless. One of those invisible living structures that are 98 per cent water and drift thousands of feet down. To have every change of the tree reverberate in you as though you were a tenuous structure made of tiny, transparent bones, something blown about in the dust and old leaves, something rackety and small, not seen, but whose minute bones chime with every sound and touch and think nothing of them.

Yellow pollen on the blanket. It's ticklish in the corner of my eye. It sticks to my skin and hair and I smell something, a thread of sweetness in the air. If I could die out into the murmur of the leaves. Most of them die to the sound of telly voices or just the clicking of the machines evaluating how close they are to going. They put the telly on in the room to keep you company, they say. You lie there hearing telly voices talking to each other as if you are already not there. You could die to *Home and Away*, or to an American sitcom, or to Jeremy Kyle, or to breakfast telly, people sitting on a couch keeping a line of chat going. All of them talking to each other as if you are gone already. You could go out to the sound of canned laughter, which might not be all that inappropriate.

To die out under the trees, when you could be taken by the wind, when you could be lifted up and tossed about the sky and maybe dropped in the graveyard so they wouldn't even have to bother with a hearse. That would be the talk of the shadowlands. To be taken up by the wind, you're that light, there's nothing to you, and dropped in a new-dug hole, all ready for the pokey worms. Chance would be a fine thing.

If being this present and no more could be what death

is. An almost invisible structure more see-through even than the finest plastic bag like the one a watch comes in. To be presence of mind with the wind for a body. But no reverie. Though I don't want to forget but I do forget. And the more time passes the more I do forget and the memories that come come as bits and pieces that I can't work out. The big one leaning over me to give me a bed bath. Swiping and swiping at me with the cloth and a line saying itself over and over in my head and in someone else's voice, someone that I know but I don't know who it is. Nooks and crannies. They say it again. Nooks and crannies. The big one swiping at me with the cloth and her breasts squashing my nose when she leans over to wring the cloth out in the basin. Then after ages when I'm lying there looking at the grey squiggles on the ceiling tiles. Nooks and crannies.

Bees visit my face. Please God let them not come now or they will be horrified at the bees and maybe keep us in for days. Or wipe at our faces with their cloths that smell of antiseptic. Let them not come now while the bees are visiting my face. Let my niece tell them, but she hasn't been for a long time. The last time she came she said that, I haven't been for a long time. I don't live near here any more, she said.

Swans have come to roost in the chestnut trees. Being mute, they don't make a sound, heads under their wings. I want to tell someone how the swans are nesting by the hundred in the horse chestnut trees, mute swans with their beaks tucked under their wings. But who could I tell? Even if I could speak who would listen to a thing like that? That patient look on, while their hands did something useful to save time. Who could I ever have told something like that to, while we sat on a couch or in the kitchen year after year at the kitchen table and kept a line of chat going.

See her? The eyes rolling. She's awful funny. Airy-fairy. But to me, oh uh-huh, oh I see what you mean. Oh aye, oh fancy. Swans. But to the others, See her? Rolling the eyes. Me saying maybe to my friend. I remember the name so well. My best friend since school. Imagine it, me saying one day at the kitchen table, have you seen the swans? They're roosting in the trees, hundreds of them. Do you know what I mean? No but look. Look at the sky, do you ever do that? Not just to see if you should take your coat. I look at it for hours. Watching the sky. Don't look at me like that, you, I'm no expecting a chariot to swing down. Them maybe giving a laugh, maybe saying, what's got into you? I am expecting though. I'm expecting, feeling the promise of something that's coming and which I'm still waiting for, now that you're dead and buried up in the new graveyard where I'll be put to be poked by the pokey worms, or will they cremate me?

Someone touches my hand. You're frozen solid. A face leans over me. She slips the brake. You'll catch your death. I move my head as much as I can. I open my mouth. She starts to wheel me away through a shower of leaves that pour and slide over my face and body. Hold me. I hear a dribble of sound near my ear. It's coming out of me. I know, she says, frozen solid. They should never have left you out here, it's a scandal. The sound comes out of me louder. My eyes roll back as she bumps me across the lawn. The dome of the tree going up in the summer dusk, the wind stirring the sheaves. Don't you worry, she says, it'll no happen again, it's a scandal so it is.

PANAGIA EVANGELISTRIA

I leave the ferry and walk along the seafront then turn up what looks like the main street going up a hill. All normal till I see a woman crawling up the street ahead of me. She's in the road close to the pavement and cars are going along next to her. Some of the people on the pavement cast her a glance. She just keeps going up the hill on her hands and knees at about the same pace as a cow, and with her bottom swaying from side to side just like a cow. She could be a nutter, but she's crawling up this dirty strip of carpet that's been laid up the side of the road with gaps in it where side streets cross. She comes to one of the gaps, looks right and left and crawls across. I hear the flats of her hands slapping on the marble slabs of the road then she reaches the next bit of carpet. I look up the road. Three more crawlers, a mother and two children. The mother stops, kneels up and puts her hands to her lower back, then shuffles forward a few steps on her knees before she slumps back down and keeps going. The children are in front of her. The first one is haring up the carpet, looking over her shoulder to see if her sister's catching up with her.

He'd love this, I'm thinking. He wouldn't believe it. I dawdle, pretending to look at the Virgin trinkets piled outside a shop. I slip my camera out of its case and hold it down at my side as if I'm just carrying it like that. I walk to the edge of the pavement and tilt my hand a bit towards the first crawler. Her big black backside. No shoes. But tights. It's boiling hot and she's wearing thirty denier tights. If you are going to crawl half a mile up a hill to get into a church, you don't take any chances with things like your legs. Though they've laddered over her knees. Her skirt has ridden up quite a long way. She's no spring chicken.

I walk slowly past her, getting quite a good shot I think, and then I get a shot of the mother and children. I go on up the hill. A couple more crawlers, both women. You wouldn't get men doing that, I'm thinking. What would it take to get a man to crawl to church on his knees? They are doing it to expiate some sin or to beg for something, or to get their man out of trouble maybe. I'll have brought wrath down on my head by secretly filming them. I should delete it. I walk faster up past the last shops. Though that's an incredibly stupid thought.

At the top of the hill the road widens into a small square in front of the church. There's a wall with a wide bank of steps running all along its length, and doors at either end of the wall. The church is quite far back behind the wall and raised so it must be up other steps. People are buying candles at a couple of stalls. Slender, seven-feet cones wrapped in spirals of sugar paper, pink, indigo and mustard. I buy one. I join the crowd that's pressing up the steps and funnelling through the doorway at the right end of the wall. He'll like the film, I think as I'm standing there, holding my paper-wrapped taper that's taller than me. He'll laugh as well at the madness when I show him.

I get my shawl out of my bag. In some countries you have to cover your bare shoulders to get in. My blouse is sleeveless but I've got the shawl, which can also be slipped up over my head in case it should need to be covered too. But for now, just over my bare shoulders, pinning my arms in to the sides where sweat trickles but no one sees. I want to make sure I get in after coming all this way, taking the ferry that leaves once a day from our island to come to this one that we've been able to see all week across the water. You could see this island almost every day, blue-misty on the horizon and not quite joined with the sea at the bottom. Leaving him to go to the beach on his own on our last day.

We stand in the noonday sun. After a few minutes there's a stirring of bodies and then it stops. I wait, feeling the slippiness between my arm and my underarm. The crowd sways, resettles. Nothing for ages, then the crowd stirs and moves one step forward. I feel sweat slip between my arm and my side under the shawl. The crowd stands. It stirs again and I see that the woman with the dyed blonde hair who was just ahead of me is now about six or seven people ahead. It's not an orderly queue. We are in a fan shape going up the steps and then there's the narrow door plugged up with people. Pushing doesn't seem right. It's not about pushing.

When the woman in front goes into her bag for her phone I flow into the temporary gap by her other elbow, sideways on so I fit. We stand. A child darts out of the crowd and I filter into the space he's left between his parents. I manage to insert my foot among all the other feet on the step just above. After a minute or two I squeeze up behind a stocky man standing on the step. My breasts don't touch the stocky man and my buttocks are maybe two inches from the chest of the tiny woman behind but I don't actually touch her. I'm not pushing. I'm flowing. I keep it up till I'm dead-centre of the crowd and much closer to the doorway at the top. We hold our tapers up in front of us, sweating.

I look around me while I'm waiting. On the far left, people are walking freely up the wide bank of steps and going through the door at that end without all this bother. I examine the crowd I'm in behind my sunglasses. Everyone in it is Greek. They are Greek-coloured which means some are creamy-bun-coloured, some are olive oil, and some are as brown as if they live out on the hills looking after a flock of sheep. I'm tanned but I don't go brown like them. Nor am I creamy-bun or olive. I'm a once pinky-white now pinky-beige person. The people walking freely through the door on the left are in my colour range, most of them. They have cameras and little rucksacks. Some of them are Greek, but those are Greek tourists maybe not that bothered about getting inside the church itself, which is what this queue must be for otherwise why? I could leave the crowd, go over and see where those others like me are going. Whether they are only getting to go into the court-yard or whether they are getting into the church itself which I've heard is beautiful. There's not much time. I got off the ferry at noon. It took me at most half an hour to get to the queue. And now it's almost one. If I leave the queue and discover that those others are only allowed into the courtyard I'll have to start at the back again and then I might lose my chance to spend time in the beautiful church and I've come all this way.

I let the shawl slip down one shoulder since I'm not actually in the church precincts yet. The crowd shifts, crushes closer. I'm getting near to the front. There's a commotion ahead. The people there are dipping their tall tapers towards a man with a face like he's seen a ghost. He grabs the top of each taper, pulls it towards him and twists. Sugar paper slides off in a ribbon and the top half of a beeswax candle, mustard-gold, is exposed. With the other hand the staring man gnashes scissors in the air then snips off a bit of the yellow rope wicks coming out of the tapers. I'm jostled, shoved forward on a heave from behind. I'm almost in range of the man's scissors. I lift my taper high and bend it towards him across the heads. I meet his eye. He's going to say, Hey, you're not Greek! You don't come in this door for the Greeks only. Out! Only he's going to say it in Greek so I won't understand and people will look round at me, and some will shake their heads and try to push me away to my proper place, saying things to me in Greek and I won't understand. The man with staring eyes looks up at my candle among all the other candles and cuts the wick.

He gnashes the scissors to free them of sticky scraps of rope.

Sweat slides between my arm and my underarm underneath the shawl. It's hard to keep my balance because the bit of the crowd I'm in is near the doorway full of faces now and they're pushing restlessly after waiting all this time, wanting to be through. I turn my head to the right for respite and I see women coming out of a tiny side door I hadn't noticed before. In and out, in and out, they're chucking armfuls of barely-burnt tapers onto a handcart that's parked there. The cart is half-full of golden wax tapers, tall as a man. The bottom ones sag down over the cart's side in droops or are broken in two so a third of their length dangles from the yellow strings down their middles. The women toss armfuls on top and the cartload of tapers wags. One or two of the tapers are still smouldering. Wisps of smoke come off them, then float up and vanish. I look away to see how near to the door I am. I wipe sweat from my lip, look back. An armful of candles is dumped on the top. They roll, settle. The candles underneath sag, all jumbled up, melting or snapped in the middle. A man appears and picks up the two wooden poles at the front of the cart and starts down a marble slope set in the steps there. The tapers on the cart rock and loll with the movement.

A shuffle and I'm squeezed forward. I'm in the coolish shadow of the doorway, entering a kind of ante-room set in the deep wall. The crowd bends to the right inside the ante-room and everyone is looking at a dark doorway that leads to another room set into the wall. I crane my neck, I'm taller than most here, and I see a cavern lit only by dozens of tapers which are set in rows inside a long brass trough. People are bursting through into the candlelit room in clumps, controlled by guardians at the door. Now I'm let in. I'm not one of them, but I've been watching to see what to do. You dip your taper towards an old woman holding a small candle in her hand. She lights yours with it, quickly, and then you go up to the trough and stick your taper in the sand at the bottom of the trough, lifting it first higher into the air, maybe a gesture of blessing, so it's lit top disappears for a second inside a brass hood, a chimney, sooty inside, and then you anchor the taper in the sand. Hail Mary, full of grace, the Lord is with thee. Blessed art thou among women and blessed is the fruit of thy womb. I've waited half an hour to say something and do some-thing. Only as I'm standing there watching the stutter of light on the end of my own candle, I realise no one else is pausing. They're sticking their candles in the sand and hurrying out into the courtyard. I realise as well that they're not lifting their candles up in some gesture of reverence into the sooty chimney. It's just that some people have to do that to get their candles over the candles in front to where there's a space at the back. And already sturdy female hands are plucking the lit tapers of those who only have just turned and gone through the door in the back wall into the daylight of the courtyard, plucking the just-lit tapers out of the sand and passing them quickly to other women who chuck them out the small side door and onto the handcart, snuffing the flames out roughly with their fingers.

The courtyard is blinding white. Marble paving slabs. Kids running about. Doves. The tourists who got in the easy way taking pictures. Two sets of marble steps going up either side to an arcaded verandah that runs along the front of the church. Four or five people are ambling up and down the set of steps on the left. Dead ahead a crowd is rammed up the other steps. These steps are carpeted red, the other steps aren't. It's a complete crush, not moving, up the steps and then halfway along the verandah to where the door into the church is. Some of the people waiting on the steps are carrying grey umbrellas against the sun. I get out my phone. Ten past one. The ferry back leaves at three. I must be on that ferry back to our island, because the high-speed ferry from there back to Athens leaves at five. Then the plane home tonight.

I've drifted into the crowd while I'm trying to decide what to do, again too much to one side. When I get to the balustrade I'll be too far out and have to squeeze to get round it onto the steps. I fall back where it's less crushy and closer to the middle. It's not about pushing, whatever else it's about. A drop of sweat slides down and tickles my waist. I look across the courtyard. I could go over. I could just go up those other steps which lead up to another doorway that I see now on the far left of the church. I could just go up and see how far those other people get in. Do they just get to go into the porch and then out again? Or are they maybe penned just down that left side of the church, while we in the crowd have full access to roam around, kneel and pray, and view all the treasures? I could leave the crowd and check but I'd lose my place and there isn't much time. There are lots of people packed behind me already. These people wouldn't be queuing in the hot sun like this for nothing, not for nothing.

I flap open one side of the shawl a little to let air under the arm. I look around under cover of my sunglasses. Lots of the women in the crowd have bare arms, a few are even wearing tank tops with their bra straps poking out. Maybe they have shawls in their bags they can get out later. I wipe sweat. I could let the shawl fall away till I get to the door of the church, I could do that. I could probably just take it off altogether. I sigh. This queue is moving in less frequent stops and starts than the first queue. I extend my lower lip and exhale over the top lip to blow cool air against my nostrils. It's not that far up to the verandah along the front of the church. The people who are strolling up the other set of steps get there in a minute or less. But already I've been standing here fifteen minutes and I've not yet reached the balustrade that curves out from the bottom of these steps.

A vague swaying passes through. We move forward as one, half a step. We're not pressed body to body at this part of the queue. That will only happen when the swathe of people is squashed together between the balustrades. We stand. A big woman in black, a woman who looks as if the clay she's made from is still soft and clammy under her clothes, keeps brushing my hipbone with her bottom. She doesn't seem to notice when she does it. Each time it happens I feel the weight of her body through her hip. I examine her behind my sunglasses. Her dress hoiks her in in four sections. Two massive sections of breast droop over in their shiny black cotton skin. A softer roll that oozes the other way, horizontal across her middle and hanging down over her pelvis. The dress is tightened again under that. Then the buttocks and thighs clad in looser cotton. It's getting hotter. We move up, one step. You can just see her being made, someone throwing great big fistfuls of clay onto the mound of her, really enjoying it, the sput sound as the clay handfuls smack onto the wodge. Then he thinks, handfuls aren't enough. He picks up an armful of clay, squeezes it against his chest with his forearms so it makes squidgy noises and the moisture in it beads out, feels how elastic it is, but also heavy, really dense and all of a piece, cool when he sinks his fingers into the depths of it. He heaves, flings. A huge great flup of clay lands top right. That'll do for a breast he thinks. That breast could feed the five thousand.

And maybe that's Mary, I think, trying to slide up onto the first step behind the nice man with the glasses, the man about fifty-five with the wife a bit younger who touches his arm every now and then. I fall back. I'm too near him like that, breathing down his neck and curving my chest in so it doesn't make contact. His wife might think it a bit funny. I blow air up over my top lip. I adjust the shawl. Maybe Mary was a Venus of Willendorf, a great whump of a woman the holy child could cling to, but not faceless like the Willendorf one. Still with the dark Mary eyes. I've reached the first step. If I sneak past the young guy with the bottle of Evian I can get a shoulder into the shade of that woman's umbrella.

In the pictures, Mary is always thin, and in some of them, almost bodiless under her flowing robes. It's rare for them to be body-conscious robes, they just fall without touching her underneath. Sometimes of course, maybe later on in art, you see her breast out, her lengthy fingers parting the bodice like fingers parting curtains to reveal a sacred treasure. The young guy's having none of it. Digging with his elbow into my waist while he looks straight ahead and chews on something. I move slightly away and back. It's not about pushing. He pushes. It's almost like Mary had pornstar plastic surgery on her breasts. He enters the pocket of space next to the grey umbrella and looks around in a yeah? way. I look down at the step in pretend above-all-that. But that's not what I feel, though that's what I would say to him to make him laugh if he were here. Mary's breast revealed by the parted bodice is more snow-globe than breast, its glass so clear you can see the blood flowing blue and the streams of milk rising up from some reservoir that's hidden away, far underground in some cavern of the body where light never goes, and the milk lies without a wind to ruffle its surface, just the odd drop falling every hundred years or so from the cavern roof in the eternal dark, and the sound of it plinking into the milk-lake and echoing. The crowd sways, presses. I shuffle left as I go up and I'm standing next to the nice man with glasses. Maybe over time, deep down in Mary's breast, stalactites and stalagmites of milk form a calcified labyrinth of lace. Over the lake glide boats woven from sub-atomic gossamer, driven by a divine wind that doesn't stir the lake's surface. Quark-sized angelic beings throng the boats, and others fly in and out of the milk-lace that soars above, carrying sparks of quantum energy that come and go, and singing alleluias that echo in the dark forevermore. The crowd sways. The woman ahead of me leans forward and puts one foot onto the edge of the step above. I put my foot where her foot had been.

I look at the Evian bottle the young guy's holding. Half-full. I think about asking him for some but people don't like sharing with a stranger. I might be infected with some-thing. I watch the children in the courtyard. They are happy just running. Some are chasing the doves, some are calling to their mothers in the crowd. The mothers shout back, it sounds like tellings-off, warnings to behave. I look down. My dusty toes, my sandals, the worn red carpet. Other shoes. Black men's shoes, proper shoes. Women's shoes with pointed toes that are suddenly squared-off just short of the ends. Women's sandals with varnished shells stuck on the straps. Maybe when it snows it's Mary's milk falling to earth and melting on the tongues of children in holy wafers. Benedictus fructus ventris tui.

The air is hot as melted glass. From out of the blue, snow. The children shriek. People meet strangers' eyes in amazement. Ave Maria, Ave! As one, we sink to our knees and hold up our tongues to receive the falling flakes. The kneeling crowd is silent. Snow hisses on hot stones, slides down brown cheeks, settles in the creases of nylon blouses and black dresses. It takes a few moments for us to realise it has stopped. It's just the hot sun again, the children running in the courtyard, and that young guy pissed off that a woman's umbrella keeps poking him in the ear. Clumsily we get to our feet. Was that a miracle? I let my weight shift from foot to foot. I check the time on my phone. After two. At this rate I'll never get into the church. At this rate I will have spent the last day of my holiday in a queue.

One step up. It's so crowded on the steps that it's impossible not to touch the others around you. I want to withdraw into myself, I don't want to feel bodies and bags bumping. I should be preparing. That's what you're supposed to use this time for, that's the function of the queue, to prepare, to be patient, maybe to open your heart to receive. If there's anything in it at all. The woman in the red-checked dress is wearing a fake flower perfume that keeps inserting itself into my nose. She's on the phone all the time. Yaaaaasas. Catarrhy voice, a smoker. Ahead of me the woman who likes her husband looks round at him, he's just beside me, and touches his arm. She has very specific eyes, the eyes of someone who is worried about someone, not him, and feels for them in a hopeless way. These people aren't just waiting to get into the church because it's a famous church. Nothing famous, not the Mona Lisa not Liz Taylor, could get people to queue like this. Sway. Up a step. Up another step, a bonus. Maybe Liz Taylor, a chance to see how badly she's aged in the actual altered flesh. The red-and-white checked woman gets her phone out again.

Its ring is a sample of a baby gooing. They are queuing for a blessing or a healing, maybe the bishop is here today, maybe there's a relic of a holy toenail that's only revealed on this particular day, maybe this is the given day to come and ask for mercy for someone that you're worried about in a hopeless way. Sweat trickles. I flap the shawl in the tiny arc of space available.

A change in the voices behind me then a surge in the crowd that forces me against the balustrade. A woman catches her balance by grasping my forearm where it's resting along the top of my bag. She says something, probably sorry, and I answer with a smile so she doesn't know I'm foreign. People are looking back and down. They are parting, though there's no room to part. Something is coming up the red carpet through the parted crowd. So this is where crawlers win out. She comes up, cow-like. Her hair's been badly done in rollers so you can still see the shape of where each roller was, and the grey lines at her scalp between each roller-shape where the hair dye hasn't reached. Up she comes on hands and knees, the people parting in front of the rollered hair and reforming behind the pantyhosed feet. She'll be along the verandah in a minute, in the church, all blessed and forgiven, and down at the dock with time for a coffee before the ferry comes in. We resettle, sweat. I see another man drinking freely from a bottle of water. I swallow.

Holy Mary, mother of God, pray for us sinners, now and at the hour of our death. Over and over again in my head without me wanting it. I'm high enough up the steps now that if I turn I can see over the wall of the courtyard below and beyond that to the sea. Pray for us sinners. Now and at the hour of our death. I lean an arm on the balustrade and look at the sea for as long as I can before it seems to irritate the people behind me that I am staring over their heads like that. Now and at the hour of our death. I face the church. I wipe sweat from my lip. Who thinks anything now like at the hour of our death? That hour that must be watched for and prayed over so that the passage into death is safely accomplished. That was a strange and morbid obsession of the past. Hail Mary full of grace the Lord is with thee blessed art thou among women and blessed is the fruit of thy womb Jesus holy Mary mother of God pray for us sinners now and at the hour of our death amen.

I'm not even Catholic. I'm not Greek Orthodox and not even Catholic. Again. Hail Mary full of grace the Lord is with thee while I stand, sweat, slightly flap the shawl in the space available, sigh, sway, wipe my hand across the back of my soaking neck, look at the legs in front, at nothing, look round at the crowd now and at the hour of our death. Amen. A small man, some of the men around here are hobbit-height, a sweet old man, his face carved into flat pans by deep lines, and with solemn brown eyes. Looks like a peasant still living a neolithic lifestyle on some barely inhabited island, somewhere where they fast properly before Easter and travel by donkey and spend the evenings sitting in front of their houses watching the dusk coming like an event. A life that lasts for aeons because slow, with not many thoughts to mar the peace between the ears. Sex of course when young, and maybe now what he worries most about is the donkey. Lord, I need another donkey, thy will be done. Except he's probably a TV salesman. Another step up. I'm near the top. I flap the shawl. I think about water.

Sounds are coming out of the church. It's a voice singing, a deep man's voice. He stops, starts again. Maybe there's a mass in progress, if they call it that. The people on the steps are mostly women, but quite a few men, mostly with women, their wives or maybe sisters, and even one or two young men. Women with toddlers in frilly ankle socks. Old women with hard faces and forceful eyes. That aggro guy in his cool T-shirt and dark glasses who's quite a few people ahead of me now. Middle-aged women of all kinds and shapes. And a girl. It's her neck bowing that catches my eye first. She's tall and has to bow her neck to talk to her companions, also girls of college age. Long black hair, the front two strands of it caught back with a bobble over the rest of the hair so you can see the oval of her face clearly. A girl with such a graceful outline it's as if God figure-skated her into existence. She half-turns to talk to a girl just behind her. A bony nose with a wobble in the middle. Dark eyes held as if by light vibrating wires in their sockets. A tiny medieval mouth. She senses someone looking and glances at me. I freeze. I'm hoping the dark glasses make it seem as if I'm looking past her to where you can see the top of the hill behind the church. She looks away. But maybe you can see by the angle of my head that I'm looking at her. I angle my head more towards the hill then slide my eyes round so I can look at her from the side. We shuffle forward.

I'm just below the last step. Soon I'll be in the arcaded verandah, in the shade, and in the final stretch to the church. It's quarter past two. The ferry leaves at three.

She is the most beautiful girl I've ever seen but not in the way expected. Maybe it's a beauty that would only be apparent on these steps, not in the street or in her class where the boys don't pay her any attention. It's not a sexual beauty. Of course she probably works in a strip joint to fund her way through college. I glance again. I have to keep taking her in. That bow to the head and the gentle intelligence that seems to permeate her arms. She's the apple of her father's eye. He can't bear anyone to touch her as if she's just another girl. She's tuned like an instrument and loving, you can tell, bowing her head to her companions and letting them slip words into her ear. She looks my way again. I'm glad I'm not a man. It's so hard for men to get a good look at anyone.

Someone is asking me something. I shake my head and look away. She says something again, louder. I have to respond. I'm sorry, I say, I don't speak Greek. She says something else. I smile, look at the bowed girl. I think of something, turn back to the woman. My cover is blown anyway. Do you speak English? Little, she says. I think of the best version, word it. Why are we waiting here? She puts her head on one side. We wait to enter the church? Sorry, she says. I look round at those closest. Does anyone speak English? No one pays any attention. Then, ahead of me, the aggro young guy says Panahia Evangelistria, most holy icon of Greece. I nod. Panahia Evangelistria, you don't know her? No, I didn't know she was here, I say. He looks as if he doesn't believe it or he doesn't understand. I don't know her, I say, is she very old? We move forward, he a bit further than me. Before Byzantine, he says. I wish he didn't have such a loud voice. I see, thank you, I say. He shakes his head as he scans the press of people. I wipe sweat from my lips. What does it mean, that name? I ask. What? he says loudly. The name Panahia Evan   ? He tuts. Is the Holy Mother. She has make many miracles here, very holy. I see, I say. I nod. He shrugs and bobs forward between two middle-aged women. They complain behind his back.

The priest starts singing again inside the church. Kyrie eleison. Words I know. Then words I don't know. Then again, Kyrie eleison. Lord have mercy. We shuffle closer to the door. I check the time on my phone. Half past two. The ferry leaves at three. I shift my weight. I look from side to side and back down at the rammed people on the steps. Am I going to have to leave now after all this time? I must be on that ferry or I'll miss the other ferry to Athens and miss my plane. I glance quickly at the bowed girl. Cream-bun coloured. Gentle in a way that's not fashionable. Not timid; bowed. I tap my hand on top of my bag. I must be on that ferry. The crowd is stirring. A woman is making her way through holding her hand up and arguing as she goes. They don't want to let her past but she pushes on, answering over her shoulder to a hairy man who starts shouting at her. She's holding up a white ferry ticket right in front of my face. I read the English on it under the Greek. She's on my ferry. And she's using it as an excuse to get to the front, see the sacred icon and get back down to the port. The woman who asked me something speaks crossly to her. But whatever she's saying the ticket-woman just keeps yakking and shoving, causing dissension at every step. What's more, two more women, arm in arm, and babbling back at the crowd around them, follow her, evidently using the same argument.

The crowd shivers restlessly. I check the time on my phone. I must see the icon because I've waited all this time to do something in this church. I go up on tiptoes. I can see into the church over the heads of the people who are entering chaotically, turning left and then moving out of sight. Dead ahead behind a red rope is a bank of candles, mustard-gold beeswax, set into a tray of sand. Behind that in the dimness I can see hundreds of silver icon lamps hanging in garlands from the ceiling and pillars. We pour forward, people breaking into shouts. The reflections from the gold and silver and the winking of the candles flashes in my eyes above the bobbing heads. I hear the chanting of the priest loud now through a microphone. I need to get back to the ferry. I wipe sweat off my face. I must see this most holy icon of Greece, this Virgin Mary, and I must light a candle like everyone else.

Twenty to three. I'm not going to make it. I have to leave now, to run all the way back down the hill. I'm at the door of the church. Now I can see gold and silver symbols hanging from all the icon lamps, votive offerings of thanks or maybe to remind God what people are asking for. There are silver legs and arms, a gold ship, a silver donkey, a house, a sprinkling of silver hearts, silver cut-out women in old-fashioned skirt suits or dresses, a cradle, a car. The crowd is in turmoil. I can hardly keep my eyes on the things inside the church because there's a bunfight with people heaving each other aside and shoving arms under each other's noses to get to the pile of mustard-gold candles laid out on the left and slip the payment through the slot in a wooden box. They are taking the candles and they're going round the corner of the candle-table further to the left to where there's a man guarding what must be the icon. She's set in a lectern at an angle, just like a book on a lectern-stand, and she's behind glass, the size of say an art book. There's a smell of sour cheese and incense. Elbows dig into me. I can't see the icon behind the glass only that the worshippers go up to her, cross themselves, but not like Catholics, and kiss the glass. Then they turn right to the bank of lit candles, and stick their own candles in the sand. It's all happening so fast. I must get a candle. I can't get into my bag, there's too much of a crush. I find some change in my pocket, and I've got something over two euros which I show to the woman who speaks a little English, she's just there in front of me, and I say, Is this OK? picking up a candle and showing her the money while people jostle from behind. Ah too much. she says and she shows me her fingers, three, four, so I pick up three candles, even though I need only one candle, to focus, to speak to God if there is one but no, I take three candles which only confuses things, and now this minibus of a woman, middle-aged, with badly-plucked eyebrows, sticks her elbow round the front of me and uses it to hoik my whole body back and propel herself forward. She's beside me now, poking away at my kidney, pushing me against the table piled with candles and sticking her other elbow into someone else. They're having none of it, Kyrie eleison, so she uses both elbows as clubs to pummel me and the other person and then she kicks me in the leg as well which might be a mistake and I must get to the icon but it's not about pushing. I can't do it like this because it's not about pushing, I just can't and so I weave backwards and to the right to get away from the jammed-up crowd by the candles. The priest chants, Kyrie eleison, the crowd thrusts past me with its arms, and I move against the flow to where there's a gap on the right just inside the door and I stand there against a red rope and I'm not going to see the Virgin after all this waiting and hoping. A hand comes to rest on my shoulder. A woman maybe ten years older than me. She rests her hand on my shoulder and she smiles. We stand there in a bit of fairly free space and she pats my shoulder and drops her hand. People surge past choppily. They're all gesturing at the minibus of a woman still shovelling her way to the front and I move a bit further away again from the troublemaker and the woman behind me puts her hand on my shoulder again and she sings a bit of something, maybe a hymn. She sings quietly, her eyes smiling directly up at me while she rests her hand on my shoulder and squeezes it slightly every now and then. I look down into her singing eyes and I have to blink to stop tears coming into my eyes. I feel myself starting to smile back at her. I'd like to sing back at her. She puts her her hand in the small of my back and I go forward, past the scrum by the candles and round the corner. I'm propelled by the flow of the crowd towards the icon and now it's almost my turn. Kyrie eleison. The woman two in front does the cross I don't know how to do, bends, kisses the glass surface, mutters something, goes. The woman in front bends, does the special cross, kisses. Now it's me. Eleison. It's my turn to kiss the holiest icon in the whole of Greece. I stand in front of the icon angled like a book on a lectern and all I can see behind the glass is jewellery. Pearl necklaces, diamond necklaces, brooches, rings, sapphires, chains of gold, dangly earrings with topaz and ruby, all tangled up and flung in any old how. It's like some crazy shop window. I search frantically for the Virgin among all the chains and precious stones while people press behind me, she must be there if you know where to look and I have to see her, but there are too many people behind me pressing, so I make the sign of the cross the only way I know how, a bit furtively, and plant a full kiss, a too smacking, not reverential enough kiss on the glass front of the display case feeling that the voices mounting behind me are saying, Hey, she's not one of us, she doesn't know what she's doing. And I turn and hurry to the bank of candles and light my three and steady them in the sand and look at the frail flames, willing them not to go out, in case that would be a sign, though that's a stupid thought, and clasp my hands and say what I have to say to one of the frail flames, the chosen one, and I quickly turn, Kyrie eleison following me in a deep man's voice and I run out of the church and down the other set of steps, the empty ones, across the courtyard and through the door and down the street with the strip of carpet, running with my heart in my mouth to catch the boat.